THE GREAT DIVORCE

GREAT
DIVORCE

THE GREAT DIVORCE

David Loy Frishkorn

gatekeeper press

Columbus, Ohio

This book is a work of fiction. The names, characters and events in this book are the products of the author's imagination or are used fictitiously. Any similarity to real persons living or dead is coincidental and not intended by the author.

The Great Divorce

Published by Gatekeeper Press
2167 Stringtown Rd, Suite 109
Columbus, OH 43123-2989
www.GatekeeperPress.com

ISBN (paperback): 9781642374209
eISBN: 9781642373554

Printed in the United States of America

Author's Note

Dedicated to my family, spouse Jack, daughters
Jessica and Jasmine, grandsons Silas, Anderson and
Callan, sons-in-law Brian and Ron, as well as many
friends who supported me in this process of creating
my first presentable work of fiction. I hope the
reading public is as supportive and receptive of my
work as my family has been in this literary journey.

This is truly a work of fiction and speculation. Many
acquaintances will undoubtedly wonder if they
inspired a name or two, here and there throughout
the book. Many characters and names are indeed
inspired by specific interactions with individuals
or an amalgam of interactions with numerous
people in my life. The only true intent in this book
is to borrow inspirational names or behaviors,
not to try to represent any particular individual.

Special thanks to my editor Zachary Bell for his relentless attention to detail and consistency as well as his continuous efforts to limit my tendency to report information through monologues.

CHAPTER *One* – *Prologue*

On this typical, crisp New England morning, Don Lasserman squinted groggily through mildly crusted eyelids, trying to ascertain the source of the persistent, annoying, mechanical, droning sound. He knew it was his bedside alarm clock. He just didn't know where it was. He could vaguely recall stabbing at it with a fist just a short ten minutes previous, but where the contraption had landed, he had no clue. He had half a mind to just let it buzz on merrily, but, if he didn't silence it within the next ten seconds or so, it was bound to rouse Maria, his beautiful wife of thirty-four years, sleeping peacefully beside him. She was close to the other side of the California king mattress, wrapped in their expensive, thousand thread count, Egyptian cotton, paisley-print sheets. For some reason, he recalled-and it bothered him that he recalled it-that they had purchased this particular bedding set at Bloomingdale's a few years earlier and the cashier was a very young and attractive Jewish woman with deep, dark, vibrant oval eyes, heavy eyebrows, a pronounced but stylish nose, perfectly coiffed sandalwood hair in a short flip, full and wide lips expertly painted scarlet to match her medium length nails, very fair but not pale skin, and yes, a pair of the largest breasts he had seen in some time, and there was much to be seen. All this he recalled vividly, but what stuck in his mind the most now, as it did when they made the purchase, was how uncannily bizarre it felt to be buying Egyptian cotton sheets from a Jewish clerk in midtown Manhattan. When would that Middle Eastern tension ever end? When would he learn to stop assigning labels and drawing unfounded conclusions? Why was Einat, the clerk, studying his credit card so closely and scrutinizing his slightly saggy and wrinkled, sixty-four-year old, splotchy pink face? Was it just careful credit card security procedures? Or was there something more in her piercing gaze? So many things to ponder as the alarm buzzed on persistently somewhere nearby.

With great effort, he slung his heavy, arthritic right arm over and reached for the floor. With a minimum of fumbling he located the offensive apparatus and tugged at it forcefully, causing the droning noise to cease as the plug flew from the outlet. Don dropped the device and rolled onto his back staring triumphantly at the coffered ceiling with its inlaid fresco copy of some masterwork of centuries gone by. Maria breathed comfortably and restfully to his right, seemingly oblivious to his struggle with, and vanquish over, the dreaded, buzz-breathing, dragon-esque Westclox now dead in a heap on the bamboo hardwood floor.

As he lay there contemplating Rembrandt's or Caravaggio's mimicked brushstrokes, Don's mind was most pre-occupied with how much he really didn't want to get out of bed. It wasn't that he wasn't fully awake now. He had gone to bed shortly after 10 p.m. and turned the alarm off at 6:30, then again at 6:40. And it wasn't as if he had some debilitating malady that was restricting his movements, other than mild arthritis not unusual for a man approaching sixty-five. It was just that he seemed to have lost the zeal for life that he had so thoroughly enjoyed for most of his years. The last few years really seemed to drain all his energy, and it was more than the increasingly monotonous routine aspect of his cushy, bureaucratic position at a top-tier investment firm. It was as if the entire ambience of life, of the world around him, had lost its appeal, its vibrancy, its raison d'être.

*****

Halfway across the country, Don's twin brother Daniel, was experiencing much the same thoughts and melancholy feelings that morning. No, that wasn't exactly true anymore. He wasn't halfway across the country; not the country that Don and Maria called home. It was as if Daniel lived in a neighboring, yet so very distant and different, country. It was a land that Don barely recognized, though it was the land where he was born and raised. But this is where Daniel lived, so Don knew the place existed, although he doubted that he would ever again visit that place. In fact, the two brothers hadn't spoken at all in the last two years — since Ted, Don and Maria's youngest child and only son, had gone off to visit Uncle Daniel and never returned.

But this morning, Daniel lay in his own full-size bed covered with tattered patchwork quilts produced by an ancestor long since forgotten and dwelled on his own reasons for not wanting to get out of bed. His life was a much simpler life than that of his twin brother. Daniel worked intermittently at one of the local chicken-processing plants. Sometimes, he didn't work due to a company slowdown or a temporary layoff as a disciplinary measure for his latest form of aberrant behavior. Sometimes, he didn't work due to an alcoholic bender. Or sometimes, he didn't work just because he didn't feel like it, or because he had somehow managed to lure the latest, unwitting, barely-legal street hustler back to his cabin for the weekend, and he didn't want her to leave come Monday morning. But this was a Friday morning, and, better than that, it was payday. Daniel had much to look forward to as he had nine days of pay coming in this check; one of his better performances of late. Yet, even without any bed company for distraction, Daniel felt no sense of urgency to rise. He seemed distracted with an achy forlorn of days gone by, days that could never be replaced or replicated.

Not that Daniel's life had ever been much different than it was now, but at one time, it was more balanced and had more sense of purpose. At nineteen, he married his college sweetheart, Amanda, after a courtship of just a few months, fewer actual dates but lots and lots of sex. They were married for forty years and raised three children in this remote western Arkansas village of Harrisburg. Marriage and fatherhood certainly brought a level of stability and structure, but, honestly, it didn't put much restriction on his lifelong pursuits of cheap alcohol, recreational drugs, rapid-fire guns, and loose women. When Amanda passed away four years ago from a savage form of cervical cancer, their two older children, Daniel Jr. and Nathaniel, were already grown and out of the house on their own. Their youngest child, Emily, was still living at home at the age of 33, but, due to her autism, it was very apparent that Daniel was unable to care for her. After Amanda's funeral, Emily went back to Stamford, Connecticut, with Uncle Don and Aunt Maria and had no contact with her father after that time of separation. Left on his own in his cabin, Daniel's life evolved from weekend benders and holing up in some sleazy, roadside motel to bringing beer, vodka, and moonshine into the house, hooking up with enterprising young girls online and giving them the run of the house until one of them tired of the other. Then, he'd start all over with the next one, occasionally going to work de-boning chickens but only to make ends meet.

But right now, Daniel's melancholia kept him paralyzed in bed. Did he miss Amanda? Did he miss his children? Perhaps he was finally missing his twin brother? They had been close most of their lives, and the last two years with no contact had been, well, different for lack of a better descriptor. "I wonder whatever happened to Leslie Ann," Daniel mused as a funny, faded memory crept into his consciousness. At sixteen, Don had dated Leslie Ann for several months and she was staying over at the Lasserman house one weekend when Luke and Mavis were visiting Mavis' aging mother suffering with dementia at the Willow Care nursing home in Willow Springs,

Missouri. Mavis openly disapproved of Leslie Ann at least partially due to the fact that she was of mixed ethnicity—the daughter of a stunning and voluptuous black woman who worked as a home caregiver for the elderly and a scrawny, anemic-looking white man who occasionally drove long-distance freight haulers. On this particular day of Daniel's reminiscence, seventeen-year old Leslie Ann awoke from a nap on Mavis' sunporch sofa and heard water running in the shower. Hoping to surprise Don, she shed her cutoff jean shorts and pale-yellow halter top and slipped into the steamy shower. Daniel was quite gleefully surprised as a wet, eager, female mouth enveloped his soft cock. Daniel made no attempt to correct her as he heard Don searching for Leslie Ann. But Leslie Ann stood up right away when she heard Don calling from the bedroom and let out a small yelp of surprise. Don rushed in to investigate and even though there was a long, awkward moment, not one of them rushed to escape the situation. After several seconds and a few back-and-forth glances between all parties, Don dropped his shorts as well. The rest of that Saturday afternoon was pure delight and Daniel felt a stiffening in his jeans now with the memory. It was his first of many threesomes, but his only one with another guy. Daniel doubted if his more prim and proper twin had ever had another such experience and his face flushed a bit as he envisioned his and his brother's naked bodies roaming liberally over and into Leslie Ann. Again, whatever happened to her? He thought her family moved away not long after that weekend, but he couldn't recall. As Daniel mulled on his current feelings of loss and despair, he finally came to the same conclusion as his twin, a world and lifestyle away: life had simply lost its appeal, its vibrancy, its reason for being. Life today wasn't what it had been back then, back before these trying and emotional times leading up to the great divorce.

CHAPTER *Two*

onald and Daniel had both been average students at Nettleton High in Jonesboro, Arkansas, but Don's passion for track and field, particularly the 100 and 200-meter sprints, secured him a partial scholarship to Arkansas State where he earned a Bachelor of Science in business administration. Entering college, Don was six feet tall, lean, with wavy, brown hair, and piercing grey eyes. During the college years, he worked on building upper body strength, which created the most noticeable distinction between him and his twin who remained thin as a rail. Upon graduation, Don moved to Cincinnati where he had been recruited by Proctor & Gamble as an entry-level brand manager. Don loved his work and the company and stayed there for seven years, taking night classes at Xavier University's Williams

College of Business. When he received his M.B.A. with a concentration in business intelligence, he received many enticing offers but decided on an entry-level position at Morgan Stanley, working in mergers and acquisitions. This job would keep him in Cincinnati where he had recently started dating Maria Stevens, a tall, beautiful blonde and a recent Xavier graduate with a Bachelor of Arts in liberal studies. They met by happenstance in the Gallagher Student Center where they were both buying books and supplies for upcoming classes. "You're going to love that book," Maria said as she spied a copy of Kurt Vonnegut's latest book, *Breakfast of Champions* in Don's shopping basket. "I finished it about a month ago," she continued. "The main character sort of reminded me of my father. At first you don't know if he's mentally ill or just a bit quirky." She laughed softly and a bit sadly.

Don leaned in to examine her book selections. "I've not heard of that one," he said pointing at Jacqueline Susann's *Once is Not Enough*. Maria looked him over quickly but appraisingly and then said, "I don't doubt it. It's about a young woman, her naivety, manipulation, deception, and, of course, sex." Again, a subtle laugh, but this one much more endearing. "I was entranced with it the moment I read Jane O'Reilly's scathing review in the *New York*

Times and can't wait to read it." Don knew he was going to like spending time with this girl.

They had now been dating a little over a year and Don knew this was not the time to move away. Maria had recently started work as an intake counselor at Talbert House and was excited about her budding career in social services and helping people. Don greatly admired Maria's commitment and dedication to families in need and to people in general. There was no way he could ask her to move away from that at this time.

It had been a good career decision and personal decision for Don. After almost three years of dating, they married and almost immediately started on a family. Jessica was born just fifteen months after they married, and, right around the same time, Don was promoted to the vice president level at Morgan Stanley. Life was very good for the young Lasserman family of Cincinnati. They lived in the chic Mount Adams section of Cincinnati and Don was enjoying the pinnacle of his career success as an investment banker in one of America's top second-tier cities. They tried to make extended family visits to Arkansas at least every other month so their infant daughter could know her grandparents and cousins. Don's parents still lived in Jonesboro as did his only sibling, twin brother Daniel. Luke and Mavis

Lasserman were not very doting grandparents, or, perhaps, they were just more used to having Daniel's two sons and daughter around as the latter spent most of their time at their grandparents' tiny home. Daniel worked sporadically and occasionally disappeared for a few days at a time. His bride, Amanda, worked steadily at two jobs; diner waitress for the breakfast shift and then as a nursing assistant for a gastroenterologist whose office hours didn't start until 10 a.m. So, Luke, an electrician, and Mavis, a substitute school teacher, often filled in on the parenting duties for Daniel's brood. Luke would often go to work early so he could be home early to pick the boys up from school if Mavis had been called to duty that day. Unfortunately, baby Jessica did not receive the proper attention she deserved due to the competing attention of tending to their other granddaughter, Emily, youngest child of Daniel and Amanda, who was also a special needs child.

Maria's parents lived just about an hour away from Cincinnati in Dayton, Ohio. Her father, Wilfred, was a mature parent and had retired from his executive position at Dayton Corrugated Packaging Company shortly after Maria and Don married. Maria's mother, Evalynne, was a stay-at-home mother, a job that she found very unfulfilling, although she was extremely good at it. Maria was an only child and had been born to Wilfred and Evalynne when he was 40 and she had just turned 22. Evalynne had doted excessively on Maria as a child and continued the same when presented with her first grandchild, Jessica. And, of course, Evalynne was a loving and devoted grandmother to Maria's next two children; Jasmine, born three years after Jessica; and Theodore, the baby and Evalynne's only grandson. Ted was two years younger than Jasmine and five years younger than Jessica. The entire family thoroughly enjoyed life in Cincinnati — first living in the Brewery District of the Over-the-Rhine neighborhood where they had purchased and renovated a duplex unit. But as Jessica approached school age, Maria was pregnant with Ted, and Don's career was progressing well. So, they found and purchased a newer and larger single-family Victorian-style home in Mount Adams, an especially-desirable school district. Now, they had been in Mount Adams for ten years and felt fully at home. A Victorian-era carriage house on a neighboring property had been put up for sale a few years ago, and Don and Maria had purchased and renovated it as a second home for Maria's mother, Evalynne, who frequently traveled from Dayton by herself to spend several days or weeks with her precious grandchildren. Wilfred, who was 73 when Ted was born, didn't care much for car trips anymore and so didn't visit as often. Now, in his eighties, Wilfred detested travel even more. "Three days away from home takes me three weeks to recover," he often bellowed. So once Don and Maria had presented Evalynne with the fully-updated carriage house, it didn't take much persuasion for Wilfred to sell their home in Dayton and move to Mount Adams permanently. Unfortunately, Wilfred passed away within a year of the move at the age of 83 following a brief struggle with pancreatic cancer.

The Cincinnati Lassermans were quite content. The household was full of energy and activity, and it really helped having Grandma Eva right next door as a built-in babysitter, cook, or errand-runner as needed. Evalynne had never learned any employable work skills and was just as happy to continue the previously-mundane activities she had done all her adult life: cooking, cleaning, shopping, and caretaking for anyone who needed her attention. She realized she had never really hated doing this drudgery; she just resented being unappreciated. This living arrangement was perfectly fine with all the Lassermans. Don's work kept him away from the house twelve hours a day when he was in Cincy, and much of the time he was away on business trips working on the latest merger or divestiture deal. He was often in New York as many a deal culminated in the great financial capital of the world. Maria's world was extremely full as well. After several good years of development work at Talbert House, she had moved over to the Greater Cincinnati Coalition for the Homeless as Director of Operations. Within two years, she was named Executive Director, a position that didn't pay all that well but required a substantial amount of her time and energy. She was more happy to give the energy than the time as she wanted to spend as much time with her growing family as she could. But with the help of her mother, Grandma Eva, she was able to make it to almost all major events of her children. Jessica, lean and lanky with long limbs and flowing chestnut hair, had been active in high school track and field, like her father, and continued to participate at Oberlin College where she was majoring in East Asian Studies with a minor in Economics. Maria attended nearly every significant high school track and field event when Jessica participated, but not very many at Oberlin as it was nearly four hours away. To Jessica, it was just as well, because her passions were shifting away from sports and more into her studies. She had just completed a study abroad program in Beijing the summer between her sophomore and junior years, and it was her intent to move to China or Hong Kong following graduation and dedicate herself to promulgating the best and truest aspects of capitalism in the officially communist country. Jessica beamed with joy and enthusiasm about Beijing when she would call home twice a month during her summer program. "I've met the nicest people." "I've tried the most interesting and delightful food." "I helped an old woman find her way home and it was the most deplorable, yet charming, living situation I've ever seen."

Their second daughter Jasmine, as tall and blonde as her mother, was also deeply involved in extracurricular activities. A horseback riding camp experience when she was twelve ignited a fervor for all animals but especially horses. Her current dream was to become one of the world's top thoroughbred trainers. At sixteen, she secured a part-time job at the racing stables at Turfway Park across the Ohio River in Florence, Kentucky. Her enthusiasm for working with and being around the animals sometimes obscured her common sense- at least, according to her parents. If Jasmine could have her way, she would transition to full-time stable work upon high school graduation and apprentice her way through the field of training. But her parents were keen on her obtaining a college education, so, at least for the present time, they had compromised on a plan; she would attend the University of Louisville with a focus on Equine Business.

Theodore, or Ted as most of the family called him, was also active with the typical grade school and middle school activities. Of average height and build with curly blond hair, he participated in youth soccer and Little League baseball. He joined the swim team and the wrestling team in junior high. He tried the math team, the chess team and the economics club, but he never seemed to click with any of the groups. Nonetheless, he was happy to participate and try new things. Nearing sixteen, his parents expected his interest to turn to dating, but, so far, he had shown no interest. Perhaps it was attributable to his mild acne or his general social discomforts, but they saw no reason for concern at this point. As Grandma Eva repeatedly assured them, "He's just a late bloomer."

The summer after Ted finished his junior year of high school, Don took Maria away for an unusual 'parents-only' long weekend. They left Cincinnati on a Thursday morning and flew to New York's LaGuardia airport. A limo whisked them into midtown where they checked in to the New York Marriot Marquis in Times Square and pampered themselves at the resident spa. That evening they had an early steak dinner at Joe Allen's on 46th Street and took in an evening performance of *The Producers* at St. James

Theater. On Friday, they visited the Museum of Modern Art on 53rd Street and then a luscious French lunch at Jean-Georges on Central Park West before hitting the Metropolitan Museum of Art for the afternoon. Then back to the hotel to tidy up before dinner at Sardi's and then an evening performance of *Rent* at the Nederlander Theater. Saturday morning started with a raucous round of experienced and comfortable lovemaking, their second round since arriving in New York, followed by breakfast at the hotel's Crossroads American Restaurant. Don suggested they head to Fifth Avenue for some shopping which prompted the following exchange.

"Shopping? With you? What on earth has gotten into you?" queried Maria, somewhat incredulously.

"What do you mean? Is it that unusual to be spending quality time with the love of my life in the greatest city in the world?" replied Don gazing directly into her seaweed green eyes and beaming like a high school boy who just got his first real kiss.

"Yes, actually, it is quite unusual. Appreciated, but unusual. What's going on? Is it something medical? Financial?"

Don was nearly laughing as he replied, "No, no, I'm fine, you're fine, we're fine. I just wanted you to have the best taste of New York City."

"Because?"

He hesitated, struggling for the right words, then resumed, "Well, the firm has offered me a substantial promotion to Managing Director of the Wealth Management group, and..."

"That's wonderful, Don," interrupted Maria, "I'm sure it will mean even more time away from home, but we can manage. We always do. And the kids are almost grown now."

"No, you didn't let me finish. The new position will actually mean *less* travel, although some serious hours in the office. The catch is that the position is here in Manhattan."

"Oh," she replied as she focused on some gum on the sidewalk and then exhaled, "That's a lot to think about. I've never envisioned living in such a large city. It's a lot to take in. And we have to think about the children. And my mother."

"As you just said," he sang, "the kids are nearly grown. Jessica is going into her senior year at Oberlin and will likely be off to Asia once she graduates. Jasmine starts at the University of Louisville in the fall. And she hardly notices anything with less than four legs anymore. And Ted, well Ted will probably be the toughest as he's going into his senior high school year. But, if he doesn't want to move, perhaps he and your mother can stay in Mount Adams for the upcoming school year and then catch up with us next spring. Let's at least discuss the pros and cons of this offer and see what accommodations we can come up with."

"I should have known from the past two days of pampering that something was coming, but I can tell how much you really want this, so we can discuss it," she said noting the boyishly eager grin on his face, "but first I want to make the most of Fifth Avenue today. That should tell me how much you want this to happen," she said playfully while, finishing her second mimosa.

Don signed the check, and they walked up Seventh Avenue to 47th Street, heading east towards 5th Avenue. Maria did a lot of window-shopping along the way as they navigated through the famous diamond district, but, fortunately for Don and their bank account, most shops had very little on display in the windows and all shops were closed for the Sabbath. Once on Fifth, they breezed through Saks before heading a couple blocks north to the Cartier store. Don admired Maria's restraint but wisely noted a few things in which she showed great interest. "It's good to plan ahead for birthdays and holidays," he thought. Still without packages, they continued north to Sergio Rossi where Maria simply couldn't resist a pair of Godiva tea rose pumps, a coordinated nude silk, and a Mermaid crystals clutch. High on the thrill of her own purchases, she insisted that they spend considerable time and money in Hugo Boss, just a few blocks farther north, buying something suitable for her husband. They ordered a new, three-piece suit for Don and gathered several silk twill ties and three French-cuffed, Kent collar dress shirts in white, blue, and a soft yellow. Don knew part of the reason Maria insisted on these purchases; she wanted to assuage any guilt she might have from the two grand they spent at Sergio Rossi, but he also took it as a good sign that she was coming around to the New York move. And he was right. Although they didn't discuss any specific aspects of the potential move for the rest of this romantic weekend jaunt, when he arrived home from work in Cincinnati the following Tuesday, he found his beautiful wife with a scrumptious homemade meal of London broil, thin-sliced broiled red potatoes, and grilled asparagus-one of his favorite meals. Without any sort of prelude, she kissed him softly but assertively at the door, took his computer bag and jacket, and lead him to the massive, oak-plank dining room table.

The first words she spoke since he walked through the door were, "I've decided we should live in lower Fairfield County in Connecticut or Westchester County in New York. I'm partial to Stamford on the Fairfield side and Ryebrook on the

Westchester side. Both have good train service to Grand Central Terminal. I'm not planning to work per se, but I do want to be involved in charitable activities and volunteering. Pour me some Cabernet and let's eat." She looked at his stunned face and let a smile creep easily on to her own. And then, they both laughed. Don simply said "Agreed", enjoyed the fabulous meal, and they retired early for some meaningful cuddle and sex time before drifting off to sleep.

Ted was spending the night in the carriage house with Grandma Eva, Jasmine was away at a horse care camp for the next three weeks, and Jessica was doing her study abroad semester in China. Maria had not clued her mother or youngest child into any of the unfolding events but had requested they both arrive at the main house by seven a.m. for a family breakfast with her and Don. Maria was concerned how each of them would take the news about the move to New York. Her mother had never lived outside the state of Ohio and had never traveled very much either. Maria was sure her mother would find the prospect of living in or near the great metropolis too intimidating, and she would find reasons to delay or prevent a move with the family. Likewise, Maria believed Ted would be intimidated by the move and would stall or outright refuse. She and Don had discussed this and were prepared to accommodate both

Evalynne and Ted by keeping the carriage house for at least the next year until Ted went to college the following fall.

Evalynne arrived at the main house around 6:30 a.m. to help with the breakfast preparations. Maria was determined to have all of Ted's favorites: French toast, link sausages, whole-wheat toast, and eggs sunny side up. She had also baked one of Evalynne's favorites, a cauliflower and egg casserole. Ted came over to the main house around seven, and, by then, Don was dressed for work and had joined them in the kitchen. Everyone filled their plates with their favorite breakfast foods and sat down at the French provincial table in the east-facing kitchen nook that Grandma Eva lovingly referred to as the solarium. The perfect, sunny, summery, early morning should have made the conversation easy, but both Don and Maria seemed to be struggling with the right opening words, as they were so concerned about the potential reactions from son and grandmother. After a few awkward false starts to get to the heart of the matter, the normally-reticent Ted chimed in, "You're trying to tell us you want to move to New York, aren't you?" There was a brief pause that seemed to suck most of the air from the room before Ted continued, "Gram and I figured it out while you were in New York City for the long weekend. It just seemed like an unusual outing for you two and you both sounded kind of, let's say squirrelly, on the phone each evening, so we figured something was up. It didn't take much deductive super power to conclude your next big promotion would be to New York. So, we'd better be right, because Gram and I have already made up long lists of things we want to do when living there."

Maria and Don were stunned as they returned blank faces to the sly smiles coming from their only son and Maria's mother, so Evalynne picked up where Ted had left off. "Yes, I'd like to do a bit of traveling before I get much older, and the options from New York will be so much more convenient than from Ohio. And, the Red Hat Society, which as you know I joined following Wilfred's passing, has several active chapters in the greater tristate area. I'm looking forward to expanding horizons and developing new friendships."

It was Ted's turn again to add to his parents' awe-stricken faces. "I have thoroughly enjoyed my involvement in drama club and the high school theatrical productions the last two years and I would so love to attend a real Broadway performance or two. I'm thinking of a career in stage management and there's no better place in the world to pursue this than New York City," he said beaming.

Both parents were still dumbstruck with the overwhelming simplicity of their task of convincing the two perceived hard sells that they still sat speechless and unmoving. After several seconds of giddiness and shocked silence, Maria simply looked at Don and said, "I guess I've got a lot of work and planning to do to get this family headed east." They all laughed and enjoyed their plates of delicious breakfast treats with light and easy conversation about their new life in the big city. Don finished his meal first and headed off to the office to make his acceptance of the promotion official. Eventually, Ted and Grandma Eva busied themselves with cleaning up the kitchen and tidying other rooms while Maria called realtors: one in Mount Adams and one in Stamford, Connecticut.

CHAPTER *Three*

Daniel Lasserman's life after high school followed a dramatically different path than his brother's. His high school academic success was similar to that of Don, but Daniel chose to spend his non-school hours hanging with his boys rather than the track field. Hence, there were no scholarships offered, and Luke and Mavis Lasserman barely had enough extra money to help one son with college expenses, let alone two, but they did the best they could. Mavis tried to be as fair as possible with her treatment of the boys for life after high school, as she had throughout their lives. Since Don received a partial, but fairly generous, scholarship to Arkansas State, he did not require much extra cash for college, but what was required was still beyond the Lasserman's means. Rather than direct all of their extra efforts towards Don's shortfall, or extend beyond what she and Luke could reasonably afford, Mavis drafted a budget that started with what she felt comfortable from her perspective over the next four years. Once she identified that monthly amount and gained Luke's concurrence, she explained to the twins what their contribution would be. Mavis would provide an equal monthly stipend for Don and Daniel. Don's would of course go towards the tuition gap at Arkansas State. Daniel had not yet made any post-high school plans, so Mavis said she would put his stipend into a dedicated savings account controlled by her and they would only withdraw funds towards education-related expenses. Both sons agreed, and Don focused on applying for Pell grants and education loans now that he knew what the net shortfall would be.

Daniel, on the other hand, had no plan yet as to what he was going to do, so he started giving it some thought. First, he spoke to the owner of the local Ace Hardware where he had been working part-time since his junior year to see if his hours could be expanded following graduation. They could, so Daniel felt good with that first step and deferred thinking much further than the end of summer. But summer did end and by the time the pleasant weather started to recede, so did Daniel's hours at the hardware store. Mr. Jeffries, the store owner, assured Daniel the hours were likely to increase for the upcoming Christmas season, but then he would likely have to cut back again until the Spring season. Luke advised his son to start giving some thought to a more stable future, so Daniel did and got a catalog from several area community colleges and schools. After some deliberation, Daniel enrolled in the Criminal Justice program at Black River Technical College in Pocahontas, Arkansas, an easy half hour commute from their home in Jonesboro. Luke had recently purchased a new-to-him 1970 Ford F-150, so Daniel became the proud recipient of his father's weathered 1964 Ford Econoline van, which would rack up tens of thousands of additional miles over the next year and a half as Daniel did the daily commute to Black River in Pocahontas.

Daniel had enrolled in the college's Associates program for Criminal Justice and worked consistently to ensure steady progress towards his degree goal. However, he was a healthy and adventurous young man, so extracurricular activities were commonplace, including billiards, bars and babes. One such babe was Amanda Winters from nearby Walnut Ridge. Amanda, a raven-haired and buxom beauty with large, oval, green eyes and full pink lips, was taking her final classes to complete her one-year technical program in healthcare when she encountered Daniel in her father's pool hall after classes one spring day. The chemistry was instantaneous, and the two were inseparable during all the free time they could find.

At the end of the semester, the third in Daniel's four-semester program, he informed his parents he was leaving in a few days. He had enlisted in the Army and would soon start his basic training at Fort Leonard Wood in Missouri. His father, Luke, was flabbergasted and couldn't understand why Daniel would enlist, especially since the draft had recently been eliminated and Vietnam war activities were rapidly winding down. Mother Mavis was also shaken, but she focused mostly on why Daniel would abandon his college program with just one semester to go. Couldn't he just finish that and then go into the service if he really wanted to? Daniel had no real answers to any of their concerns. He just steadfastly stuck by his decision, and, within days, he was off to basic training and several weeks without any direct communications.

After the fact, Mavis would opine that she should not have been surprised when a stranger knocked on their door roughly a month after Daniel left for Fort Leonard Wood. That stranger was Amanda Winters and that stranger had news. Amanda, now three months pregnant, had not heard from Daniel since the end of the school semester and had no way to contact him. It was only through her recollections of conversational snippets with Daniel that she was able to piece together that his parents lived in Jonesboro, and their names were Luke and Mavis. Daniel did not talk much about his home life, and, quite frankly, at the times he did, she hadn't paid much attention. Like many their age, they were in love and obsessed with the overwhelming joy and instant gratification of sex; lots of sex. Now she was pregnant and alone. Her parents did not yet know of her predicament, and Amanda didn't want to take any next steps without consulting with the baby's father. She was utterly devastated when Mavis and Luke informed her that Daniel had abruptly enlisted in the Army and was away at basic training. Though Mavis was noticeably disappointed and disapproving of her son's actions, both the pregnancy and the abandonment, she quickly resumed her natural position of the person in charge and insisted that Amanda move in to Daniel's bedroom right then and there. Daniel would be home from basic training for a long weekend in about two weeks. Mavis would arrange for Amanda's family to come to Jonesboro that weekend and there would be a small, but official, wedding ceremony, following which Amanda would continue to live with Luke and Mavis until such time that Daniel was able to plan and provide for his own family's needs. So, by the will of Mavis, Daniel's life was cast on a new path; one which he never openly regretted, but one in which he was not the primary decision-maker. In his mind, later, this justified his endless drinking, gambling, and fornicating.

Daniel returned for the anticipated long weekend of leave, and he went along with all of his mother's plans for the wedding, for Amanda, and for the baby. For their part, Amanda's parents were extremely accommodating, mostly because all the potential problems of a teenage mother had been removed from their hands, and they simply preferred their own lives to be simple. Amanda was their oldest child of four. They figured they had their hands full with the other three, and, at this point, a pregnant teenager was not the best role model for her rapidly maturing siblings. Luke's brother, a justice of the peace, performed the ceremony in Luke and Amanda's backyard in front of an aboveground, circular swimming pool. The reception consisted of cold cuts and beer at two wooden picnic tables and benches, one of which justice of the peace Uncle Fred had brought with him from his house just four blocks away. The wedding party consisted of the bride and groom, their respective parents, Uncle Fred and Aunt Martha, and one other special invitee, Daniel's twin brother Don who had driven in from Cincinnati where he was doing a summer internship at Proctor and Gamble.

Amanda and Don bonded immediately. In Don, Amanda saw all the qualities she adored and lusted for in Daniel, but far fewer of the flaws. Don seemed to exude empathy, responsibility and accountability. Her new husband was severely lacking in all these areas. But young Amanda reasoned that if Don could embody these qualities, she could instill them in Daniel over time. She was hopeful and optimistic for their future. The next few months passed quickly and uneventfully. Daniel Jr. was born a week before Christmas and three months before his father would be able to return from Fort Leonard Hood to Jonesboro. Amanda was grateful that the pregnancy and delivery had both gone smoothly. As an added bonus, the whole ordeal had given her great insight into doctors, nurses, hospitals and procedures that further excited her passion for a career in healthcare. She had shared much of her dreams for the future with Mavis, who was now more like a mother and sister to her than her own family. Mavis confided that she had a little money put away for Daniel's education expenses, and she didn't see any reason why those meager funds couldn't serve as seed money for Amanda's continuing education to become a nurse.

Furthermore, Mavis reasoned, Daniel was really getting the best education through his Army stint.

When Daniel did return to Jonesboro in March, he was thrilled to see his firstborn son and ecstatic to be reunited with his lovely and voluptuous young bride. So, it really came as no surprise to Mavis when Amanda shared with her in June that she was again pregnant. Mavis realized that her son and daughter-in-law were driven far more by hormones than sense and that she needed to take a firmer hand in their lives, so she set in motion to give up her full-time elementary school teaching position after the upcoming fall semester to focus on daycare for her soon-to-be two grandchildren. This, she reasoned, would allow Amanda to pursue her nursing degree. Mavis also insisted that Amanda get on a birth control pill regimen, as her reliance on condoms with Daniel was obviously not effective.

So, life went on for the Jonesboro Lassermans. Daniel and Amanda's second son, Nathaniel, was born two days after Daniel Junior's first birthday. Daniel appeared to be a normal doting and proud father, often cuddling with his two infant sons when he was home on leave; one of whom he simply referred to as Junior and the other one, Little One. Amanda, now working part-time as a diner waitress, enrolled in a two-year nursing program at Arkansas

State where she enjoyed the periodic encounters with her brother-in-law, Don. They shared occasional lunches as well as rides home to Luke and Mavis' 1950's ranch home, now bursting at the seams with two small boys, two large boys, and the bride of one. Don had given up his bedroom to be a nursery for Daniel Junior and Nathaniel; his now former-room was between his parents' and his brother's. Don didn't need much and had converted the family's single-car garage into an adequate student, bachelor pad. Mavis worried excessively about the space heaters that Don used in the winter months, but her husband, an electrician by trade, assured her that he had taken all necessary precautions with the wiring and fuses. Now that the garage was dedicated as additional living space, one more vehicle was added to the bulging car lot in the Lassermans' driveway and side yard. The driveway could only accommodate two vehicles—Luke's Ford F-150 and Mavis' trusty 1971 bright red Ford Pinto wagon which she had purchased new and was now displaced from its garage residence. This, of course, displaced the Ford Econoline van, which Luke had handed down to Daniel and in which Daniel Junior and Nathaniel were both conceived. Don had acquired a well-used, 1959 red-and-white Ford Fairlane convertible when he started at Arkansas State, and he still drove it occasionally. Most of the time he used the Ford Econoline now that Daniel was deployed, and the van was infinitely more reliable than the much older convertible. So, the ragtop spent much of its declining years in the backyard, under a large white pine.

The following summer, Daniel returned to Jonesboro having completed his two-year Army commitment with an honorable discharge. He started working part-time at the hardware store again, but Luke pulled him aside after a few months to convince Daniel that he needed to focus on a more stable and lucrative future. Mavis really, really wanted him to return to Black River Technical for his final semester of his criminal justice program, but Daniel said the Army had convinced him there was no such thing as justice. He refused to elaborate on this position, but it was clear his interest in criminal justice had waned. Only later would they all learn that he was now leaning more towards criminal than justice.

The only positive step forward for Daniel at this time in his life was the joy and pride he felt in his young family. Luke and Mavis were never candidates for parents of the year, but they had been attentive and loving as well as honest and forthright with their sons. Their interactions with their sons and their activities in the community made it clear to all how much they valued being parents. For this reason, Daniel was equally comfortable in his role of father and comfortable making do with the limited resources they had, just as his parents had done when raising him and Don. After his parents failed to convince him to resume his studies, Daniel was fortunate to find a flexible part-time job at a local pharmacy just two doors down the street from the hardware store. His job was to deliver prescriptions to shut-ins, the elderly, or anyone else who just needed or preferred the gratis delivery service. The pharmacist, Jake, was Luke's half-brother and a first cousin of the hardware store owner, so Daniel was allowed to use the hardware store van for his pharmacy deliveries. The hardware store van was much more presentable than Daniel's twelve-year old Econoline, so it was a win-win for everyone. At this job, Daniel was paid $1.35 per hour, which was fifty cents less than he was now making at the hardware store, but he did receive occasional tips from his deliveries. After a while, however, to help assuage his feelings of inadequacy and lack of control over his own destiny, Daniel started helping himself to his own sort of tips. Several of his regular customers received prescriptions for Darvon, Valium, Ritalin, and a new-to-the-market drug, Percocet. At first, Daniel was just taking one pill from many of the prescription bottles, banking on the likelihood that no one would notice one missing pill. However, as his alleyway sales--mostly to Vietnam War veterans--of the painkillers and Quaaludes blossomed, he became more aggressive with his pilfering. At just twenty-four years old, Daniel waved good-bye to Amanda, their young sons, and his parents as he was led away for his next two-year stint, this one in Arkansas' Tucker unit of the Department of Corrections, nearly a three-hour drive away.

By the time Daniel returned to Jonesboro, his eldest son was starting first grade, and Nathaniel was in kindergarten. They had changed so much in such a short time even though the time didn't feel all that short to Daniel. Amanda, somewhat resigned to her lot in life, was now working as a nurse at the Baptist Clinic and contributing greatly to the Lasserman family income, which had been extremely helpful since Mavis had given up teaching to be a full-time grandmother. Now that the boys were in school, she hoped to be returning to the teaching world soon. Amanda was extremely happy to have Daniel home, so it was only natural that she was, again, quickly pregnant with their third child. However, due to the extremely generous policies and benefits at the Baptist Clinic, coupled with Mavis opting to serve as a substitute teacher rather than seek a full-time position, the family was able to get by financially and provide proper childcare during the necessary hours. Luke was also able to help. He had recently taken on an apprentice, Billy, a recent technical school graduate; Billy was brilliant, aggressive, and pleasant with the customers. Due to Billy's success and attitude, Luke was able to be more flexible in his work schedule and fill in as daycare provider when absolutely necessary. For his part, Daniel could also chip in with daycare when needed, assuming he could be found. Following his release from prison, he found it impossible to find local employment. In this town, everyone knew everyone else's business, so his time in prison was no secret and a considerable obstacle to securing employment. Luke tried to keep Daniel busy helping out at his electrician business, but many customers were intimidated by Daniel's presence, so Luke could only keep him busy in the stockroom, out of sight of customers; there was only so much work to do back there. Daniel often went missing but could easily be found at any one of a handful of nearby bars. He had sworn off the illegal drug trade but compensated for his lack of success, his lack of future prospects, and his abundance of idle time by drinking excessively and hustling pool when he was near sober.

Luke and Mavis' household and life were certainly full. Amanda and Daniel had moved out to the garage apartment that Don created during his undergraduate college years, but it was really too small and not warm enough for the small boys in the winter, so Daniel Jr. and Nathaniel were usually in the house with Grandma Mavis. In addition to the permanent live-ins, Don and his bride Maria would come to visit every few weeks. They now had a baby girl, Jessica, who was adorable and precious, but Mavis just felt so tired all the time that she couldn't fully enjoy the wonders of her only granddaughter. And now, Amanda was pregnant yet again. Would life ever get simpler and happier?

Turns out that it could, even though it was precipitated by the death of Grandpa George, Luke's father. George had been in declining health for years, basically, the last decade since his second wife, Marybeth, had left him. George had met Marybeth at Vince's Bar and Grill on Route 18 just east of the Jonesboro city limits where she was a waitress. George had never visited Vince's, but he noticed it one day on his drive home from the Bowman Cemetery in nearby Bowman where his first wife, Elvira, had recently taken up residence. Elvira was the love of his life but had unfortunately died of cervical cancer within two years of giving birth to Luke. George stopped in at Vince's Bar and Grill for coffee and a grilled cheese sandwich. Before long, Marybeth was his regular waitress, and, before too much longer, she became wife number two. Their only child, Jake, was born within a year of marrying and was almost five years younger than Luke. They were a happy and industrious family for over thirty years until Marybeth met Jerry, a pharmaceutical rep who called on Jake's pharmacy. It was quite the scandal around town, so it was fortunate for everyone when Jerry was assigned to a new sales territory, and he and Marybeth left Arkansas for Chicago. That was nearly ten years ago when George was sixty-four. At that point, George felt too old for dating, too disinterested to work, and too downtrodden to do much of anything else. So, he sold his too-large Jonesboro home filled with too many sad memories of Elvira and angry memories relative to Marybeth and built a small, simple, A-frame cottage on an acre-and-a-half pond outside Harrisburg, Arkansas, about a forty-minute drive from Jonesboro. Here, George had everything he could want or need in his semi-reclusive state. The pond was large enough for some good bass fishing. The twelve-acre plot of land was largely wooded and provided hunting opportunities for turkeys, rabbits, and even the occasional deer. His most frequent visitor while living in Harrisburg was Daniel who often brought Daniel Junior and Nathaniel, though he seldom brought his baby girl, Emily, or her mother, Amanda. Daniel enjoyed hunting and fishing with his grandfather, but he also enjoyed leaving the two young boys with their great-grandfather for hours, sometimes overnight, while he made the hour-drive to Memphis, Tennessee. Memphis had plenty of adult extracurricular activities to tantalize the wayward Daniel, and he often took full advantage of them.

Luke and his brother Jake had no reason to expect the death of their father; he was only in his mid-seventies and in apparent good health, but they had expected that when George passed on he would likely leave the cabin to Daniel. So, when the day finally arrived, following a massive cerebral hemorrhage, Luke and Jake were surprised that George had left the cabin to the two of them. It was a fairly straightforward will directing that all of his assets be divided equally between the two of them. After assessing George's assets, his sons found that other than the cabin and surrounding property, their father held quite a few stocks and bonds as well as an interest in some oil fields in Oklahoma that he had purchased with an old Army buddy when they returned from Korea fifty years previous. Although the cabin and land comprised over sixty percent of the asset value, Luke and Jake agreed to split the assets along those lines. Luke would get the cabin and land; Jake got everything else. Jake readily agreed to this, because his brother told him he intended to deed the cabin and land to Daniel. It was meaningful to him and would have the added benefit of providing a separate living space for Daniel and his family. There was added benefit to Uncle Jake as well. Although he loved his nephew, Jake thought it would be better for all involved if Daniel was no longer residing in Jonesboro. His presence in the small city was a constant reminder to everyone, especially customers of Jake's pharmacy, of Daniel's days shortchanging drug deliveries, profiting greatly from illegal alleyway drug sales, and ultimately spending time in prison. Jake believed his own life and stature in the community would be greatly improved if Daniel were out of sight. And Harrisburg, Arkansas, was a wonderful place to be out of sight. Luke called his other son, Don, and laid out his rationale for essentially directing all of his inheritance from his father to his other son and bypassing Don altogether. Luke explained how much he and Don's mother really needed to get Daniel, Amanda and the children out of the house, and how much greater Daniel's need for assistance in life was than Don's. And then, finally, Luke explained that he and Mavis had used all of their extra money and assets to help Don through college and Daniel had not enjoyed the same benefit. Luke failed to explain that he and Mavis had in reality spent an amount equal to what they had spent on Don to get Amanda through nursing school. Don concurred with his father's rationale and rarely gave the deferential treatment another thought, especially as he continued his career successes and widened the economic, social, and cultural gap between himself and his parents and brother.

Daniel moved his family to Harrisburg, and Amanda changed her work hours at the Baptist Clinic to the night shift so she could be home during the day with the children, even though the boys needed her less and less as they grew older. Emily, by now diagnosed with mild autism, needed more care so she wanted to be close by during the day. The boys were quite responsible and could tend to everyday needs during the night if their father was insufficiently sober. Amanda didn't really mind the forty-five-minute drive to the hospital as it gave her a much-needed break from the increasing bickering with Daniel, but she did worry about the extra time taken away from her children. She so wished that Daniel would drink less and get a steady job. His meager efforts at part-time, day labor jobs were insufficient to help the family much, especially since he was most often paid in cash, and the cash rarely made it past the closest bar, pool hall, or package store on Daniel's way home. Amanda often hoped that her husband could be more like his twin, Don, who was now a successful executive of some sort for a banking firm that really wasn't a bank; however, she would never, ever say this to Daniel. And her expectations were not set that high. She knew Daniel didn't have the education nor the ambition to be like his brother, but if Daniel would just get a steady job, it would help the family budget and maybe cut down on his drinking.

Amanda's hopes found purchase during their second year of living in Harrisburg. A poultry-processing plant about twenty minutes away from the cabin was greatly expanding their operations and doing a massive hiring drive. One of the shift managers, Paul Rutterby, was an old Army acquaintance of Daniel's. Paul was from somewhere near Atlanta, but they had met early on during basic training at Fort Leonard Wood and had remained good friends. Paul had sowed his own wild oats and indulged in a plethora of drinking and smoking activities before settling down with Becky at the age of 30. Now, with much support from Becky and *Friends of Bill*, Paul was the epitome of lower middle-class success. He was a member of the vestry at their local Episcopal parish, working full-time at Pardo's Poultry, and helping to coach Pop Warner football, even though his only child, Aidy, was a girl and only three years old, too young to play yet. Amanda believed Paul was an excellent role model and mentor for Daniel, so she didn't hesitate to call him and beg him to find a way to get Daniel a job at the chicken plant when she learned of their hiring drive.

From Paul's perspective, he was actually glad to secure a job for Daniel. Paul had long wanted the right opportunity to make a positive difference in Daniel's life and here it was. He would be supervising Daniel eight hours a day. Another hour would be taken up in Daniel's roundtrip commute. If Paul could get Daniel to enroll his young sons in Pop Warner, then Paul could likely leverage Daniel into helping with the league. All of this was intended to reduce, if not eliminate, the available time for Daniel to get into trouble. Paul, nearly born-again, fervently believed that Daniel was basically a good person led astray by the devil himself during Daniel's abundant idle hours. Amanda fully supported Paul's vision and the two of them felt rightfully proud as the plan seem to take hold. Daniel had always loved his sons, and the Pop Warner activities and interactions rekindled the love that he had felt when they were born. For two years, the plan seemed on solid footing. Daniel worked the day shift, 7 a.m. to 3 p.m. then helped at Pop Warner football with his boys until 5 p.m. He would then drive the boys home for dinner and homework. Daughter Emily was enrolled in a special program, and Amanda would pick her up mid-afternoon and take her home where the two of them would spend time together making the evening meal and doing household chores. The entire family always tried to have dinner together, and it was supremely and serenely enjoyable as the dining table was set up in the front main windows of the A-frame overlooking the pond and woods. The children ate their meals while watching ducks, geese, ground hogs, rabbits, deer and various birds. Once, the calm of the dinnertime was abruptly disrupted as Emily shrieked and pointed excitedly. Nathaniel was the first to pinpoint the source of her agitation and directed his older brother and parents to the black bear making its way toward the west end of the pond. Despite the potential threat brought on by such a site, Amanda felt peaceful and content with their life in Harrisburg and was glad the family was growing and moving forward in such a positive direction. Daniel, however, had jumped up from the table and retrieved his shotgun. "No, Daniel, let it be. Emily is enjoying this so much," Amanda pleaded. "It's going to go through our god-damn garbage and who's going to clean it up?" barked Daniel, already sensing the lower back pain likely to come from clearing the yard of strewn trash. As his parents continued disagreeing about whether or not to chase off the bear, seven-year old Nathaniel finally interrupted, "Don't worry about the garbage. Your yelling has scared off the bear." His parents stared at him, and then out the window where they saw the bear ambling off at a hurried pace. Daniel put his shotgun back in the gun rack and then went out for a drive in his pick-up.

Amanda usually left the cabin at 10 p.m. on work nights for her drive to Jonesboro to start her night shift at 11 p.m. By then, the children were fast asleep, and Daniel was well on his way to sleep as well. She couldn't remember the last time they had bickered or argued other than about the bear. A teenage girl who lived about a mile down the road would walk to the Lasserman cabin in the morning on her way to the school bus and take care of the three little ones after Daniel left for the poultry plant until Amanda got home from the hospital. Life was so good now that Daniel was working full-time and engaged in healthy endeavors with his children. The Lassermans would even occasionally visit Paul and Becky's Episcopal church on Sunday mornings. All this contentment, stability, and harmony ended abruptly when Paul innocently commented to Daniel during a periodic, mandatory performance review, that he was so happy Amanda had called him two years earlier and begged Paul to find work for her husband. Daniel's ego was battered and bruised by

this revelation. He went back to work after the performance discussion without any comment to Paul,
but he did not go to Pop Warner after work. Instead,
he went to the Dew Drop Inn roadside tavern, and
he stayed there. He didn't return home until 10 a.m.
the next morning. By then, Amanda was beside herself with concern. She didn't understand why she
had been called to pick up the boys at Pop Warner.
She didn't understand why her husband didn't come
home for dinner. She didn't understand why she had
to take a personal day and miss her work shift. And
she didn't understand why the sheriff refused to do
anything about her missing spouse who was not yet
missing for the required twenty-four hours.

When Daniel did show up in the morning, she
rushed to greet him, but he pushed her aside on his
way to their bedroom. She followed anxiously trying
to gather any information or insight. He slapped her
and spat, "You didn't think a worthless fuck like me
could find work on my own?" She knew instantly that
her best efforts for the family had been detected and
were backfiring on her. She also knew not to press the
conversation and simply left the room. They never
discussed it again. And Daniel did not return to the
chicken plant for two years and only then did he do
so due to the persistent nagging of Paul who now felt
responsible for all his friend's failings. In fact, Paul

now a full-fledged, Bible verse-spouting, born-again Christian, believed it was his life's mission to put Daniel on the proper path forward. And so, after two years' absence from the plant, Daniel returned and set upon a work/life balance that continued through the rest of his working life...periodically de-boning chickens, constantly drinking, and opportunistically chasing pussy. Paul's best efforts to shape Daniel merely became enablers as he was always covering for his friend at work and extending second chances over and over again.

CHAPTER *Four*

By the time Don and Daniel Lasserman turned fifty years old, Don and Maria were enjoying a highly successful social life in Cincinnati. Don always felt emotionally close to his family and wanted to share his success with his parents and brother. He and Maria arranged for a small, elegant dinner at the Ivy Hills Country Club where they had been members for the past six years. As the dinner arrangements were becoming more crystalized, Don realized that what he viewed as simple but elegant would undoubtedly be seen as extravagant and garish by his brother; so he scrapped the sit-down dinner in favor of an indoor BBQ buffet, but still at Ivy Hills. This turned out to be a very wise decision. Don's parents, Luke and Mavis, arrived on Thursday before the event with granddaughter Emily, now twenty-four years old. Emily's father, Daniel, had little patience for dealing with his daughter's autistic symptoms and behaviors, so it had become increasingly common over time for Amanda to leave Emily with her in-laws for days at a time. In fact, Amanda herself spent a fair amount of time at her in-laws. She justified these actions, because she still worked at the Baptist Clinic, which was just a few minutes' drive from Luke and Mavis' home and because there were better educational and social integration support systems for Emily in Jonesboro than in Harrisburg. Daniel and Amanda's sons had been reasonably self-sufficient since their early teenage years, as they often had to fend for themselves during their father's drinking binges and their sister's need for care from their mother. Now that Daniel was turning fifty, Daniel Junior was just weeks away from turning thirty, and Nathaniel was just a year behind his older brother. Both boys were grown, educated, married, and had fathered children. Daniel Junior was so inspired by his mother's dedication to others, that he followed her example into the medical field and currently served as one of the few male nurses at Le Bonheur Children's Hospital in Memphis. It was at the hospital that he met Brigette Harley, a beautiful and extremely extroverted redhead, with deep green eyes framed by the cutest dork glasses Daniel Junior had ever seen on a woman. Brigette was now a full-fledged pediatrician and the mother of Rebecca, just thirteen months old.

Nathaniel, typically going by Nate now, had been attracted to science and was fortunate to gain a prized Pathways Internship spot at NASA's George C. Marshall Space Flight Center in Huntsville, Alabama. During his junior year in high school, Nate won the annual science fair and the father of another student was so impressed with Nate's work that he mentioned it to his brother who worked at Marshall. Months later, the uncle was in Harrisburg visiting his brother and his family, and they invited Nate to join them one Saturday afternoon. The uncle was so impressed with Nate's knowledge and curiosity, that they struck up a mentoring relationship on the spot that continued throughout the uncle's life. Nate worked his way through college, participated in all Pathways programs at the Space Center, and now worked there full-time as a thermal-protection systems engineer. Along the way, Nate met and married Donna Sunderland, a cheerleader at the University of Alabama where he had played football, second string, but still football for the Crimson Tide. Donna had been raised Jewish, or, as she put it, "Jewish light", and this intrigued Nate. She had assumed he was Jewish when they first started dating and was surprised when he said he was barely Christian. His grandparents had belonged to an Episcopal church in Jonesboro, but he had never known either of his parents to go to church, and his grandparents rarely attended. Donna said, "With a name like Lasserman, there must be some Jewish lineage somewhere in your background." They both agreed to look into it someday, but, for now, they intended to keep religion out of their lives and out of the children's upbringing. Although Nate was saddled with a great deal of college loans, he couldn't have been happier. He was enjoying the career of his dreams. He was married to his beautiful and talented college sweetheart. He had two healthy young boys; three-year old twins. And, he was far away from Harrisburg, Arkansas, and all the problems he left behind there, namely, his father.

Nate, Donna, and the boys, Luke and Wayne, named for their great-grandfathers, drove from Huntsville to Cincinnati for Don and Daniel's 50th birthday celebration. Even though the drive would take a little over six hours, Nate and Donna whole-heartedly agreed that six hours in a car with two 3-year old boys was preferable over the expense and hassles of flying. Air travel had become quite challenging since the terrorist attacks of September 11th and having toddlers in tow only added to the stress levels for the parents and other passengers. Besides, they had recently splurged on their first new car, a new model from Ford called the Freestyle. It wasn't as large as a Dodge Caravan, but it was more masculine than the old station wagons, and had plenty of room for two car seats, the accompanying childhood accessories, and several suitcases. The drive to Cincinnati would be their first chance to test the new vehicle on a long road trip. And Nate was excited to see his Uncle Don and his family. Nate and Donna had married impetuously at the local city hall and had never had a real wedding or reception, so this event in Cincinnati would be the first opportunity for Nate to introduce Donna to his aunt and uncle and their three children, all of whom were many years younger than Nate.

Daniel Junior and his family would also be driving to Cincinnati from Memphis but by way of Harrisburg. They were taking Daniel and Amanda with them on this long weekend outing. It wasn't that Daniel Sr. or Amanda couldn't do the drive themselves, but Daniel Junior knew the long drive would be better with himself, his bride, and their baby girl as buffers between his parents. Daniel Junior couldn't say that his parents fought often or violently; it was more of an ongoing, uncomfortable truce where both parties gravitated towards actions that would help them avoid the other. For nearly twenty years, Amanda spent several days a week, sometimes the whole week, at Daniel's parents' home in Jonesboro, which was close to her job and convenient for the care of their autistic daughter, Emily. Amanda and Emily almost always came home to Harrisburg for the weekends; Daniel was almost always there, and they both acted civil, especially around their children. Daniel Junior could even remember times when they seemed almost like a normal family and would enjoy their dinner views of the pond, the woods, and the animals. Now that Daniel Junior and Nate had moved away, he hoped that the weekend dinner rituals continued, because his sister Emily so enjoyed the wildlife visiting the pond in the evenings. Daniel Junior knew that his sister was traveling with their grandparents to Cincinnati from Jonesboro a day earlier than the rest of the family, so his parents would be driving by themselves. He couldn't imagine his parents alone in a car together for eight hours. Brigette tried to convince him that the time alone together might be beneficial for his parents, but Daniel Junior only foresaw disaster and persuaded Brigette to make the detour to his parents' cabin home just to help ensure the weekend would unfold as uneventfully as possible.

All of the Lassermans were in the Cincinnati neighborhood of Mount Adams by early afternoon on Saturday. Luke, Mavis, and Emily had arrived in time for dinner the night before, and twenty-four old Emily was so enjoying all her cousins, especially Jessica, who was now eighteen and closest in age to Emily. Jessica was cordial and pleasant with Emily but found it terribly difficult to relate to her autistic, older cousin. Ted, on the other hand, though only thirteen, was extremely patient and understanding with Emily. By early Saturday, the two of them had even worked out some sort of secret code that was only witnessed by others as a raised-eyebrow glance from Ted which would send Emily into a sustained fit of laughter. That part was enjoyed by everyone, but inevitably following the laughter, came a huge mood swing, and Emily could only be comforted by her Grandma Mavis. For her part, Grandma Mavis was getting anxious for her daughter-in-law to arrive so that the attention that Emily required could be shared between the two of them.

Grandma Eva, Maria's mother, had taken on the role of general caretaker for the weekend and was ensuring that food was ready when needed, clothes were being washed and pressed, and schedules were being kept. Eva was quite fond of Mavis, her son-in-law's mother. The two of them had quite a lot in common; close in age, becoming mothers young in life, undying devotion to their grandchildren. But Eva did worry that Mavis always seemed so tired.

Eva and Mavis met for the first time almost twenty years previous at Don and Maria's wedding. The two got along easily from their very first meeting, but even then, Eva worried about Mavis' state of being. Unlike Eva who was the perpetual optimist and Pollyanna, Mavis carried herself in a somewhat bedraggled state. She wasn't a pessimist or a downer in any way, just consistently tired or overwhelmed. Eva believed there were many likely causes for the way Mavis plodded through life. One cause was likely the extra twenty or thirty pounds that Mavis carried on her five-foot-four frame. Another factor was that Mavis, unlike Eva, had a career outside the home. Mavis only subbed as a teacher one or two days per week, but, still, it was a burden that Eva had never carried. And then, of course, was the added responsibility of three grandchildren hovering around her all the time. At the time of Maria's wedding, Mavis had two grandsons, ages 10 and 11, running in and out and all around her all the time, as well as a five-year old granddaughter who never strayed far from her grandmother; in fact, she sat on her lap as much and as often as possible. Eva had desperately wanted to be a grandmother some day in the near future, but when she considered how heavy that role seemed to weigh on Mavis at this time, she wondered if grandparenting was as wonderful as she envisioned. Now, Eva was that grandmother that she wanted to be. Her three treasures were well beyond toddler years. Jessica was eighteen and a freshman at Oberlin College. Jasmine was sixteen, an excellent student, and totally dedicated to horses. And Teddy, her youngest grandchild at thirteen, was a shy and quiet boy, but definitely the light of her life. Eva and Teddy had always been close, but since her husband Wilfred died two years ago, grandma and grandson were nearly constant companions and cohorts.

Nate, Donna, and the twin toddlers arrived at lunchtime on Saturday. Uncle Don was thrilled to get reacquainted with his youngest nephew and meet his wife and babies. Don commented that Donna was so beautiful and reminded him of his mother Mavis when she was younger. Don explained that while his mother was nearly half a foot shorter than Donna, and that their respective blonde and auburn hair set them apart, they both had deep, green eyes as well as shapely, sharp angular noses and wide smiles. Nate said he recalled seeing pictures of his grandmother as a young woman but since the pictures were only in black-and-white and faded, fuzzy, silver prints, he had never noticed the resemblances to his wife.

The last to arrive that day were Daniel and Amanda driven by Daniel Junior with his young family. Grandma Eva adored Amanda, always had, but she generally kept her distance from Daniel. She was never a fan of alcohol consumption, and Daniel's excessive intake was more than sufficient to cause Eva to give wide berth. She could never fathom how someone she found so repulsive could be surrounded by so many wonderful people. She reasoned that perhaps everyone in Daniel's inner and outer circles needed to be extra wonderful to compensate for Daniel's boorish and often obnoxious drunken states of being. And she also could never fathom how her son-in-law and his twin brother could look so similar yet not possibly be more different in personality and behavior. Mavis had once told her that Don and Daniel, while always close growing up, had shown clear signs of distinct personalities at a young age. Even as infants, Mavis said, Don was the easier to care for and the one more likely to find contentment in toys, activities, playmates, and parental attention. Daniel always seemed to need more care and attention but also exhibited far less curiosity and imagination. As teenagers, Mavis was not sure which son to worry about more. When not at school or the track field, Don was frequently engrossed in increasingly dangerous activities; at least they were dangerous in a mother's eyes. Don loved his BMX bike, his skateboards, kayaking, rock climbing, trail hiking, and riding. And she worried more when he got his first

car, a 1959 Ford Fairlane convertible, and then, due to
a major transmission failure on the Ford, his second
car less than a year later; a very-used 1965 Plymouth
Barracuda, which he always seemed to be driving at
its limits. Mavis could hear that car from three blocks
away, a very loud and annoying sound, but also the
most comforting sound as she knew he was returning home safe once again. She was silently thankful
when the transmission dropped just after high school
graduation and that ferocious mechanical beast was
hauled away to the scrap yard. The Fairlane sat at
the back of their yard, behind the garage, as Don and
Luke always insisted they could repair it.

With Daniel, Mavis never had worries of this
nature. He was much more predictable and far less
adventurous, at least relative to extreme sports and
fast cars, than his twin brother was. Daniel preferred to 'just hang' as he put it nearly every day
when Mavis asked what he was doing or where he
was going. This usually meant the Walgreen's parking lot on Highland Drive, which was convenient
to a neighborhood grocery store that sold beer and
rolling papers. Mavis didn't know how Daniel and
his friends convinced college-age boys to buy beer
for them, but she preferred it to an alternative route
she learned about later when a bar maid friend of
her called with shocking news. Just down the road

from Walgreen's, on Industrial Drive, was a local bar and grill frequented by shift workers at the nearby metal fabrication plants. Daniel and his posse were seen combing through the bottle bins behind the bar at night and aggregating the liquid remnants of any bottle. A few drops from several dozen empty beer bottles would quickly add up a full bottle or two. The same with discarded wine and liquor bottles. Mavis was horrified at the thought of the rodents and roaches that must pore over those same bottles before and during they boys' reclamation activities and offered to buy beer for her fifteen-year old son if he would vow to never climb in a garbage receptacle again. Luke, however, disagreed with this approach, negated the offer, grounded Daniel for two months, and actually put him to work every Saturday morning collecting garbage working for Luke's high school friend Kevin Laymon who now ran a garbage collection business.

"But, dad," Daniel had whined, "Mom says it's not a problem. I'm just being a kid."

"It's not often that I disagree with your mother, but I think this will be one of the important lessons in your life. You need to be responsible and doing hard work for Mr. Laymon will serve you well." Luke calmly implored, not knowing if his heavy-handed approach would work or stick. Daniel stomped off to his room in a rage and popped two screws on the bedroom door hinge with the force of his slamming.

Luke figured that more exposure to more disgusting garbage would dissuade his son from collecting and drinking bar patrons' leftovers. If this approach was successful, Luke and Mavis never knew, but at least they never caught him at it again.

The entire crew of Lassermans, thirteen in all, plus Maria's mother Eva, Daniel Junior's baby Rebecca, and Nate's three-year old toddler twins, arrived at Ivy Hills promptly at six p.m. The club had decorated a private room following suggestions from Eva to make it resemble a Hawaiian luau. The buffet tables were skirted with grass. The entrees included a suckling pig in addition to chicken, grilled pineapples, and poi, which Mavis remarked tasty a bit like grits that had been reheated the third time. The servers, male and female, wore grass skirts mimicking the buffet tables. And everyone received a greeting with a lei upon entering the room. Don Ho strummed his ukulele via a CD in the background. Just as the cocktail hour was ending, and the family was making their way to their seats, a tall, lean, muscular black man with wisps of gray at his temples and a Hollywood-perfect smile of large, perfectly-straight teeth entered the room and strode right up to Don Lasserman. The two embraced warmly and chatted and laughed for many seconds before Don walked the man to the long banquet table to introduce him to his twin brother and other family members.

"I'd like you to meet my twin brother Daniel," Don said as they arrived at the table. "And this is his darling wife Amanda." Amanda rose to shake the man's hand, unlike her husband who not only had not risen when the guest arrived but also did not receive the man's proffered hand. The man shook Amanda's hand warmly as he also bent in for a formal peck on her cheek. Amanda blushed. Don then went around the table indicating the names and relationships of the others, his parents, his nephews, their families.

"Everyone, this is a very good friend of mine, Congressman Richard Adamo. I'll be serving as campaign chair for his upcoming re-election campaign next year." Don beamed as he panned the table with all his family. Everyone was dutifully impressed and clapping politely except for one twin brother now substantially inebriated.

"Congressman?" Daniel managed to articulate despite his drunken slurs. "I thought you were the hostess, or whatever you call it when you're a man."

Don moved to silence his twin, but Amanda beat him to it. "Daniel, that's ridiculous! You apologize to this wonderful, gracious man right now!"

"What do I have to apologize for?" Daniel confusedly pondered. "Blacks only dress up when they're serving white people."

"Richard, I am so, so sorry. I'm afraid my brother has been drinking too much in celebration of our half century mark," Don said to his friend while grasping his arm to guide him from the room. But the Congressman had another plan. He slipped from Don's loose grip and made his way directly to Daniel, still seated and unaware of the tension he had created. Congressman Adamo placed his left hand on Daniel's right shoulder, leaned in, and said, "In fact, it is my pleasure and honor to be of service to all the people of Ohio, including the white ones." He smiled, and with his right hand he reached for Amanda's right hand to pull her in for another cheek peck as he repeated, "a pleasure and an honor".

With that, the congressional representative left the room and the room immediately fell into disarray as Daniel's parents, wife, and children all lit into him with one castigation after another. Don deflated as he sat down next to his wife who reached for his hand and patted it comfortingly. Don was equally disappointed and boiling with rage at his brother's behavior, but years of experience taught him that all the finger-pointing and shaming of Daniel going on around him right now was of no use. This was simply

who his brother was when he was drunk and who he
would continue to be. Daniel would most likely have
no recollection of it in the morning and certainly no
remorse.

CHAPTER *Five*

I f Don ever worried that his friendship and status with the Congressman was in jeopardy, he needn't have. A week after the birthday celebration, Don and Richard were at a charity fundraiser at the University of Cincinnati Cancer Institute where Adamo, actually *Dr.* Adamo, had been on staff as on oncologist years before he entered the political arena to realize his passion of fixing the country's inefficient and super-expensive health care system. Don tried his best to apologize again for his brother's conduct at the birthday fete, but the Congressman simply said there was no need and not to mention it again. And neither of them ever did. Their friendship continued and thrived along with the highly successful re-election bid. Adamo won his third congressional term with fifty-eight percent of the vote with the remaining forty-two percent being split between two other candidates. Three months after the election, Ohio's junior senator died in a boating accident while on vacation with his family in St. John, U.S. Virgin Islands. The governor named Congressman Adamo to serve out the senator's remaining term, and, thus, Senator Richard Adamo was created.

Barely getting his feet wet as the newest member of the Senate, Adamo was stupefied when the national chairwoman of his party called on him one sun-filled, early Spring day with a request for a lunch date. They met at the Charlie Palmer Steak restaurant on Constitution Avenue where Chairwoman Bushwick had arranged a private and secluded table. After normal social bantering, Chairwoman Bushwick leaned in close and said, "Richard, we want you on the ticket next year." She never took her eyes from his. The chairwoman stood just five feet, four inches tall, but anyone who knew her knew not to underestimate her strength and determination. Her soft, blemish-free, light brown skin could pass for black, Hispanic, or well-tanned Caucasian, but her tight Afro belied her true roots, and her deep, black eyes were known to make many a journalist quiver when trying to get the upper hand in an interview.

"I'm flabbergasted, Charlene. I've never thought about the vice-presidency. I'm still rather new at this. And we don't even have a presidential candidate yet," murmured Adamo, while also barely maintaining her intense gaze.

That intense gaze intensified as she spoke deliberately and pleadingly, "Actually, I'm hoping we do have a presidential candidate. We want *you* on the *top* of the ticket."

Now Adamo broke the gaze as he slowly straightened and looked around for something else to focus on. Charlene remained silent and intent and let Richard take his time gathering his thoughts and concerns. At long last, Adamo let out a breath that had been held too long and simply said, "Let me think about it." The party chairwoman nodded and said, "We'll be in touch soon then." She stood, shook Adamo's hand, made some sort of sign to the maître d who nodded affirmatively, and she strolled out of the restaurant and into a waiting town car that whisked her away immediately. Freshman Senator Adamo sat alone pensively for many minutes after Charlene left. The waiter brought two more iced teas before Adamo called his wife to ensure she had no plans for the evening. She assured him she would be at home but also conveyed that the children would not be home until later as they were at a school play rehearsal until 8 p.m. A small, but promising, smile intruded upon his russet-colored lips as he said, "Perfect" into his new smartphone and tapped it off. Late that afternoon, in his office in the Russell Senate Office Building, just up the street from Charlie Palmer Steak, Adamo received a shock via an unexpected phone call. His secretary seemed somewhat nervous as she buzzed him on the intercom. "President Rinehart, for you, sir." Rinehart was not the current president, but the last president from Adamo's own party who completed his two terms seven years previous. Adamo pushed the first line button on his office phone.

"President Rinehart, what a surprise, I just…"

"Call me Bill," the former president bellowed in his mild southern drawl. "I'm hoping we'll be working quite closely in the months ahead." Adamo could picture Rinehart's perpetually smiling face, strawberry-tinted, plump cheeks, massive bleach-white teeth, and ocean of wavy white hair as the man spoke.

"Sir, uh Bill, I don't…"

"Bushwick tells me she had a very productive lunch with you today and we're all very excited," the former president continued as though he had not heard Adamo's attempt to speak.

"Bill, I need to…"

"Yes, yes, of course. Discuss it with your family. Think about it overnight and we'll talk again in the morning." And with that, his new close ally was gone for the time being.

Adamo left the office without answering his secretary's numerous questions as to what the former president had called about. He arrived home much earlier than his usual time and well before dinner was ready. Normally, Makayla might have been alarmed to see her husband arrive at such a time, but she had astutely detected something exciting in his voice during their phone discussion earlier this afternoon. When she heard the garage door in operation, she fixed his usual dirty martini, using his favorite Hangar One vodka, and had it and herself waiting in the library.

She embraced him, pointed him to a seat on the sofa in front of his martini, and grabbed her own cocktail glass. She sat in the armchair perpendicular to his position and said, "Tell me all about it."

He looked at his wife of twenty-six years, her rich cocoa skin, her manicured and lacquered nails, her soft, full, red lips, her tight body reflecting her Pilates addiction, her seductive and imploring, dark brown eyes, and said, "They want me to run for president."

Makayla dropped her glass and her jaw at the same time. The broken glass also broke the flow of their conversation as paper towels, a broom, and a dustpan were secured and put to work. Following this commotion, they returned to the commotion that had triggered this one and discussed the pros and cons for over an hour.

Finally, Makayla asked, "So, what are you going to tell Rinehart in the morning?"

"I still don't know. It's all so much, so soon, so overwhelming. What do you think?"

"Let's call Don," she suggested. So, they did. Despite the Lassermans having moved to Connecticut and Don being at least as busy as an elected official, the Adamos had remained in close contact with their good friends from Cincinnati. Don was elated to hear from his treasured friend. Their friendship had started quite innocuously. One Saturday morning, nearly twenty years ago, Don had shown up at Ivy Hills for his usual eight a.m. tee time. It was eerily quiet at the club and only one other member from his foursome was there. So, he waited. At the same time, Dr. Richard Adamo had shown up at the club as a guest, and he was seated at the bar with a glass of orange juice waiting for his foursome. Eventually, one other doctor from his foursome showed up, but he, too, was a guest. The resident golf pro reported that there was a multi-car crash out on I-275 near the Route 32 interchange that had created a huge backup, so anyone traveling to the club from the east or south was going to be very late. Don had come in on Route 32 from the west, and Adamo had traveled down

Route 50 from his home in Milford to the north. After confirming that there were no serious injuries in the crash, the two half-foursomes got together, created an impromptu foursome, and played their round of golf that day. Don and Richard got along famously from the first tee, and their families became close and remained close to this day.

"To what do I owe this honor, Senator?" teased Don on the phone from his study in Stamford. Richard had placed the call via speakerphone and Makayla spoke first with vigor. "Don, they want him to run for president."

Several seconds of silence ensued before Richard queried, "So what do you think?"

Don replied with hope in his voice, "Do I get to help with the campaign?"

"Want to be my northeast chair?" Adamo answered.

"Then I say let's get started!" exhorted Don. The three of them talked for several more minutes about concerns, potential pitfalls, even potential campaign slogans, before disconnecting.

"So, future first lady, what's on the menu tonight?" asked Adamo playfully.

"Oh, I didn't prepare anything," she replied coolly. "I'll order Chinese to be here for when the kids get home."

And with that they returned to their everyday life.

It wasn't Rinehart who called in the morning, but Bushwick. She called Adamo's office at exactly ten a.m. and asked if he was ready with his decision. Adamo had many questions, which she answered, and he had a few conditions, which she readily agreed to, and then they were off. Off the phone, and off and running. The next nineteen months were a blur in Adamo's mind. There were so many meetings, speeches, rallies, debates, then a convention and more meetings, speeches, rallies and debates. And so, so much travel. Adamo literally had trouble remembering what city was before him when he spoke at rallies. Fortunately, Makayla proved to be quite the trooper for the campaign trail and she always seemed to know where they were on any given day. Makayla had taken leave from her law firm to be on the campaign trail, and her mother, Lenora, a retired social worker and widow, moved into her daughter's home to be full-time caretaker of her grandchildren when Richard and Makayla couldn't be there. Not that they needed much care. The three teenagers were involved in nearly every sport and activity at school, so Lenora sometimes felt she was just their housekeeper, preparing meals for the refrigerator, doing laundry, and tidying up their bedrooms. But she was grateful for the few moments, here and there, that she could capture with her two granddaughters and grandson.

Don and his family were with the Adamos at the Hilton Cincinnati on Netherland Plaza on election night to hear the returns. Just fifteen minutes after the CNN announcement that Adamo would be president, Don's phone rang displaying a familiar number, one he hadn't seen in months. Ever since the debacle at their joint fiftieth birthday celebration, Don and his twin, Daniel, only spoke infrequently, only briefly, and never about anything meaningful, certainly never about the party fiasco or an apology. Don had no sooner hit the talk button and said, "Hello, brother," before being confronted with, "You must be awfully proud of yourself getting that damn waiter elected president. God help us." And with that, Daniel hung up. Don looked quizzically at the phone for many seconds before chalking it up to another drunken stupor and rant before rejoining his family and the Adamos in the celebration.

The next eight years passed rather professionally and calmly. President Adamo served admirably with no major scandals in his administration and achieved many notable achievements despite an adversarial Congress that presented obstacles at every opportunity. Entering office on the heels of a massive recession caused by lax regulations in the financial industry and great greed of corporate and banking executives, Adamo and his team enacted prudent financial industry controls and turned the economy around. In fact, the eight years of the Adamo Administration turned out to be one of the most productive and profitable economic periods of American history.

Significant gains were also made in areas of foreign diplomacy and global trade and cooperation, ultimately even including the normalization of travel and diplomatic relations with long-time pariah, Cuba, as well as mandated improvements in immigration, especially for children of illegal immigrants who were born in America. President Adamo and Congress agreed that these individuals should not be under ongoing threat of deportation, and in fact, should have a reasonable path to citizenship. Adamo significantly curtailed American troop involvement in a long-running Middle East war following the September 11, 2001 terrorist attacks in New York City, Washington, DC, and Pennsylvania. A key mastermind of the terrorist attacks was finally tracked down and killed and terrorist activities were largely kept away from the American homeland throughout Adamo's tenure. Adamo advocated for many improvements in areas of fuel efficiency standards, use of renewable resources for fuel, reductions in dependencies on foreign oil, and global agreements on mitigating effects of climate change. Advancements were also made on many social issues, such as increased funding for birth control education and services, same-sex marriage rights for gays and lesbians, and inclusive dialogue for transgender individuals and their equal rights.

A key party platform plank that was realized early in the Adamo first term was health care for all. For too long over twenty million Americans lacked health care insurance due to unaffordable access and unreasonable restrictions related to pre-existing conditions and discriminatory definitions relative to various health conditions, including mental health. The successful passage of the Accessibility Defined and Advanced Medical Opportunities for All Health Care Act was a major struggle for Congress and the public. Many compromises and accommodations were comprehended in the final version of the bill. Health care administration was left in the hands of the health insurance industry and more flexibility and authority was provided for the insurers to define and pay claims. And there was an effort to help make medical education more affordable and effective, hence the 'medical opportunities' portion of the Act. The intent was to bring more qualified health care workers into the profession and to reduce the educational debt burden for medical professionals, which then had to be recouped through the cost of the health care they provided. The health care act also included limitations on malpractice suits and a process to pursue such claims.

However, many lobbyists and special interest groups effectively convinced a sizable percentage of the American public that the Health Care Act would cost them money. They basically painted 'affordable health care' for all as yet another government social welfare program built on the backs of hard-working, everyday Americans to benefit historically dependent and undeserving others, the others being seen as immigrants, poor, unemployed, disabled and welfare recipients. Furthermore, the fact that the official name of the Act included an acronym actually spelling out ADAMO was just like waving raw meat in front of Adamo's rabid detractors. Although the President always maintained that he was not aware of the inadvertent acronym at the time of design and passage, it was too late to mitigate the damage caused by the now-labeled Adamocare.

Repeal of Adamocare became a rallying cry for the opposition and further fertilized the seeds of resentment that had been sown during the presidential campaign. Although no serious and credible opposition candidates ever expressed blatant racist statements during the many debates or other speaking opportunities, the country did see the rise of many new faces in the local and state political arenas, and even in national circles, that had close ties to organizations with radical racist views or beliefs of supremacy of one race over all others. The political atmosphere did not present an outright attack along racist lines, but there was a simmering boil just below the surface. Many of these new faces browbeat some of the old guard in the opposition party to create a 'Repeal Adamocare' at all costs movement. They viewed Adamocare, as well as all the other social advances and globalization gains enabled by Adamo as coming at the expense of hard working, every day, mostly white, Americans.

During the Adamo years, Don continued working as a Managing Director at Morgan Stanley in New York and also as a non-paid, casual advisor to his friend, the President. His twin brother, Daniel, continued his sporadic work schedule at the poultry-processing plant and rarely spoke to Don. When he did, he was always drunk and always had some deep-seated, emotional complaint about the President, his policies, his conduct, his appearance, really anything associated with President Richard Adamo. Don also tried to engage in conversation on less volatile topics, including the well-being of

Daniel's wife, children and grandchildren, but Daniel seemed to have lost interest in such trivial matters and would always resort to condemning Adamo for anything and everything he perceived to be wrong in the world. Occasionally, Don would try to engage in deeper dialogue with Daniel to try to get to the root cause of his political complaint or concerns, but these efforts were futile.

"What about the President's speech last night did you find offensive, Daniel?" Don would inquire.

"He's got no business laying out a military strategy for our boys in Afghanistan. Why can't he just leave them alone to do their job?" Daniel would lament.

"As President, he's commander-in-chief of the military. It's his job to define the strategy."

"He ain't got no business being commander-in-chief. He should stick to something he's better suited for."

"Like what, Daniel? It's a big job," Don would explain with growing annoyance.

"He seems fine at the White House Christmas tour I saw last year. Of course, his wife did most of the talking." said Daniel, referring to the traditional behind-the-scenes holiday special focusing on the White House decorations and entertainment events.

"Daniel, have you ever considered that you just don't like the President because he's black?" inquired Don.

"Don't you go calling me a racist again. I grew up just like you, and you know we lived in a racially-mixed neighborhood. We used to play with some of them boys."

"I didn't call you a racist, but I think you might have some racist tendencies. I think we all do, but we must do what we can to overcome such internal biases," explained Don as patiently as he could.

And so their occasional conversations would go, centered around whatever latest trigger had set Daniel afire. In reality, Daniel really didn't consider himself to be a racist. It was true that he had played with some of them boys as a child in their Jonesboro neighborhood. And it was true that he considered this a happy part of his troubled childhood. Many of his teenage crowd, including the bar dumpster-diving troop, were black. He even drank from the same dirty beer bottles and liquor bottles. Many of his Army buddies were black and he had no issues serving with them, except for the one lieutenant colonel at Fort Leonard Wood, but he was just an ass, not because he was black. And at the poultry plant, he worked side-by-side with some of them and enjoyed break room banter with them, even shooting pool with them after work at whatever pool hall or road-side bar they might end up in. In fact, if he was being honest about it, at least twice that he could recall, he'd ended up with a black girl at one of the Memphis whorehouses when none of his usual white girls was available. Yes, in Daniel's mind, he was certainly one of the least racist people he knew.

Of course, Daniel's view of the world was rather limited and his interactions with blacks was almost always in a manner that did not cause him any discomfort. His world did not include blacks in a position of authority that might directly affect him, except, again, that Army lieutenant colonel at the base so many years ago who was just a bad person, not a bad black person. At the chicken plant, Daniel worked *with* blacks, but he would never work *under* one. Daniel didn't foresee this as any sort of future threat, because the plant was owned and run by a traditional white family of many generations. He also simply couldn't envision blacks in a management position near him. If Daniel could step back and objectively assess his views of blacks, he would eventually see that he was indeed okay with blacks as long as they conformed to his expectations of them, and he certainly didn't expect, or accept, that one of them would be living and ruling in the White House.

During the eight Adamo years, the collective Lasserman family experienced quite a few ups and downs. The Stamford Lassermans were thriving. Don commuted into Manhattan daily, usually via Metro North Railroad, but, if he had a special need, like picking up a client or heading to one of the New York City airports during the day, he would take advantage of one of the firm's chauffeured town cars. Don owned several cars. One was a jet-black BMW M5 coupe that he enjoyed driving on fall and spring weekends. One was a silver 2016 Mercedes GLE 350 which he used in the winter months or when Maria or the kids accompanied him. And his special, favorite car was a professionally-restored, frame-off restoration, yellow 1965 Plymouth Barracuda with bright red and orange flames on the hood, fenders and doors. As a teenager, Don had a white '65 'Cuda that he ran hard, and he had always fantasized about the paint and color scheme that he now owned. His wife still drove, occasionally, her red 1999 Mazda Miata MX-5 that she had received from Don as a special gift for her fortieth birthday back when they lived in Cincinnati. Maria would never part with that car. For everyday needs, she typically used Don's GLE or the M5 if the GLE was not available. She had never driven the 'Cuda because she did not want to risk any damage to her husband's primary materialistic pride and joy, but also because she had never learned to drive a stick shift. Don had special-ordered the automatic transmission for her Miata which came standard with a 5-speed stick shift. He also ordered his 2014 M5 with the highly engineered, dual-clutch, seven-speed, automatic transmission with manual shift paddles so his wife could drive the car if needed, but he could still enjoy the thrill of speed and shift control for his weekend driving pleasures.

Teddy, or Ted, as he had preferred as an adult, was the only one of Don and Maria's three children to do any of his growing up in the North Stamford home they had purchased ten years ago. Ted had attended Westhill High School for his senior year and moved out of the Stamford house when he left for Boston University to pursue a BFA in Stage Management. It was debatable who was more traumatized by Ted going off to college—his mother, Grandma Eva, or Ted himself. They all cried-a lot-and even stalwart Don shed a tear or two as he, his wife, and mother-in-law drove away from BU's main campus in the Kenmore neighborhood of Boston, not far from the famed Fenway Park. To everyone's happy surprise, Ted took well to college and dormitory life. His roommate was a nerdy, science geek, pale and skinny with a witch's nose and a wizard's glasses, from Springfield, Massachusetts. He and Ted respected each other's insularity while simultaneously being there for unspoken support for one another when the highly charged, extroverted forces of the campus and its hormone-laden residents became too much for one or both of them. Ted and his roommate, Brad, were always together when not in classes. They ate meals together, visited the bookstore together, went to the library and computer lab together. Maria was pleased that her son had a new best friend, possibly his only friend, and his first best friend, not counting Grandma Eva. The Lassermans visited their son in Boston about every three weeks. Maria preferred to stay at the Residence Inn by Marriott in Boston's Back Bay area, not far from Ted's university and convenient to all the cultural activities that Beantown had to offer. She liked this location, because it was easy to get into and out of, which was important on the occasions when she drove if Don couldn't get away from some commitment in Stamford or Manhattan. Grandma Eva never missed an opportunity to come along.

Ted's coming out to his family was both remarkable and unremarkable. It was remarkable, because it happened in an instant, and it happened to all of them, including Ted, at the same time. It was unremarkable, because it happened without a single word being said and acceptance occurring with simple knowing nods and smiles. It was during one of the family's Boston visits; actually, it was Thanksgiving weekend of Ted's sophomore year, while Brad was at home in Springfield with his family. Ted had wanted to stay at the University over the Thanksgiving break due to some schoolwork he was behind on as well as a stage backdrop that needed his attention. Maria and Eva were happy to have a reprieve from the usual, lengthy feast preparation for a change. Besides, there was a new Cezanne exhibit at the art museum that Don, Eva, and Maria wanted to see.

They had all enjoyed a fantastic meal of turkey and the traditional holiday accompaniments at Parker's downtown the previous day, and this evening, they enjoyed a fine Italian meal at Davio's on Arlington before heading across Boston Common to attend a performance of The Nutcracker at the Boston Opera House. The Boston Ballet was phenomenal, and everyone was thoroughly enjoying the performance. At intermission, the family headed to the bar for drinks and snacks when the coming-out event happened just like a script from a cheesy romcom movie. Ted was surveying the snack options when he reached to his side with his right hand expecting to grasp his grandmother's hand. Instead, as he turned he found he was holding the left hand of a tall, lithe, beautiful young man about his own age. Their eyes locked. Their entwined fingers did likewise. Neither moved or breathed, for several seconds. Finally, the stranger, unaware of Ted's family standing slack-jawed just feet away, said, "Hey, I'm Jamie. I'm with some friends up in the balcony, and there are empty seats nearby if you want to join us." Ted blushed, thought about the proposal for three seconds, then turned and began to speak in a pleading voice, "Mom, is it..." Maria smiled and said, "We'll see you out front after the ballet," and as she, her mother, and husband turned to return to the orchestra section, they all had eyes glistening with joy like dew on the morning grass. They had always known Ted to be quiet, somewhat reclusive, so it was fulfilling to see that unspoken veil of secrecy being shattered and his enigmatic personality blossoming to life.

After the ballet, Don, Maria and Grandma Eva met Ted and Jamie out front as agreed. From there, they took a short walk to jm Curley pub for drinks, snacks, and a highly anticipated conversation. They had never seen Ted in such a lively and animated way.

Maria began, "Did you boys enjoy the second act?"

And from there, Jamie took over, "Oh my yes. I've been so looking forward to this performance. I'm a dancer myself, studying at the Boston Conservancy. I'm so happy I came tonight." And with that last sentence, Jamie glanced at Ted and squeezed his hand under the table.

"I'm surprised you didn't go home for the holiday break," Grandma Eva said. "Is your home far from Boston?"

"My parents live in Tampa," Jamie stated, "but they took advantage of the long weekend to visit my grandparents in our native St. Lucia. My mom's parents live in Soufriere, and my dad's mother lives in Castries. So, they're busy driving the island this weekend to visit all the relatives."

"It's a beautiful island," offered Don.

"And I love the Pitons," added Maria.

Don continued, "It's a shame you're not able to be visiting your grandparents and cousins."

"Yeah, I miss them, and it would have been nice to visit, but it's a long and expensive trip from here. And the weekend here is turning out to be very enjoyable," responded Jamie, and with that, there was another hand squeeze under the table.

After drinks, some bar snacks, and over an hour of additional conversation, Don, Maria, and Grandma Eva all hugged Ted good-night and headed outside to get a cab back to the hotel. They made plans to go to the Museum of Fine Art in the morning, and it was Grandma Eva who leaned back towards her grandson and his new friend and said, "Jamie, we'd be delighted if you'd join us tomorrow." Ted beamed with delight and hugged his grandmother once again as Jamie replied that he would indeed be joining the family.

The next year was full of momentous events for the Stamford Lassermans. In May, they returned to the Cincinnati area, along with Grandma Eva, to attend their middle child's college graduation. Jasmine had completed her equine business studies at the University of Louisville and had already been offered a full-time job at Claiborne Farm in nearby Paris, Kentucky. Following their trip to Louisville, Don and Maria took a three-week trip to Asia with plenty of time in Hong Kong to visit their oldest child. Jessica had been living in Hong Kong for nearly three years, was working for the Bank of China as a financial analyst, and was greatly enjoying all of her work experiences. But she was also enjoying her social life. Jessica was thrilled to surprise her parents by introducing them to her fiancé Alex Yip, or more completely, Alex Yip Yiu Kwok, a Hong Kong resident. Jessica herself had been surprised the night before her parents' arrival when Alex popped the question at one of their favorite restaurants in Kowloon. Alex said he wanted to have some official status when he got to meet her mom and dad.

"Mom, Dad, this is Alex, my boyfriend," Jessica started. Alex quickly interrupted with a smile, "Fiancé as of yesterday."

Maria was first to recover her proper speaking voice after the delightful surprise. "Alex, we are so happy to meet you." And Don promptly followed suit by embracing Alex closely and whispering loudly in his ear, "You'd better be good to my little girl." They all laughed comfortably and then headed off to lunch at The Peak Lookout restaurant.

In October of that year, Don's mother Mavis, went to bed after bidding the last of the trick-or-treaters good-night and simply stopped breathing. While the official cause of death was listed as respiratory failure, her doctor told Luke it was as if she was just too tired to go on. Both sons and all the grandchildren traveled to Jonesboro for the funeral. Even Jessica came all the way from Hong Kong with Alex. Luke was more withdrawn than Don or Daniel had ever seen their father, and they were both concerned about his state of being. Jessica pleaded with her grandfather to spend some time with her and her fiancé. "Grandpa, I would so love for you to drive us around Jonesboro and show us some of the local sights and maybe even where your electrical shop used to be. This is Alex' first trip to America." "Your father or Uncle Daniel can take you," was all Luke could muster before assertively affixing himself to a rocking chair on the front porch where he sat, he rocked, he stared.

For their part, the brothers bickered constantly when not consoling their father or greeting mourners. Daniel was particularly agitated that President Adamo appeared to be headed towards certain re-election in just a few days. Daniel's agitation was only amplified when, ten days later, his brother and family returned to Jonesboro two days after Election Day to arrange their father's unexpected funeral. Daniel's wife, Amanda, and their autistic daughter, Emily, had been staying with Luke and Mavis the week Mavis passed away. After her funeral, Amanda and Emily went to their cabin home in Harrisburg with Daniel. Two days later, Luke slumped over in his rocking chair on the front porch. "He was dead of heart failure before the EMTs arrived. It was as if his heart was broken, and there was no reason for it to keep beating," stated the neighbor from across the street who found Luke when he returned home from work. It was impossible to ascertain Daniel's state of mind over his father's passing, but he somehow seemed to blame it on the President. President Adamo had been re-elected with fifty-three percent of the popular vote and a near landslide in the Electoral College the day before Luke died. Daniel was convinced the country was doomed, and he kept spouting how horrible his life had become under Adamo, though he could site no specifics when pressed by Don.

Amanda Lasserman was only fifty-six years old when her in-laws passed away, but, without their support, she could not imagine how to care for Emily and keep her nursing job. Her husband, Daniel, could only be depended on to deliver disappointment, although his daily routines had become more predictable. Most days now, he would actually work a full day, then stop at one of a handful of bars or pool halls, almost like he had one favorite for each day of the week, and then he would somehow make it back to the cabin and sleep until the next morning. Amanda had long ago ceased preparing any meals for Daniel and assumed he just found sufficient nourishment somewhere.

So, Amanda took an early retirement from the Baptist Clinic in order to stay home to care for Emily. And for the next two years, Amanda simply cared for herself and her daughter. She prepared meals just for the two of them and tolerated Daniel for the limited interactions they had. Weekends were a fifty-fifty crapshoot as to whether or not Daniel would be around the cabin or shacking up somewhere in Memphis. Amanda missed Jonesboro, but she really did enjoy the cabin and most especially the newfound joy that Emily always demonstrated when watching wild animals at the pond. Amanda did not want to take Emily away from that as it seemed to be her only joy in life following the death of her grandparents.

But Amanda's plan for a peaceful, stable future for her daughter did not go as planned. Just a little over a year after her father-in-law's funeral, Amanda took ill. After cursory treatment at an emergency clinic in Harrisburg, the doctors found what they suspected to be cervical cancer, and she asked to be taken to Baptist Cancer Center in Memphis where she would be close to her eldest son and his family. Amanda hoped her daughter-in-law would be willing to take Emily in until Amanda recovered and was able to care for her daughter on her own. Brigette not only graciously agreed to take in her husband's thirty-three-year-old autistic sister, but she also insisted they hire a full-time home nurse who could assist with Amanda's care. The nurse would also help with the general care of Emily as well as Daniel Junior and Brigette's own children, nine-year old Rebecca and four-year old Tanya. This arrangement went on for six months while Amanda did her best to fight the cancer. Emily was often tense and unsettled during her mother's hospital stays but calmer when Amanda was at home in her son's house. Daniel Junior was well aware of Emily's endless fascination with the wild animals at the pond outside their cabin home, so he would take Emily to the Memphis Zoo as often as he could to help dissipate the brewing tensions within his home. Emily particularly enjoyed the giraffes, flamingoes, and, of course, bears, as they were one of her special delights when she would see them by the pond at home. During these six months, Daniel the elder would stop by on most weekends to check on the well-being of his wife and daughter, but seldom stayed for more than an hour and never spent the night in his son's home. Amanda passed away in early December, less than a month after her fifty-eighth birthday.

It was at Amanda's funeral that Brigette confided to her husband's Aunt Maria that she was concerned for the future of Emily. Daniel Junior and Brigette had been happy to provide a home for Emily for the past six months with the support of the home nursing aide, but Brigette didn't think they could sustain that for much longer. She worried that Emily would have to be placed in an assisted-living facility since her father had shown little interest in his daughter or ability to provide the care and attention she required. Aunt Maria patted her hand and told her not to worry; they would work something out. That evening at the hotel, Maria asked Don if they could take Emily in. At first, Don hesitated and then listed many reasons that Emily required better care than they could provide. But Maria persisted and cited her social work background, her years of volunteer work including the Southfield Development Center in neighboring Darien, Connecticut, and her current void of responsibilities now that Ted was out of the house and living in Arlington with Jamie where they both worked at theater jobs in Boston. Don, always a quick study, grasped that his loving and beautiful wife was really pleading with him to help her fill her emptiness now that all their children were grown and on their own. Furthermore, he knew his wife was lonely at home, especially when her mother, Grandma Eva, was traveling with one of her women's groups, which was now more often than not. He wasn't sure what life would be like with a four-year old child living in a thirty-three-old woman's body around the house, but he was willing to give it a try.

As so life continued on peacefully for the Stamford Lassermans, including Emily, for the next two years; the final two years of the Adamo presidency. Emily took easily to living in Stamford. She gravitated easily and often to Grandma Eva who possibly reminded her of her other grandmother, the late Mavis. Emily would usually throw minor tantrums when Eva would leave for yet another tourism sojourn. Emily's transition was also made easier by the large koi pond Don and Maria had on their property. It wasn't visible from their kitchen table, but it was just a short walk behind the pool to a shady seating area around the pond filled with the bright orange and mottled white fish. Emily loved to sit there and watch the fish, the ubiquitous squirrels and chipmunks, the occasional ground hog, and the many ducks and other birds that would make appearances from time-to-time. Grandma Eva was alarmed when Emily emitted a loud, shrill shriek one day as a giant blue heron swooped down and grabbed one of the smaller fishes in its beak. But Eva sighed with relief and broke into a bit of laughter as she realized Emily was squealing with delight, not fear. Maria stayed home now as full-time caregiver for Emily and never regretted her commitment to do so. For Maria, in a way, it was like having a younger sister that she never had. It was rare that she felt sorry for herself that she was an only child, but it was so fulfilling to have a pseudo-sibling in Emily. Don was being called upon for advice less and less by his friend, the President, and when Adamo did call upon him, it was usually related to social matters of golf, travel, dining, or post-term residency. Don was

growing confident that his friend would take up residence in Connecticut or nearby Manhattan following
the next president's inauguration.

Life in the South was mostly peaceful for the
Daniel Lasserman family as well. Daniel Junior and
his wife Brigette welcomed a third daughter, Melanie,
and moved to a larger home in Memphis. They
purchased, and were actively renovating, a turn-
of-the-twentieth century, four-bedroom, American
Craftsman style, southern charmer in the Central
Gardens neighborhood just a few minutes' drive up
Poplar Avenue from the hospital where they both
worked. Nate and wife Donna had become quintes-
sential soccer parents in Huntsville to their twin sons
who were now driving age. And life was generally
good for Daniel Sr. It had not been a difficult transition for him following the death of his wife. From
an outsider's perspective, you might assume that he
had always been a bachelor. Although Daniel did not
particularly enjoy working at the poultry-processing
plant, it had become an intrinsic part of his routine
life: work, drink, sleep, repeat; fuck on weekends.

Daniel may not have realized it, but he really
didn't need to work. When his parents died four
years earlier, twin brother Don served as executor of
their estate. Their parents were not wealthy, but they
had owned their home for nearly five decades and it

had been paid off years ago. Somewhere along the way, Don didn't even know they had done it, Luke and Mavis had purchased two vacant lots adjacent to Luke's electric business, probably with dreams of future expansion in mind. Both the homestead and the electric shop with its adjacent vacant lots were now worth considerably more than when purchased. After settling all debts, Luke and Mavis' net estate was worth a bit more than six hundred thousand dollars. By the time, Don and his local lawyer were able to liquidate the real estate and move towards settling the estate, Amanda had died. Don knew Amanda had always handled the bills for herself and Daniel and he doubted that Daniel would be able to learn these new basic skills. So, Don had the lawyer put all of Daniel's share into a blind trust for Daniel's benefit and arranged for all of Daniel's bills to be directed to the trust for satisfaction. Daniel had very few bills. He had inherited the cabin and land from his grandfather and his life was very, very simple. So, Don had the property taxes, utilities, even gas station credit card paid directly by the trust. He doubted very much whether his brother ever gave a thought to how the bills were mysteriously paid, just as he probably had no recollection of the conversation that Don and the lawyer had with him when they estab-lished this arrangement and asked him to sign several documents. As for his share of the estate, Don had established trusts for each of his three children that they could access when they turned twenty-five. This would complement similar trusts he and Maria had established for their own estate.

If Daniel became aware of his trust fortune, he probably would have squandered it, some on whiskey and women, but probably also a substantial amount on his new burgeoning passion: Alexander Haight. The political and social tension that started growing significantly with President Adamo's first term was now in full bloom as the end of his presidency was in sight. Alexander Haight was considered a dark horse candidate, but he continually confounded his adversaries by deflecting any and all criticism cast his way. Haight was an extremely wealthy, secretive man who controlled his family's conglomerate of industrial and real estate holdings from his lofty office in Salt Lake City. Haight had no political experience and was disdained by both predominant political parties, so most political pundits discounted his chances of success, severely underestimating the appeal that his outsider status had with many Americans. Those same political pundits believed that Haight's crass and combative style would also prevent his ascension to the presidency. Once again, they were not connecting with the potential appeal that this style would have with a large number of disenfranchised Americans who had been wary of Washington's ability to govern and after nearly eight years of progressive policies. These policies brought change that they could not comprehend and they were downright frustrated and angry with the whole of Washington politics.

From the perspective of his opponents, Haight became synonymous with two primary negative traits. One was lying. During speeches and debates, Haight simply seemed to make up 'facts' that were convenient to his position. He didn't seem to care that fact-checkers would define these as outright lies within hours, or even minutes, of him spouting them. Haight even lied about his own ancestry. At a rally in California, he claimed to be a direct descendant of Henry Haight, a prominent nineteenth century pioneer, San Francisco banker, and namesake of Haight Street of Haight-Ashbury fame. At a debate in Rochester, New York, he claimed to be a direct descendant of Henry Huntly Haight, a nephew of the San Francisco Haight and a native of Rochester who went on to become the tenth governor of California. Haight would often site this familial connection as proof of his ability to govern. But, while in Charlottesville, Virginia, weeks later, candidate Haight claimed to be a descendant of another

Alexander Haight, a prominent Virginia plantation owner prior to the Civil War. Such disjointed claims incensed his detractors and sent the fact-checkers into frenzied research loops, but his supporters didn't seem to care one way or another. Haight was a master at inciting his supporters, mostly men like Daniel, at rallies. Daniel had traveled to several Haight rallies throughout the South and Midwest. He loved the fervor and message coming from candidate Haight, but he also found that there were many women of his standards attending these rallies. His motel rooms frequently devolved into dens of drunken debauchery with loose women and their male and female friends coming and going for hours. Daniel felt happy and excited for the future.

Alexander Haight's other negative trait was his willingness to use minorities as scapegoats. He ridiculed blacks, Hispanics, gays, the disabled, the super-rich. It was staggering to see that he could get away with attacking the super-rich since he was one of them. He could convince his supporters that he wasn't really one of them not matter how much money he had. And no one knew exactly how much money he had as he was steadfastly secretive about his finances and those of his companies and family. His penchant for scapegoating and his reluctance to denounce many known hate groups and their actions lead to a prevalent chant at opponent rallies: 'Haight Equals Hate.' But this chant did little more than fire up both Haight's opponents and supporters; both camps severely entrenched in their unequivocal, closed-minded beliefs. Haight's supporters were so entranced with his style and outsider status that even when numerous allegations of sexual harassment surfaced, they stood by their man. Two dozen women claimed to have suffered abuse at the hands, and more, of the wealthy neophyte politician. Two women even claimed they were raped, and one even produced an audio recording of a voice mail wherein Alexander Haight was bragging to a colleague about his conquest of her. His lemming-like supporters didn't flinch in their adoration of the man. As Daniel Lasserman said at one point, "At least we know we're not electing some homo to the White House."

Alexander Haight did become his reluctant party's nominee. Many in the party had scoffed at his candidacy, and then downright opposed him as he gained political strength, and then finally tried awkwardly to embrace him as his trajectory proved unstoppable. The opposing party's candidate, anointed by President Adamo, was the country's first Hispanic presidential candidate and a former governor of New Mexico. The opposing party, like the cadre of political pundits, grossly underestimated the frustration of many Americans following their perceived persecution under Adamo's presidency. After eight years of black rule, they simply were not going to acquiesce to brown rule. What these Americans wanted was a straight-talking, white man who was not part of the politics-as-usual Washington machine. Haight clearly saw this yearning and exploited it like a virtuoso. Alexander Haight won the general election in an extremely close race to the shock of many who never opened their eyes to this outrageous possibility. By Inauguration Day, over two months later, many of the shocked were still refusing to accept the results. One of these individuals was Evalynne Stevens, Don Lasserman's mother-in-law, better known as Grandma Eva.

Like so many progressive and liberal-leaning individuals, Eva Stevens attended dozens of 'No Hate / No Haight' rallies in and around New York City and Connecticut in the weeks following the election and her participation pace ratcheted up after Inauguration Day. On the day after the inauguration, Eva traveled to Washington in a bus caravan with members of one of her women's groups to attend the largest gathering of women at any political or social rally. Many of the women had foregone their travel quests in favor of the hugely popular No Haight rallies. Eva was feverish in her No Hate beliefs, and it was an added bonus to be in the fight alongside so many of her friends. For the next two months, Eva was always on the phone, writing to elected officials, or participating in a march or rally. Eva, her circle of friends, and so many other Americans just couldn't get their minds around this new, unfathomable, unacceptable reality, so they did, in reality, simply refuse to accept it. In mid-March, Eva was at a lunchtime rally in nearby Wilton, Connecticut, actually at the speaker's podium at the time, when she toppled over on the stage. She was rushed to the closest hospital in Norwalk where she was pronounced dead of a brain aneurysm. It was as if her brain literally exploded with the angst of a Haight presidency. Evalynne Stevens was just shy of her eightieth birthday.

Jasmine came to Stamford for the funeral with her fiancé Gregory, a certified public accountant at a local firm in Lexington, not far from Jasmine's job at Claiborne Farm in Paris, Kentucky. Jessica and her husband came all the way from Hong Kong. Both she and Jasmine did not say they were coming 'home' as neither of them had ever lived in Stamford, but it was an opportunity to introduce their significant others to their siblings as well as pay respects to their beloved grandmother. Ted came home from Boston, and he brought Jamie with him. While the two had not been apart for a day since they met, they had not yet married. Marriage for same-sex couples was a relatively new right that came during President Adamo's second term.

Ted brought up the marriage topic with Jamie once by innocently asking, "Jamie, do you think we'll want to get married someday?"

Jamie had patted Ted's hand softly and pecked him on the cheek before responding, "Of course I think we'll want to, but we're only twenty-four, Ted. Let's keep things going the way they are and focus on building our careers in the theater before getting serious about marriage. I suppose next you'll want to talk about children." Ted joined Jamie in a subtle laugh at the last suggestion and never brought up the marriage topic again.

Maria was so happy to have Jamie there, as he was a great comfort for Ted who was emotionally devastated by the loss of his lifelong best friend. Even though Ted and Grandma Eva spent less time together once he went off to college, they still talked on the phone or FaceTime nearly every day, only missing a day here and there when Grandma Eva was traveling in an inconvenient time zone.

Grandma Eva's funeral was spectacular. The Red Hat Society had assisted with many of the arrangements and they were in full attendance at the wake and the funeral mass at St. Paul's on the Green in nearby Norwalk. The beautiful stone church was barely a hundred years old, but it was built in the Decorated Gothic style mimicking a typical thirteenth century English church. None of the Lassermans were particularly religious, but following Ted's coming out experience with the family a few years earlier, both Eva and Maria had sought out the local chapter of PFLAG at Fairfield County's Triangle Community Center, not so much for support, but for an extended sense of community. Through PFLAG they were introduced to the community at St. Paul's, a particularly gay-friendly Episcopal faith community. Grandma Eva was also fond of and a volunteer at the Seabury Academy for Music and Arts on the grounds at St. Paul's. An added benefit of attending services at St. Paul's had been the effect it had on Emily. Though she occasionally had difficulty sitting through an entire hour of service, at the sound of the pipe organ she stopped fidgeting and began clapping, sometimes wildly. If any of the other parishioners found her behavior disturbing they never let it be known. Both Eva and Maria believed the church community to be sincerely welcoming and tolerant, towards not only the gay community, but all people, including Emily with her autism. Don would attend occasionally with Eva, Maria, and Emily if it wasn't peak golfing season.

At the conclusion of the funeral mass, Grandma Eva's coffin was taken away to a crematorium in Stamford while the church community hosted a light lunch in the church's basement social hall. The entire family descended the stairs to the hall where the buffet lunch was elegantly displayed. Everyone enjoyed a much-needed laugh when Emily shouted Bingo when they got to their table. The Lassermans had attended a few drag queen bingo events in this church hall when Ted and Jamie were in town for one holiday or another, and Emily was always so excited when there was a bingo winner. She had been frightened at the first shout of Bingo, but once everyone started clapping she became quite animated. Emily always loved clapping.

Ted did his best to maintain his composure during the service and the lunch. Maria looked at him with adoration and heartache. She could clearly see her darling baby boy, so sweet, so innocent, so shy. But she could also see a fine young man. He had grown his soft blond hair longer since college, and he sported a close-cropped goatee. Her heart ached to see his deep green eyes glistening with tears and pain but warmed when she saw how comforted he was in Jamie's embrace. Ted's eyes, the color of juniper, reflected her own, but the natural curl of his long golden tresses came from his father, though nowadays Don kept what little was left of his hair trimmed quite close to mitigate the visual effects of balding and silvering.

All of the Lassermans returned to the Stamford home and spent another two days together. The national news was brimming with executive orders cascading from the Oval Office; apparently, the White House was intending to undo much of what President Adamo had put in place. There were actions targeting transgender rights, immigration policies, environment regulations, abortion funding, progressive educational initiatives, and limitations on state welfare subsidies. Don, Maria, and Ted shared with Jessica, Jasmine, and the spouses how Grandma Eva would rail against each of these actions, make phone calls, march at rallies. The girls had not had a chance to see this aspect of their grandmother. They could only recall the pleasant, home-body woman who helped with their homework, cooked many of their meals, attended all of their school plays, gymnastic trials and dance recitals, and in general, ensured their busy teenage lives ran on schedule. Ted, living much closer and sharing all of Grandma Eva's political viewpoints, knew this aspect of their grandmother's latter years quite well. He shared a story of how their grandmother actually hung up the phone on their Uncle Daniel a few days after Christmas when Daniel called to chide his twin brother about President-Elect Haight's plans to rid the country of Muslims and Mexicans. Don and Maria were out for the day with Emily, so Grandma Eva said she would let them know he called. But Uncle Daniel was fired up and liquored up, and he just needed to gloat in one fashion or another. He began blathering about how great Haight was and how great the future would be for America. Grandma Eva listened for twenty or thirty seconds before saying, "Daniel, I'll do my best to remember to tell my son-in-law that his only brother called to inquire about his well-being. But I will relay none of your hateful, racist, narrow-minded rant. Good day!" and with that she clicked the phone off, turned to Ted and Jamie and simply said, "Turd!" She walked from the kitchen leaving Ted and Jamie giggling to themselves about what they just witnessed and heard. Jessica and Jasmine giggled themselves as their brother relayed this story and insight into their grandmother.

On the third day, Jessica and Alex had an early return flight to Hong Kong, so Don drove them to JFK airport in the Mercedes SUV. Jasmine and Greg had a flight to Cincinnati a few hours later, but when it was time to take them to Westchester Airport in neighboring White Plains, Don had not yet returned so Maria drove them in the BMW M5. As usual, she was nervous when driving the powerful machine, but the Westchester Airport wasn't far, and she made it back to the house without incident just before Don returned from the JFK drop off.

Ted and Jamie were both between theater gigs at the moment, so they planned to stay on in Stamford for a bit longer. Jamie had only visited New York City twice before, during brief visits to the Lasserman home, so he and Ted wanted to take advantage of all New York City had to offer. For over three weeks, they followed a fairly regular regimen. They arose early, had breakfast with Don, Maria, and Emily, and went for a walk around the neighborhood. They both loved all the spring blooms of forsythia, azaleas, daffodils, and tulips. They then caught a 10 a.m. Metro North train into Grand Central, visited the Museum of Modern Art, the Metropolitan Museum of Art, the Guggenheim, the Whitney, the Frick, or the Morgan, had lunch at one of the museums or a nearby café, and traveled to Times Square to get discount show tickets at the TKTS booth at 47th Street and Seventh Avenue. After that, they grabbed a light dinner at one of the many restaurants in the Theater District (their favorite was 44 & X on Tenth Avenue), and proceeded to their evening show: Wicked, Come From Away, A Doll's House Part 2, War Paint, whatever else they could find on- or off-Broadway, before finally catching a Stamford-bound train around 11 p.m.. There were some notable exceptions to their routine. On Wednesdays, they would take in an afternoon matinee show if there was something they wanted to see. And on Friday evenings, Jamie often insisted they visit one of the many gay bars in Greenwich Village. Jamie like the Duplex and the Monster. Ted loathed these outings. He didn't care for the bar scene, and he really hated the stress of rushing back to Grand Central to get the last train home. Jamie thrived on the attention he received in the bars while Ted usually sulked in the background. Jamie was extremely extroverted and usually wore loud colors, reflective of his Caribbean island homeland and upbringing. Mondays, they would normally spend most of the day with Maria and Emily, as many museums and theaters were closed on Mondays, some on Tuesdays.

In mid-April, Jamie received a call from his dance troupe manager informing him that there would be tryouts for a production at the Shubert Theater in two days. Performing at the Shubert would be an important rung on Jamie's dance career ladder, and Ted knew this was an opportunity not to be missed, so he began to get ready for the train ride back to Boston.

Ted was surprised when Jamie said, "You should stay here for a while. Your mother really enjoys having you home, and I'm going to be really tied up with the audition and the rehearsals, assuming I make the cut. If I don't make the cut, I'll come right back."

Ted felt disappointed and a little bit scared. He and Jamie had never gone to bed without the other since the night they met at a performance of The Nutcracker in Boston five-and-a-half years ago, but he certainly couldn't argue that his mother enjoyed having him home and that he was probably more of an aid in her grieving process than he realized. He also wasn't sure how intense his own grieving process would be once he left the home of his dear grandmother, but the loneliness would undoubtedly overwhelm him in their tiny apartment. He and Jamie hugged for several minutes at the Stamford train station the next morning waiting for Jamie's Amtrak train to Boston's South Station. From there, Jamie would get on a Red Line T for two stops and then change at Park Street to a Green Line train for the short ride to Arlington. If all went as scheduled, Jamie would be back in their apartment before lunchtime.

Ted and Jamie spoke by phone at least once every day and texted constantly throughout the days. The second day, Jamie had his tryout for the upcoming production of Dirty Dancing.

"I really danced my ass off out there, Ted," Jamie extolled on their nightly phone call. "and I think one of the producers winked at me as I left the stage, so that seems good. But they told us not to expect final word for a few days."

Ted playfully reassured Jamie, "If you danced your ass off out there I'm sure there was more than one wink. Let me know as soon as you hear from them. I'll get the champagne ready."

Thankfully, just a few days later, Jamie called Ted to report that he got the job and would be beginning rehearsals immediately as the show would start in late June, just eight weeks away.

"I'll be on a train tomorrow morning and we can celebrate at the Stella," Ted crowed.

"Whoa, slow down stallion," Jamie said calmly. "Rehearsals start right away and our schedule is going to be grueling. I'll be lucky if I get back to the apartment before midnight and I'll need to be up by 6 to get back to rehearsals. I'm not going to be very good company."

"But I miss you so much and want to celebrate with you," Ted implored.

"I know, sweetie, but we'll have time to celebrate when my schedule settles down. And I'm sure you are a tremendous comfort and help to your mother right now. Just stay there for a couple more weeks and we'll figure it out from there," Jamie explained in a paternalistic tone.

Ted really wanted to be with Jamie to celebrate, but Jamie was adamant that Ted should stay in Stamford with his parents for now. Ted's next work commitment wasn't until a production of Shear Madness at the Charles Playhouse scheduled to open in September, although Ted would be required to be there for set up and rehearsals in late July. So, he agreed with Jamie that he should stay in Stamford for the time being. But his heart was aching terribly. The next day, Ted was as despondent as Maria had seen him since he arrived for Grandma Eva's funeral. He literally moped around the house, didn't eat much, and wouldn't even humor his autistic cousin Emily with their secret code words and facial expressions. Don arrived home for dinner at a reasonable time and the four of them sat down to an easy and delicious meal of spaghetti and meatballs, one of Ted's lifelong favorites. Maria had learned most of her cooking skills from her own mother, but she had altered the sauce recipe over the years with input from Don's mother, Mavis. Consequently, Maria's contemporary version of spaghetti and meatballs was not only Ted's favorite, but it was also one of Emily's. Don picked up on Ted's mood immediately after sitting down at the table.

"Doing okay, son?" Don queried softly, assuming his melancholia was attributable to the death of his grandmother just a month previous.

"I'm fine. I just miss Jamie a lot. He landed this new dance gig in Dirty Dancing, and, traditionally, we celebrate when either of us gets news of a new job. He thinks I should stay here for now," responded Ted meekly and with the strain of distress evident in his voice.

Don hated to see his only son in such emotional distress. He said, "I see," as he fumbled for his Samsung 8 in his pocket. Thirty seconds later father said to son, "Amtrak has a Northeast Regional train from Stamford to Boston at 8:45. Gives us enough time to finish dinner and get to the station."

Ted couldn't control his smile as he shoveled a huge twirl of spaghetti into his mouth. Maria reached over and squeezed her husband's hand displaying her own smile of joy. And, to everyone's surprise, Emily started clapping loudly and wildly. Ted packed a few things into his backpack, and his dad drove him to the train station in the '65 'Cuda as a special treat for both of them. The classic Barracuda had last been out of its garage in October when Don drove it to Norwalk for a car show at the city's Calf Pasture Beach, although Don fired it up at least twice a month during the winter months. The last award that the car had won had also been in Norwalk the year before but at the Lockwood-Mathews Mansion's annual Father's Day car show. Ted had not been home for Father's Day that year, and Don was grateful to relate the experience to his son with the award ribbon hanging in the car.

Once settled in on the train, Ted pulled his iPhone out several times to send Jamie a text to say he was on his way. But he kept putting it back without sending any texts. He hadn't heard from Jamie since noon, so he figured his boyfriend must be as busy with the dance rehearsals as he said he was going to be. Also, based on yesterday's phone exchange, Ted assumed Jamie would again try to convince him to stay with his parents for now, and he didn't want to be dissuaded from his quest. And, finally, Ted also found a great deal of excitement and anticipation in the idea of surprising his lover with his unannounced arrival. The Amtrak train was scheduled to arrive in South Station at twenty minutes after midnight, but there were several minor delays along the route, so the actual arrival time was closer to one o'clock. The last Red Line subway train departed from the station at 12:43. Fortunately, Ted had the Uber app, so he clicked for a ride to Arlington. It was just after 1:30 in the morning when Ted unlocked the door of their second-floor apartment.

All was quiet, so Ted assumed Jamie was sound asleep. As quietly as he could, he used the bathroom, disrobed there, turned out the bathroom light and made his way down the short, carpeted hallway to their bedroom without turning on any lights. Ted's usual side of the bed was the one closest to the door, so he sat down on that edge of the bed to lay down. He was pleased to feel Jamie's warm body against his butt as he moved into the bed. Jamie must take some comfort in sleeping in Ted's space when he's not there. Now Ted was moving gingerly as he lay down and cuddled up behind Jamie's back. He reached around Jamie to run his right hand down Jamie's smooth, muscular chest and encountered curly hairs. What the fuck! Ted reached for the Toy Story night-stand light as he quickly jumped from the bed. The soft glow of Buzz Lightyear revealed Ted and Jamie's good friend Tim still sleeping on the far side of the bed. Tim's smooth pink chest was nestled up against Jamie's lean, muscular, mocha-colored dance frame lying prostrate in the middle of their king-sized bed. Jamie too was still fast asleep. The only body in the bed that was attempting to rouse was the one Ted has just inadvertently spooned; Tim's boyfriend Gerry. Through barely-opening eyes in a groggy, just-awakening voice, Gerry smiled, grabbed Ted's cock and with a slight tug, pleaded, "Teddy, come join us."

Ted jumped back two steps slapping Gerry's clinging fingers away. The growing commotion brought both Tim and Jamie out of their slumber, and it was a cacophonous scene as bare bodies lunged to and fro; Tim attempting to cover up, Gerry attempting to pull Ted in, and Jamie attempting to reach Ted to offer some lame explanation.

There was no doubt it would be lame, because as Jamie's naked body grasped for Ted, he stammered, "Honey, it's not what you think." Really? Lame. Very lame. Ted had no words and, therefore, offered none. He raced for the bathroom where he had left his backpack and clothes on the floor. Jamie was literally on his heels, but Ted managed to beat him to the bathroom and lock the door. While Ted frantically put on his clothes, Jamie kept banging on the door with cries of, "Please, let me explain, please." Ted swung the door open and shoved Jamie aside with his backpack and hauled ass down the stairs without even a glance back. When he got to the street he just ran for several blocks before stopping to assess his predicament and his options. The options were few, but he knew he didn't belong on the streets of their neighborhood at two o'clock in the morning. Once again, Uber came to the rescue and took Ted to the only place he could think of at this time of night; back to the train station. There wouldn't be an Amtrak to Stamford until six a.m., so Ted sat and partially dozed on and off for three hours. By the time the train station was coming to life, Ted had processed more of his situation. He had thought he could wait until he knew Jamie was at rehearsal and go to the apartment and collect some of his things. But he eventually nixed this idea, because he didn't want to risk running into his former good friends and Jamie's bedmates of just hours ago. Ted knew Tim worked part-time as a bartender on weekends, but, in his current state of mind, he couldn't recall what Gerry did. There was a very good likelihood that they might still be in the apartment, partially because Ted thought they didn't have day jobs to take them away and partially because Ted believed Jamie would ask them to stay there in case Ted returned. Ted didn't want to see them. In fact, Ted didn't want to see anyone, or be around anyone except his Grandma Eva. Since that wasn't possible, the only thing Ted could think to do was to return to his parents' home in Stamford and be as close to his grandmother as possible. He wasn't even sure he could open up to his parents about this. Was he embarrassed? Angry? Disappointed? Depressed? Confused? Hurt? Vengeful? Scared? Yes, the answer was yes.

Ted arrived at the Stamford house a little before 10 a.m. He had texted his mother from the train, so

she was expecting him, but she couldn't have foreseen his forlorn state. Maria knew her son didn't like
confrontation, so she did her best to not barrage him
with questions. The most information she got from
Ted was, "Mom, he was in bed asleep, but he wasn't
alone." Maria hoped her husband would be a better
comforter for Ted on this topic, but she didn't think
so. She was right. When Don got home from the
office, he listened and then hugged Ted as much as
Ted would allow, but Ted retired to his room early
and they didn't see him until breakfast the next day
which was Saturday. Don and Maria had plans to
take Emily to the Bronx Zoo and begged Ted to join
them, but he declined. They also offered to change
their plans and stay with him, but he said the thing
he needed the most was some alone time. He was
wrong. After his parents left the house, Ted realized
he had never felt so alone. He went to his grandmother's room and cried, just cried. He then wan-
dered the rest of the house and the backyard koi pond
and, before long, he was wallowing in self-pity and
self-loathing. He reasoned that this wouldn't have
happened if he'd been a better lover, a better person,
and that personal self-loathing seeded thoughts of
hating Jamie, Gerry, and Tim, and soon, in his mind,
the entire gay community. Just after lunchtime, the
house phone rang, and Ted answered it hesitantly,

thinking it might be Jamie since Ted had turned his cell phone off after his Uber ride when he left their apartment. It wasn't Jamie. It was Uncle Daniel. Ted was not really close to his uncle, but he had a fondness for him since he was so similar to his father in appearance, if not demeanor. Also, Uncle Daniel was the father of Daniel Junior, Nate, and Emily, and Ted cherished all of his cousins. Uncle Daniel was in his usual mood of wanting to rub his brother's face in what Daniel thought was President Haight's latest act of courage or leadership in restoring America's stature on the world stage. But Ted was in no mood for such trivial nonsense. Ted was spiraling downward in the most important, emotional whirlpool in the history of man. He needed to unload all his feelings with someone and he had been too embarrassed to share intimate details with his parents. Ted told his uncle of the scene in his apartment, his feelings of hurt and betrayal, of his shame of being gay, which was part of what he felt at this moment. That last revelation triggered something in Uncle Daniel's mind, and even though Daniel was a self-centered drunk, at some level, his heart was generous, and he wanted to do right by his nephew.

"Say Teddy, have you ever heard of pray-the-gay-away ministries?" asked Daniel.

"I've heard of them, but they're just a scam. You can't pray something like that away," replied Ted.

"Maybe, maybe. But I've got this old buddy down here, a guy your dad and I went to high school with. We called him Preacher Bob even way back then because he was always spouting scripture in class. Anyway, he's got a church in Jonesboro and they minister to the gays who want it to go away. You might want to come down and check it. Couldn't hurt," offered Uncle Daniel.

Ted really didn't want any part of an anti-gay minister, but his uncle's suggestion that 'it couldn't hurt' rolled around in his mind for the rest of the weekend and he really had no other plan for his life for right now. He had told Uncle Daniel thanks, but no thanks, but by Monday morning, he was seriously considering it, and by Tuesday morning, he was on a bus heading to Arkansas. He had waited until after his father left for work and his mother took Emily to their monthly manicures and hair styling appointments, so he wouldn't have to explain what he was doing or where he was going. It was the beginning of May when he arrived in Jonesboro a few days later. With no other plan or prospects, he went directly to the church that Uncle Daniel had described. Preacher Bob was stern and strict but ebullient about the prospects of setting Ted on a promising life path in service of Jesus Christ. Ted was skeptical but had no will or energy to argue or protest.

For over three weeks, he followed the established routines. There were lectures about the sins of homosexuals. There were bible studies extolling the virtues of a celibate life. There were slide shows featuring video clips of straight porn where Preacher Bob and his male staff all attended and watched with eager anticipation as Ted and the other boys viewed the videos clad only in their underwear. There were slide shows that featured man-on-man sex videos and Preacher Bob and his staff would slap any boy's aroused penis in his briefs with a ruler. There were prayer circles and assigned support buddies. And then, eventually, there was electro-convulsive therapy to be administered by one of the staff 'doctors.' Ted doubted that Dr. Pete was a licensed doctor, and he was sure he didn't want shock therapy even if Dr. Pete was legit. Ted fled. His heart ached for Jamie, despite the orgy he had seen in his bed. His heart ached for his departed grandmother. His heart yearned for his parents but brimmed with a belief that he had let them down. Ted ached in every physical, psychological and emotional sense, but believed he had no one to help him through this. His mother or father called his cell phone every other day to make sure he was all right, but he never told them where he was. He lied and said he was back in Boston working things out with Jamie, and they had no reason to doubt this. Ted felt as though he had nowhere to go, too angry to go back to Boston, too embarrassed to go to Stamford, too uncomfortable to live with Uncle Daniel, so he lived on the streets of Jonesboro, and ended up doing what a young man needs to do to get by living on the streets. Ted was on the streets for less than a month, but in that time, he was introduced to hustling and drugs, concepts foreign to him and things he was ill equipped to handle. Ted died of an opioid overdose after being raped by a trick on his twenty-fifth birthday, ironically in an alleyway where Uncle Daniel had once sold illegal painkillers.

Rationally, Don knew his brother was not directly or specifically to blame for Ted's death, but he also knew he would always consider Daniel generally responsible for this outcome. Daniel called Don about a month after Ted's death and just started bemoaning the fact that former President Adamo said some non-flattering things about President Haight in an interview on 60 Minutes. Daniel didn't even reference Ted or inquire how Don was feeling. He was just singularly focused on the mission of President Haight as though he were a modern-day messiah. Don followed his mother-in-law's example of dealing with Daniel and just hung up on him, never accepting another call from him. A week later, Jamie called the Stamford house, and Maria answered the phone. He was looking for Ted, unaware of what had transpired. Not sure what to say, and being her mother's daughter, Maria simply hung up the phone. Jamie never phoned again.

For the next two years, the Haight Administration bumbled along from one misguided anti-social reform to the next, from one controversy to the next, and from one scandal to the next. Congress was not obeying the will of the President and he had no ability or desire to cooperate or compromise with them. Consequently, nothing was getting done and the country was falling into greater disarray relative to social interactions and political discourse. The various social media outlets and technologies made it way too easy for any citizen, any politician, any president, to dump half-baked ideas or outright hateful messages on the general American public who seemed to be getting more and more of their news and views from trendy social media outlets than from trustworthy, fact-checked news bureaus. The No Hate / No Haight resistance movement did not waver. The chasm between the two primary political parties grew ever deeper. The gap between rich and poor grew ever wider.

In the midst of all this federal government ineptitude, Haight was dealing with a number of issues of his own. The media had been obsessed with likely interference in the U.S. election process by a foreign government, but as that investigation grew it also became clear that the new president and his businesses had alleged ties to the same government. Proving the allegations would be extremely difficult, even though Congress had established a special counsel to lead an investigation, but it would likely take months, if not years, to get to the bottom of the issues. There was also the lingering specter of numerous sexual harassment allegations that preceded the president's election to office. His approach to these matters was consistent denial and to brand all accusers as liars or whores. It was proving extremely difficult to get any of these allegations to bring down the president either. His supporters simply regurgitated the pablum fed to them by the president and became angrier and angrier with his detractors, including the media.

However, Haight came under intense scrutiny for another matter that his opponents hoped would be easier and quicker to investigate. In an effort to protect his personal investments and businesses in the event he should be successful in his bid for the presidency, Haight and his family and his businesses engaged in some reorganizations and other business moves that the Securities Exchange Commission believed constituted insider trading. His detractors believed the audit trail for such questionable trans-actions would be easy to document and hold up in court. His supporters, naturally, believed this was nothing more than a witch-hunt designed to derail their movement. A further and unexpected compli-cation in this investigation, however, was that one of Haight's closest financial advisors, Vincent Posner, was found dead in his Salt Lake City home just a few days after the election and just a few days before news of the SEC insider trading investigation was made public. The death was ruled an accident, but questions remained, and conspiracy theories pro-liferated. Posner's body had been found in his tool shed with three different bottles of pesticides open, one of which had been spilled. The autopsy indicated severe chemical burns inside Posner's nose, throat, and lung tissues, as well as extensive and numerous skin burns. Without access to Posner, it appeared the SEC investigation might also grind to an inconclu-sive end.

As a candidate, Haight had made innumerable promises on the campaign trail and fully intended to fulfill them in one way or another as president, at least within his own mind. Since he was so prolific at spouting off on any topic at any time without the benefit of much serious thought or understanding, it was nearly impossible to define his real position on any matter. His campaign rhetoric was designed to reach out to anyone feeling disenfranchised with the dysfunctionality of the federal government. He told any and every group he was put in front of exactly what they wanted to hear. He was a master at absolving the disenfranchised of any responsibility for their own plights and identifying false scapegoats who became targets for their wrath; first verbal and theoretical, then confrontational and impractical, and occasionally downright hurtful and violent. He told Midwest, rural, economically struggling groups that he and he alone, could solve all their problems. He would revive the auto industry by requiring all automobile jobs to return to America and imposing huge tariffs on any imports. He told unemployed steelworkers and coal miners that he would undo burdensome regulations and open up long-dormant mines and steel plants putting them all back to work in well-paying, union-protected jobs. He told Southwest ranchers that he would protect their lands and erect an impenetrable wall along the border with Mexico. He told Northwest ranchers they would have free and open access to federal lands for cattle grazing. And he told nearly everyone that nothing was their fault or in their control. No matter what their concern was, the blame could be placed at the feet of any one of many scapegoats. Immigrants were a threat to jobs. Muslims were a threat to national security. Blacks were a threat to effective police operations. Gays were a threat to family structure and American values. And yet he told the gay community that he was a far better friend to them than his political opponent. He told black audiences that he would help bring jobs, security, and family stability to their neighborhoods. He told immigrants that he would enact policies to help them stop living in fear of deportation. He told everyone that he was their savior, and many believed him.

As president, President Haight made various efforts to address his campaign promises, but most were half-hearted efforts that were not well thought out and were launched without any intent to work with others or make real progress through compromise. He genuinely seemed to believe that he could just say what he wanted, and it would happen. Perhaps he thought this was the role of president; basically, serve as a dictatorial mouthpiece. Perhaps he had no understanding of how bills were passed or what the role of Congress was. Perhaps he assumed everyone, literally everyone, saw the world exactly as he saw it and therefore everything he thought and spoke would automatically materialize. Perhaps he was so in love with himself that he had no ability whatsoever to process any feedback that didn't validate that self-perception. Perhaps all the preceding was true in one way or another. In any event, no progress, not even anti-progress, was happening. The only constant in the Haight Administration's approach to governing was to undo anything accomplished by the Adamo Administration. Since there had been a great deal of political entrenchment during the eight Adamo years, many of his accomplishments had been affected via executive orders, circumventing the Congressional stalemate and malaise. Since the results had not been codified by the enactment of supporting laws and policies, undoing them could be accomplished simply via countermanding executive orders from President Haight. Limited protections for children of undocumented immigrants could simply be signed away. The same with protections for transgendered individuals and family planning funding and educational initiatives and environmental programs and so many other areas that Congress refused to work on under President Adamo. The most challenging obstacle for President Haight in realizing his total anti-Adamo universe was the repeal of Adamocare. This accomplishment actually had been achieved via a great deal of hard work and compromise with all major constituents; both major political parties, both the executive and legislative branches of government, the insurers, the healthcare providers, local governments, and input from the general public. The result was a health care system that was not ideal for anyone but was regarded as the best that could be achieved at the time while doing its best to satisfy everyone. The result of this process was that the Accessibility Defined and Advanced Medical Opportunities for All Health Care Act, also known as Adamocare, was the law of the land as defined and passed by Congress, therefore President Haight was unable to simply sign it away. Congress was repeatedly unable to come up with a plan to repeal Adamocare, which caused great frustration for President Haight, further inflamed political tensions, and compounded the Administration's inability to accomplish much of its agenda.

Furthermore, the Haight Administration was significantly handicapped by numerous self-inflicted wounds via social media and verbal gaffes. Cabinet members openly disagreed with each other as well as the president. Staff came and went so regularly that the media joked the front portico of the White House had been retrofitted with a revolving door. The president himself, no stranger to social media, initiated or fueled many of the controversies. His crude and crass 'everyman' style of connecting to his political supporters only further inflamed those who felt he promulgated discrimination and division. His obsession with himself and taking credit for anything that went right was only underscored in its absurdness by the passion with which he bullied and blamed others for everything that went wrong. He thrived on media attention while castigating the media for anything he did not find favorable or which did not compliment himself or his agenda. He ordered his direct staff and cabinet members to do all the dirty work of implementing their agenda, such as announcing drastic changes to immigration policies, defunding Planned Parenthood, and enacting a controversial religious freedom policy allowing blatant discrimination against any individual based on religious grounds. Under this last policy, business owners or even individual employees, could refuse to offer service or sell goods to anyone if they claimed it was against their religious conscience. The policy was commonly known as the 'Cake Law' because it stemmed from outrage over a baker's refusal to sell a wedding cake to a gay couple, but the new policy was so broad and vague that it could be applied to denial of service to people of different faiths, races, or even genders.

Throughout all of this turmoil, the No Hate / No Haight groups only grew in strength and numbers. Each outrageous blunder by the Administration or implementation of a new divisive policy or executive order further galvanized the resistance forces. There was a marked increase in hate crime violence, even as currently loosely defined, and random shootings, burnings of black churches, and degeneration of social discourse, had become the daily norm. Ardent Haight supporters, especially the self-proclaimed Christian Right leaders, were emboldened by their moral leader and vowed an all-out civil war if Haight detractors forced him from the office of the presidency.

CHAPTER *Six*

Don and Maria Lasserman shared the viewpoint of these groups and really wanted to get more involved for their own consciences as well as the legacy left by Grandma Eva, but their deep grief over the death of their only son had all but paralyzed them in actions and communications. They rarely spoke about Ted and the circumstances that lead to his drug overdose. In fact, they rarely spoke to each other about anything anymore other than through, and about, their grown daughters and their growing families. There was no animosity, just discomfort. The barest of interaction between Don and Maria brought too much pain, suffering and questioning to the surface, so they silently, mutually acquiesced to merely co-exist and go through the motions of life.

On this typical, crisp New England morning, Don was now emerging from the shower after his victory over the earlier offensive alarm clock, he caught a glimpse of his wife stirring on her side of the bed. He sighed, walked over to her, put a hand on her shoulder, and quietly uttered, "Don't forget Emily's doctor's appointment this morning." Maria mumbled something, but he did not understand. His mission was accomplished, and the exchange between the two of them was complete, likely the only interaction they would have that day. Neither of them could have foreseen how drastically their day would change, how drastically America's day would change.

It was just after one p.m. in Don's midtown Manhattan office when his secretary, Claudia, interrupted his usual desktop lunch of a grilled chicken Caesar salad, sea salt and cracked pepper potato chips, and a Coke Zero Sugar, to tell him there were six FBI agents outside. But no sooner had she said so than they were inside staring directly into Don's utterly astonished face. Lauren Wright, special-agent-in-charge, did not bother with any background information.

"Are you Donald Lasserman?"

"Yes, what is this about?"

"We're going to need your cellphone, your computer, any other electronic or recording devices," she tersely explained. "Also, I'll need to interview you as soon as our behavioral psychologist arrives."

While she was saying all this, she guided Don to a nearby conference room and the other five agents lay siege to his office and devices. SAIC Wright told Don to stay put and she would be right back with him within minutes. Just as she was exiting the conference room, Claudia stuck her head in the door. "Don, Maria is on the line. She sounds hysterical."

Don exited the conference room despite SAIC Wright's order and grabbed the phone at Claudia's desk. "Maria, what is it?" he barked more tersely than he intended.

"What the hell is going on, Don? Emily and I just arrived home from the park, and the house is surrounded by lights and sirens. They broke down the front door, and there are FBI agents roaming all over the house. They took my cellphone, but Margie came over from next door, and I'm on her phone. What do they want?" she started crying and breathing heavily.

"I really don't know. They're here in the office, too. They haven't told me anything yet," he explained more calmly than when he first picked up the phone.

"Is this something to do with insider trading?" she queried. "What have you done?"

Don was incredulous that his wife of thirty-eight years would jump to this conclusion, but quickly processing the absurdity of the situation and the lack of any explanatory insight, he absently replied, "No, no, nothing like that. I'm sure. Unless it involves someone else at the firm, and they think I might know something. I don't know. They haven't told me anything. They've got me parked in a conference room waiting for a psychologist to arrive, so they can interview me. We'll know something soon. Please calm down and don't frighten Emily," he soothed, before adding, "I love you." He wasn't sure why he said those last three words. He was sure he hadn't said them in the past two years since Teddy's death, but he was also sure he truly meant them. What Don and Maria did not know at this point in time was how Emily's father's day was unfolding several states, and one time zone, away.

Daniel Lasserman had awoken that morning with a deep sense of loss and pain. His life had certainly had its share of sadness. His parents were now dead. His wife of forty years had passed on. His two sons were grown and on their own and only maintained minimal, necessary contact with him. His only daughter, Emily, hadn't seen him in years since she went to live with her Uncle Don and Aunt Maria who could better cope with the behavioral aspects of her autism. Daniel could admit, reluctantly when sober, that all these things troubled him a bit, but his current mental state was being shaped by much more than these personal circumstances. Daniel's sub-conscience was a human petri dish where the angst of the nation, the frustration of the Haight Administration, the despair for America's future, were fermenting into a desperate melancholy and volatile powder keg. All that was missing was a catalyst. Not even Daniel knew how close at hand that catalyst would be.

This was a Friday morning, a payday Friday. Daniel never missed paydays, and he wasn't going to miss this one. He was on time, a rarity, and shocked when his new supervisor, a guy named Randy Whittlecock-though all the crew referred to him as Littlecock-met him at the time clock. Daniel's long-time supervisor and closest friend, Paul Rutterby, had passed away just about a month earlier from an aggressive brain tumor, and he had been re-assigned to Littlecock who now said, "We need to make a stop at HR."

"We?" stammered Daniel.

"Yes, you and me," barked Whittlecock. "Let's go." So, Daniel followed Littlecock into Ben Jackson's tiny office just off the chicken-processing shop floor.

Jackson began without context or foreplay, "Daniel, we're letting you go. Here's your final paycheck, including today, your severance and your unused vacation. Your years of intermittent absences and occasional fuck-ups are almost legendary around here, but it wasn't until we were going through Paul's office files that we learned how bad you've been over time and how much Paul covered for you. If he were still alive, I'd fire him as well." Jackson stared down Daniel, "Any questions?"

Daniel stared intently back at the human resources geek before replying simply and calmly, "No." With that, Whittlecock walked Daniel to the plant exit door, took his employee badge, and closed the door behind Daniel without a word. Daniel walked purposefully towards his pickup. He got in, fumed for thirty seconds before opening his lunch box, removing the sandwich and store-bought cupcake. His mind was racing with fury and contempt. Jackson reminded him of Adamo and this is what happens when blacks get authority. He swallowed the cupcake in two bites and then removed one of two handguns from his glovebox. He placed the Glock G19 in his now-empty lunchbox. After another few contemplative seconds, Daniel walked back to the plant's employee entrance.

"Let me in, Zeke," Daniel said to his long-time friend, the day-shift security guard, "I forgot something in my locker."

"I'll have to get Littlecock to escort you, Daniel. Got orders here." And Zeke turned around to reach for the phone.

"Fuck that!" shrieked Daniel as he pulled out the Glock and shot Zeke in the back. With his left hand, he reached in to press the door opening button as Zeke slumped from his chair onto the guard station floor.

As Daniel entered his former work area, many of his former co-workers were already running from the floor having heard the single gunshot just outside the door. If they had any doubts as to their safety, the crazed look on Daniel's face erased them. Daniel raised his right hand and fired two shots before shouting, "Everybody on the floor at your station. Anyone who moves gets shot." As if to test his resolve, two workers let out screams and started to run. True to his word, Daniel shot both Fred and Debbie in their backs as they tried to flee. Their limp bodies fell to the floor and everyone else within Daniel's view planted their faces as firmly as they could against the filthy concrete floor, chicken blood and tissue clinging to their cheeks and getting in their hair. Daniel steadfastly marched down the outside aisle to the second office just twenty yards away where he found Ben Jackson cowering under his desk. Without a word, Daniel fired two rounds into Ben's head and proceeded down the aisle checking the next few offices but not finding his prey. He then started combing the work areas where his former co-workers were still face down on the floor. Every few seconds, they heard a shot; bullet number five, then number six, number seven. There was plenty of sobbing and wailing, but no one dared run and it seemed clear that he wasn't shooting at everyone. Just after his third on-the-floor target, Randy Whittlecock came flying around a corner. "What the hell is going on in here?" He stopped in his tracks when he saw Daniel. To his credit, the supervisor did not turn and run. He stood his ground. Daniel closed the fifteen yards between them in about ten frenzied strides. "Ah, Littlecock!" Daniel smiled coyly, "I'm taking back what's mine." And without any further explanation or conversation, put two shots in Whittlecock's forehead. With a bit more speed than before, Daniel returned to the work aisles to resume his task; shots number ten, eleven, twelve. Now people started to scramble, to head for any door they could. Daniel continued his quest. Three more victims. Fifteen shots total, the end of his clip, but he didn't think anyone else had been counting as he ran out the employee exit and headed for his pickup truck.

Once back inside the truck, Daniel finally wondered distractedly to himself as if in shellshock,

"What the hell have I done?" His hands were shaking. His blood was coursing boldly through his veins and pounding loudly in his temples. But after less than twenty seconds, Daniel grasped the steering wheel with both hands and let out a loud exhale that almost sounded like a battle whoop. He started the Ford, dropped it into drive, and fled the parking lot at a high rate of speed, looking forward, only forward. Towards Memphis.

Within an hour, Daniel was in Memphis. His adrenaline had kept him pumped during the fast drive but had also drained him quite a bit physically and emotionally. His shaking hands were now steady and he sported a sly grin each time he eyed the handguns on the truck seat. He spotted a diner up ahead and pulled into Rizzo's parking lot on South Main Street. He could use a cup of coffee and maybe a donut. Daniel was shocked that the parking lot was empty and became filled with paranoia. Maybe the police had been tracking him and had evacuated the area, so they could ambush him. He looked around and saw nothing, but noted the diner was not a 24-hour business, as he had assumed, but was only open for dinner. What kind of diner isn't open for breakfast? He was pissed, but the frustration reignited his adrenaline rush. He tried to relax a bit, reloaded his Glock and retrieved his Beemiller from the glovebox. He tucked both handguns in his waistband under his denim jacket and strolled three hundred feet up Mulberry Street to the ticket office of the National Civil Rights Museum. The museum was centered around the former Lorraine Motel where Reverend Martin Luther King, Jr. had been assassinated on April 4, 1968. The museum opened in 1991 and would be open for business today at 9 a.m., just about five minutes from now. A cashier was in the ticket office already beginning to sell tickets to the half-dozen or so people waiting in line for the doors to open. Daniel snidely noticed that he was the only white person in the area. As he pulled out the Glock and began point-blank firing, there was a lot of screaming and frantic running. He pointed and fired as quickly and accurately as he could and within just a few seconds he had exhausted his fifteen-round clip. All was silent again, but he couldn't tell if anyone had escaped around the corner of the first building. He didn't even contemplate searching for any survivors; he just burst into the entrance door and shot the first two workers he encountered with the first two rounds from the Beemiller. Again, silence. Daniel wondered what to do now just as he heard a distinct, and vaguely familiar, voice nearby. He sprinted and peered around the corner ready to fire when he saw the face of the legendary slain civil rights leader taunting him from a video screen. Flying into a fit of rage, Daniel re-assassinated the civil rights martyr on the screen and started smashing display cases, overturning video screens, and ripping mementos from the walls and shelves while screaming, "We'll see who shall overcome now!"

Daniel ended his fury-fueled, sixty-second, rant of destruction by striking a match to wastebasket debris or other flammables in various of the rooms. As he exited a rear door he spotted a wheel valve marked 'Water Shut-Off' so he did as suggested and shut the water off. He didn't know if it would stop all, or any, of the sprinklers, but it was worth the effort. With that done, he jogged the half block back to Rizzo's Diner where his truck still sat alone in the parking lot. Daniel intended to get in his truck and drive, but at the last second, paranoia found him, so he opted to walk a few more blocks down Main Street where he caught the Main Street Trolley headed for downtown. as he rode across town, he chuckled at the sounds of sirens that seemed to be coming from all directions.

Back in Manhattan, Don Lasserman had been waiting to be grilled by the FBI agents and their psychologist. After the initial interaction with SAIC

Lauren Wright, Don had a few minutes to tend to company business before the psychologist arrived.

"Claudia," Don called to his secretary, "please call upstairs and let Ivy and Ken know what's going on down here." Don was referring to the firm's general counsel, Ivy McKinsey, and managing partner, Ken Chenowalt.

"Already done," she replied. "Or, should I say, the FBI already did that. Dawn called me just a few minutes after the agents arrived here in your office." Claudia was referring to the general counsel's administrative assistant, Dawn Liu. "I guess agent Wright made a brief stop upstairs before heading down here to your office. Anyway, Dawn said they didn't stay long."

"Okay, thanks," said Don pensively. "Call back to Ivy's office and suggest that she come down here. I'm not sure what direction this is heading."

Within minutes the psychologist arrived and SAIC Wright ushered her and Don into the same conference room where she had parked Don earlier. Don quickly learned that this was not about insider trading or anything to do with the firm but that his twin brother had mentally snapped earlier in the day and gone on a shooting spree at the poultry-processing plant where he worked. Or, allegedly, they reassured him. The FBI told him that there were eleven victims at the plant. Four white employees had been shot, including Whittlecock, dead, Zeke, the security guard, currently in surgery for severe internal bleeding, and Fred and Debbie, the two employees who dared to run when Daniel opened fire. Their surgeries were complete, and they were expected to survive. Seven black employees had also been shot, including the HR manager Ben Jackson, dead, four other plant workers, all dead, and two other black employees currently undergoing brain surgeries.

The behavioral psychologist was trying to determine Daniel's mental state based on what little information the FBI had gathered and needed input from Don to help frame the picture. She seemed to be trying make a connection with terrorism. Don was confused, and though he admitted his brother may have some racist tendencies, he couldn't understand the speculation about terrorism or why the FBI was involved.

Even though he was overwhelmed with this shocking and tragic news, Don queried, "Why is the FBI investigating a workplace shooting? Shouldn't the Arkansas State Police be doing this? Is there something you haven't told me?"

Glances between SAIC Wright and psychologist Carmella Brown told Don he was correct, and the subtle nod from Wright to Brown told him he was about to find out what it was. SAIC Wright began, "There's been another incident in Memphis that we think may be related. Your brother is armed and on the run. Memphis is across the state boundary, hence, the justification for our leadership in this investigation."

"What else has happened?"

The psychologist didn't answer Don's question directly. She wanted to pursue a different angle first. "We've talked a bit about your brother's attitude towards African-Americans, and we're trying to determine if it's systemic, if he's targeting blacks as part of a larger initiative."

"But four of the victims at the plant were white. Why do you think this is something other than a workplace rage incident? You told me he had been fired this morning. This doesn't seem planned."

Another nod from SAIC Wright and the psychologist continued. "The incident in Memphis was at the National Civil Rights Memorial. There are nine victims, all black, five dead, three in serious condition, one with non-life-threatening wounds. The museum is substantially destroyed. It was set on fire and firefighters were kept at bay for two hours while we tried to determine if your brother was still inside or if he had set any traps."

"And?" Don inquired pensively. "Is Daniel inside? Are you sure it's Daniel?"

SAIC Wright picked up the storyline. "Your brother's pickup is sitting in a restaurant parking lot less than a block from the museum. We're still going through the rubble of the burnt sections of the museum. We've found two dead workers, both shot with a .38 caliber handgun, but no one else so far. We're still looking, but we're treating the situation as though he escaped and is on the run. We desperately need your help here."

"I don't really know what else to say. I know he frequented Memphis, so he probably knows the city well. And I know he has always enjoyed guns and has several, but I don't know what type or how many. His sons may have better insight."

"As I said earlier, we are interrogating both sons right now. In fact, we're transporting Nathaniel from Alabama to Memphis right now, so he can be easily accessible in case we need him," said Wright.

"You mean in case you corner his father and need help talking him down," Don stated coldly.

It wasn't that he didn't want the shootings stopped, or his brother stopped, but he was so tired of playing the FBI's game of mystery and holding all the cards. They had rifled through his office, his computer, his phones, looking for any interesting correspondences with Daniel or any internet searches to indicate that Don was involved or knew what Daniel was planning. Overall, they treated Don as if he was a criminal, and he worried that they must be doing the same to Maria at home.

"Yes," was all Wright said in response to Don's question about 'talking Daniel down' from a precarious situation.

Don asked if they could take a break and the agents agreed. He immediately went for a phone and called his house knowing that the FBI had taken Maria's cell phone. When he called the house, an unknown male voice answered, simply saying, "Yes?"

"This is Don Lasserman. Please put my wife on the phone." stammered Don with growing frustration.

"I'm sorry, sir. This is Agent Crandall. Mrs. Lasserman is not available right now." replied the F.B.I. agent a bit sheepishly.

"What do you mean, not available?"

"Yes, sir. She's not here."

"Not there?" demanded Don angrily, "Where could she be?"

"Sir, she and two of the agents are currently searching for your daughter." stated the agent before being interrupted by Don.

"My daughter?" Don interrupted. "Which one? When did she arrive?"

"Sir, she was here with your wife all day and when she became agitated, Mrs. Lasserman put her to bed."

Don was confused, tired, frustrated, but quickly figured out the situation. "Oh, you mean Emily. She's my niece, but she lives with us. Where is she now? You said Maria is looking for her?"

"Well, sir, we initially tried to interview your daughter, I mean niece, but Mrs. Lasserman explained she is autistic, so we abandoned the interview with her. While we were talking with Mrs. Lasserman about the situation with your brother, your niece was nearby and just started yelling and literally pulling her hair out. She seemed uncontrollable, but Mrs. Lasserman was able to calm her a bit and took her to her bedroom. When Mrs. Lasserman went to check on her about half an hour later, she was not there, and we haven't been able to find her."

"Damn it!" shrieked Don into the phone. "Of course, Emily would be upset. Daniel is her father. God only knows what the poor girl is thinking. I'm on my way right now. If my wife returns, please tell her I'm coming."

Don got off the phone and noticed that SAIC Wright was standing nearby. She must have overheard the conversation or perhaps had been briefed by the agents at the house. "Mr. Lasserman, we have a car waiting downstairs that can take you to Stamford right now. I'll go with you."

On the forty-minute drive to the Lasserman's North Stamford home, Don explained the Emily situation to SAIC Wright. "Emily is a very sweet and intelligent girl. Due to her autism, she has very limited communications skills, but she seems to be very comprehending. I can scarcely imagine how she is processing this situation about her father. Emily has lived with us since her mother died four years ago. Daniel is simply not capable of providing the basic care a child needs, let alone the special care that Emily requires. Yes, I know she's a grown woman, nearly forty years old, but she is still a child in most ways."

By the time the FBI black Chevy Suburban pulled into the Lasserman's circular drive, Don knew something unusual was going on because there was a great deal of activity at the front of the house. Men and women in dark suits and pant suits were scurrying about and speaking on radios and phones. There was a siren sounding in the near distance. SAIC Wright said to Don, "Wait here a moment while I found out what is going on." She exited the SUV and Don, ignoring her directive, alighted right behind her.

"Foster," Wright barked at one of the agents, "what's happening?"

Foster ran over to his supervisor and opened his mouth to speak but stopped short when he saw Don immediately behind her. Wright, seeing his apprehension, turned and saw Don. Her first thought was to admonish Lasserman but then just turned to Foster and said, "Go ahead, just tell us."

"Yes, sir," Foster said to Wright. "I'm afraid they've found the woman dead on a railroad track."

Don exploded in a frenzy, "What? Who? Maria? Emily?" SAIC Wright put her arm around Don's shoulder to get him to calm down just a bit.

Agent Foster continued, "The younger woman. It appears she fell from an embankment onto the tracks in front of an incoming train."

Don was pacing in a circle as the Stamford police cruiser arrived, and Maria got out from the back seat. She looked bedraggled and near exhaustion. Don ran to her and caught her in his arms as she was about to collapse. Through tears and sobs, she explained that Emily must have walked to a yard above the Metro North tracks on the New Canaan line and fell or jumped in front of a train arriving at the Talmadge Hill Station.

"But that's nearly three miles from here," protested Don.

"If you're driving," explained officer Coates who was standing at Maria's side after exiting the cruiser. "We think she walked more or less a straight line, right through the Woodway Country Club and the surrounding woods. If she followed that route it's less than two miles."

Don and Maria found that explanation insightful and plausible, but not comforting. Eventually, the coroner would rule the death an accident, but Maria always believed that it was intentional. Maria knew Emily better than anyone and totally believed that Emily fully comprehended what was being said about her father, now labeled a monster, and she simply couldn't handle the thought of being the daughter of such a man.

Don and Maria were in the dining room processing the day's tragic events when SAIC Wright interrupted their privacy. "Mr. Lasserman, I'm afraid we have a new development."

Don, still holding Maria's hand, looked up at the FBI agent, but said nothing. His eyes, however, simply conveyed, "now what?"

SAIC Wright took the cue and explained, "It appears your brother did escape the conflagration at the Civil Rights Memorial. There's a gunman holed up at Graceland threatening to blow the place up if anyone comes near. We believe it's your brother."

Don was speechless, so said nothing. He just looked at the agent imploringly. There were several long seconds of awkward and painful silence. Finally, Don asked in bewilderment, "Graceland? You mean the Elvis place?"

"Yes, sir. I'll be back as we get more information."

As the agent left the dining room, Maria broke into more sobs. Don moved his chair closer to her and they sat side-by-side in an awkward embrace. Just as Teddy's death had created a strange chasm between the couple, Emily's death was bringing them back together. Within minutes, SAIC Wright returned.

"Sir, Director Mantis is on the phone. He would like to speak to you." She was referring to FBI Director Ronald Mantis. The weary look on Don's face telegraphed, "Really?" but he kissed Maria on the top of her head and followed SAIC Wright into the adjacent kitchen.

"This is Don Lasserman," Don said when Wright handed him the cellphone.

"Mr. Lasserman. The gunman has confirmed he is your brother. He won't come out. He also hasn't made any demands." explained the director.

"And?" said Don.

"Well, sir, we'd like you to come down to Memphis to see if you can help diffuse this situation before anyone else gets hurt. He shot two black employees on his way into Graceland and all he keeps shouting from inside is 'We're taking the country back, baby.'"

Don's nerves were frayed, and his emotions drained. "Has he actually asked for me? Aren't his two sons already there?"

"Yes, sir. Both Daniel Junior and Nathaniel are now on site in Memphis. Daniel Junior, quite frankly, seems uncontrollable, and we are worried about sending him into to talk to his father. He keeps saying he just wants to kill him. Nathaniel seems much more stable and says he'll go in, but he wants you to go with him."

"Me?" shouted Don. "And why is anyone 'going in?' Can't you just smoke him out? Send in a SWAT team? This doesn't seem like normal protocol." Don was way beyond annoyed. "I need to be here with my wife. Our niece, sister of Nathaniel and Daniel Junior, has just been found dead. Do the boys know that yet? That their sister is dead?" Don's voice was continuing to rise in volume.

Director Mantis tried to calmly explain, "Sir, you are correct. It is not normal protocol. We're not even sure if it's a hostage situation or not. An employee, a twenty-year old black girl named Darla, is missing, and we're presuming she is with your brother, but he hasn't said one way or the other. We're trying our best to talk him out in order to preserve her life, if she's with him, and the president wants to ensure we don't do anything to damage the museum, so we're working this situation with very soft gloves."

Don exploded at the mention of President Haight. "The son-of-a-bitch is worried about the museum? What the fuck is wrong with him? A girl's life may be on the line, and he's worried about mementos?"

Director Mantis, not known as a fan of the president, worked his best to be professional. "Sir, I believe he is worried about the public relations disaster if the United States government accidentally causes any damage to the home of one of America's most beloved icons. I further believe..."

Don cut him off. "I get it. I get it. He's just an ass, that's all." He was about to explain again that he needed to stay in Stamford with his wife in light of the death of Emily, when Maria walked into the kitchen.

She put her arm around her husband and said, "Don, it's okay. Nate needs you. The country needs you."

"But..."

"I'll be okay. Jasmine and Greg are already on their way here. They'll be here in a couple of hours. Go stop Daniel before anything more happens." She looked into his eyes and Don knew she was resolute.

They hugged for a long time. Don turned to SAIC Wright who was standing nearby holding the cellphone with the Director on the line and just nodded.

On the ground in Memphis, just after dusk, Don huddled with his nephews. Daniel Junior was, as the FBI Director had warned him, unhinged.

"Uncle Don," Daniel Junior whined, "how could he do this to us? As usual he hasn't given any thought to how his actions affect the rest of us. He just does whatever he damn well pleases and the rest of us are stuck cleaning up his mess."

Don tried to reason with his nephew. "This is way beyond some self-centered behavior, Daniel. He seems to be carrying out some sort of ill-conceived vendetta."

Daniel broke back into the conversation. "Vendetta? The stupid son-of-a-bitch couldn't spell the word let alone comprehend its meaning. He just got his feelings hurt and someone else needs to suffer for it. I swear I'll kill him if I get my hands on him. How can I go back to my job at the hospital or even return to my neighborhood with everyone whispering behind my back about being the son of a maniacal, mass-murdering nut job?"

Daniel's rants about killing his son-of-a-bitch father made the FBI nervous. Although they may not have been disappointed with such an outcome, there was no assurance that the takedown would go the way Daniel Junior envisioned and could actually make the situation worse. Nathaniel, on the other hand, agreed with all of his brother's laments but realized the focus needed to be on resolving the current situation. After talking with the boys, Don told SAIC Wright who had accompanied him from Stamford, that he and Nate would go into the Graceland home, but only if Daniel was receptive to their entry.

Within a few moments, the FBI was able to connect with Daniel on one of the Graceland landlines. Daniel had left his personal cellphone in his truck, which was now in FBI custody, having been towed earlier from the Rizzo's Diner parking lot. Daniel seemed somewhat surreal. His voice was upbeat, but his words were bizarrely disjointed, and he was showing signs of severe paranoia; not unusual when dozens of law enforcement officers surround you, most of whom would simply love to drive a bullet through your brain. SAIC Wright handed the phone to Nate.

"Hey, little one," intoned Daniel to his second-born son. Daniel had always referred to Nate as the little one, even when he was a grown man and even though his size, through regimental workout training, had long ago dwarfed both his father and his older brother. "Seems like quite a pickle here." Daniel continued with a barely-controlled lilt in his voice.

"Dad, Uncle Don and I would like to come in and talk to you," replied Nate as calmly as he could.

"Donny boy is here?" said Daniel in a more excited tone. "Put him on the phone."

Nate handed the phone to his uncle, but Don only got as far as saying, "Daniel" before his twin brother launched into a fitful diatribe.

"Whatcha think now, Donny boy? We're taking this country back. And 'bout fucking time. What would your buddy Adamo think now? Who's in control now? I am! Haight says it's time to take our country back, and that's what we're doing, starting today," Daniel seemed to boast proudly, his barely-intelligible words interspersed with non-intelligible grunts and curses.

"Daniel," Don began again, "let me and Nate come in and talk."

"Sure, sure," said Daniel much too serenely. Don was surprised it was going to be so easy. But then Daniel shouted something nonsensical about former president Adamo, followed by "Take our country back" followed by a short list of conditions. "No cops, dammit, and no weapons."

"Of course not," Don reassured, but Daniel wasn't done yet.

"I need to know. I need to know. Just you and Nate. No funny business. Stay on the main aisles. Bring this cellphone with you, and I'll let you know where I am as you get closer."

Don was readily agreeing to everything his brother demanded when he was caught off guard by a final demand. "No weapons! If you're coming in, you've got to be naked, so I know you've got nothing on you." Don was reluctant to give into this humiliating demand, so after a few back-and-forths they settled on underwear as being acceptable.

So it was that Don Lasserman and his nephew Nate were being televised walking across the driveway of the Graceland Mansion in their boxers and briefs respectively. Agent Wilkins, presumably in charge at the Memphis site, had briefed the two Lassermans before they started on their walk of shame. Wilkins explained that they had no idea where Daniel Lasserman was inside the massive structure.

"The building is over 17,000 square feet with 23 rooms. He could be just about anywhere. The two employees he shot and killed were found right at the front door. We don't know if he shot them there or encountered them elsewhere on the grounds and dragged them there. We're also not sure exactly how long he's been here. All available law enforcement resources were focused on the shootings at the National Civil Rights Memorial across town and most tourist attractions, including Graceland, went on lockdown, so there weren't any visitors on site here by the time he got here. We haven't been inside as we don't want to endanger the missing employee. The museum director has accounted for all employees except this one." Both Don and Nate nodded in understanding and then hugged one another to marshal the strength to undertake this bizarre, inconceivable task.

Don and Nate entered the grand entrance hall and had just stepped into the large living room where they were staring at an opposing doorway framed with stained glass peacocks when the cellphone Don was holding trilled.

"We're here," was all Don said to his brother.

"Yeah, yeah, I can hear you," retorted Daniel. "Come on down to the basement. I'm in the pool room." Don absent-mindedly closed the phone and held it in his left hand.

Just as they started to turn away from the peacocks, there was a subtle creaking sound, like a door hinge, and a very subdued sob with a sharp intake of breath. Nate was closest to the peacock-framed door, which was slightly ajar, so he pulled it open. Quickly shrinking away from the door was a very frightened young black girl.

"Darla?" Nate whispered as he put his finger to his lips. The girl froze and stared at Nate, which must have been quite a surprising site for her; it's doubtful she was expecting to see a tall, handsome, white man strolling through the mansion in his underwear. He explained quietly as he reached for her hand, "We're going to head down the stairs to the basement. When we start down the stairs, you walk out the front door to the police. Keep your hands in plain sight above your head as you go out." With that, the three of them headed back through the living room to the entrance hall. Nate squeezed Darla's hand and then let go as they parted ways to head in their separate directions.

Nate and Uncle Don made as much noise as they could in their bare feet while heading down the stairs to the basement. They were trying to cover up any commotion that might occur as the police reacted to Darla's appearance should that occur before they got to their destination. They never heard anything from outside, so they assumed Darla's exit went well. At the bottom of the stairs, they saw a room with multiple TVs, but before they could decide which way to go, Daniel called to them from the room across the way. The two men clad in only their underwear walked cautiously into Elvis' billiards room.

They were surprised to see Daniel calmly shooting nine-ball. Don looked at the cellphone in his hand and belatedly realized that he had not actually needed the phone for the last several minutes. Not having a pocket to drop the phone in, he let it just drop to the floor. Daniel's face lit up at the sight of them, and he put the cue stick down on the table as he picked up the Beemiller that had been laying on the rail closest to him. With the gun in his right hand, Daniel approached his middle child for an embrace. As he wrapped his arms around his son, he quietly said, "Little One" and then held the embrace for much longer than Nate ever remembered being embraced by his father. Don remained a safe distance away around the corner of the pool table keeping a close eye on the Beemiller wagging in his brother's hand.

Eventually, Daniel released his grip on Nate and looked towards Don. "Afraid of me?" mocked Daniel. "I'm not one of them. Adamo and his kind are the enemy." Daniel looked at his brother with something approaching pity on his face mixed with fear and concern. After many silent seconds and unblinking stares, Don moved tentatively towards his brother's outstretched arms. As they embraced,

Nate was still standing close by. Nate would later recall that he wasn't really aware of the next few seconds of violent activity, but as his father closed his arms around Uncle Don, something inside Nate similar to the rage his brother had been openly sharing, was unleashed and this inner being took over with a ferocious and furious frenzy.

Making a final mental note of the gun in his father's hand, Nate rushed at his uncle and father. With full throttle he slammed into Uncle Don's back which in turn slammed the entwined brothers into the rear wall with such force that as Nate stepped back from them, his uncle bounced out of the embrace and fell to the floor, and the Beemiller flew from Daniel's grip. Before his father could react for the gun or fall to the floor, Nate's right fist, fueled by long-repressed anger, landed squarely on the side of Daniel's cheek. With a fractured mandible, broken nasal concha, and blood spurting from his left eye and nostril, Daniel fell to the floor with a thud and did not move. Nate's anger was still seething, so the pain of his bruised hand with four fractured bones- three phalanges and one metacarpal-had not yet registered. To his uncle's amazement, Nate reached into his briefs and withdrew a small plastic disk from under his scrotum. He pressed it like you would a garage door opener then spoke into it, "We're in the billiards room in the basement. No threat." With that, he threw the disk across the room and collapsed on the floor. Later, he would explain to his uncle that agent Wilkins had given him the miniature, transmitting device just before they began their walk up the mansion driveway.

Don was overwhelmed by the show of force that entered the billiards room within fifteen seconds of Nate's message. He looked on with amazement without relinquishing his position in the center of the room. Four agents carried Daniel's still comatose body from the room after securing plastic hand ties and ankle cuffs. Agent Wilkins knelt beside Nate, still sitting on the floor, spoke briefly to him, and then rose, patting Nate on the shoulder as he did so. Then Wilkins approached Don.

"Are you okay, Mr. Lasserman?"

Don thought, shook his head slightly, but then said, "I think so."

"We'll bring your clothes down and an EMT team is just outside waiting to check you and your nephew over. Thanks for your heroic efforts today. It's likely you prevented further bloodshed, and I'm certain you saved your brother's life," said the agent in a consoling tone. Don looked at him but offered no response.

After several minutes, when no one else was left in the room, Don walked over to his nephew and just stared down at him still sitting on the floor. Nate looked up at his uncle and took the proffered hand to lift him up to a standing position. The two men, still only in the underwear, looked at each other, both with moist eyes. Nate collapsed onto his uncle's chest and the tears flowed freely for two or three minutes. Then they began the processing of dressing and prepared to face the waiting FBI agents and the press conference that would likely be forthcoming after being checked out by the EMTs.

Their assumption of an awkward, but necessary, press report was correct. After a few moments huddled with Director Mantis, Agents Wilkins and Wright, and yet another FBI psychologist, Nate and Don were paraded in front of the cameras. Thankfully, the FBI Director did all the talking and fielded all questions. He referenced Nate and Don as being invaluable in bringing this nightmare to a speedy and bloodless end but offered no further explanations. He remained stoic even when persistent reporters wanted details of why the two family members had entered the mansion only in their underwear. Don wondered if this day would ever end and he wondered what his nephews were thinking. At the end of the news conference, Don's thoughts returned to his wife a thousand miles away in Connecticut, and it suddenly occurred to him that his nephews were probably still unaware of their sister's death, be it accident or suicide. The thought of breaking that news to his beleaguered and exhausted nephews brought Don to a new level of despair and grief.

But Don knew that once they were not *on* the news his nephews would be watching the news, so he needed to tell them about their sister's death in Connecticut earlier in the day. Daniel Junior and Nathaniel absorbed the news as well as they could. Perhaps it was easier when set against the backdrop of the day's activities. Nathaniel said, "One of us should tell dad." But Daniel Junior simply said, "Fuck that." And the thought faded away. After a few moments, Daniel Junior realized that he hadn't eaten since morning. As he mentioned it, Nate and Uncle Don had the same realization. Though it was now nearing 9 p.m., Daniel Junior called his wife, Brigette, and asked her to prepare a meal for all of them. He also informed her that Nate and Uncle Don would be spending the night. Don opened his mouth to protest but realized he was really too exhausted to fly to White Plains tonight, even in a government private jet. Besides, it would probably be good for the three men to have some more introspective time together. He called Maria, who assured him she was doing fine with Jasmine and Greg there and she would rest easier now knowing that he and the boys were safe.

Don turned to his oldest nephew and said, "Okay, Daniel, let's go."

Daniel Junior looked at his uncle and then his brother. Through some tears and with a shaky voice that climaxed in determined resolution, he said, "Call me DJ. I never want to hear the name Daniel again."

CHAPTER *Seven*

The next day, Don returned to his home in Connecticut. His heart and mind were awash with emotions and conflicts. Happy to be home with Maria. Sad over the death of Emily. Overjoyed to have Jasmine and Greg at home. Heartbreaking reminder that Ted is not there. Content with the role he played yesterday in bringing his brother's reign of terror to an end. Despondent that his only sibling is now in jail awaiting arraignment on multiple murder and other charges. At moments, he felt his heart would burst open with aching or with joy. And at other moments, his head felt ready to implode alternating with the desire to explode. While wallowing in this sense of no direction, no right or wrong answers, no way to bring closure to so many elements in his life, he began to marvel at his wife's state of calm and sense of purpose. So, he asked her what she was thinking and how she was managing to present herself in such a stable and competent manner.

"Oh, Don," she said as she stroked his forearm, "I'm not sure what I feel or how to act. Emily's death is so overwhelming, but I know it would have been so difficult for her to go on living knowing what her father has done. No one ever gave her credit for her intelligence or insight. Underneath that inability to communicate effectively with us was a very wonderful, caring, empathetic young woman. Remember I used to tell you how tranquil she would be at the Southfield Center? She loved to play and laugh with the children, and we always assumed it was because she herself was so childlike. But what if she really just enjoyed making the lives of those children a bit better for a few hours? Her thoughts and feelings were a lot deeper and better defined than what we could comprehend. I know she was devastated to learn what Daniel has done. And I believe she was ashamed of what he has also done to this family."

Don wrapped his arm around his grieving wife and said, "I suppose we will never know exactly what happened after she walked out of the house, but in the end, it doesn't really matter, does it? Her death, like her life, is so full of mysteries that we can never fully understand or appreciate."

"Exactly," sobbed Maria. "I miss her so already, and I know I will feel it even more when Jasmine and Greg leave to go back home in Kentucky, you go back to work, and the emptiness of the house closes in on me."

"Well, I'm sure you're right about that," Don confirmed, "but I'm not sure I'll be going back to work. Ivy called this morning before I got on the government plane in Memphis. She said I should take all the time I need to take care of things here."

"That was nice of her." Maria said in reference to the general counsel at Don's firm.

"But there's more," Don added. "She said when I do come back I need to go see her and Ken before going to my office. I'm fairly certain that means they don't want me going back to my office ever again. I'm sure they're concerned about the firm's reputation and any perceived connection with Daniel."

"Oh, Don, can they do that?" Maria sounded sympathetic and concerned for her husband.

"It's all right, Maria. It's time anyway. Don't forget, I already retired four years ago." Don was referring to his retirement at age 60, the firm's normal retirement age for senior executives, but he returned less than two months later at the firm's urging. Due to several other key resignations, or defections, the firm was left with an insufficient succession plan, and Don agreed to return short-term to help ensure a smoother transition to the next generation of leaders. That was over three years ago, and he was still there functioning as the firm's interim chief administrative officer.

Maria changed the subject. "I spoke with Father Lane late yesterday," she said referring to the pastor at St. Paul's on the Green, the Episcopal church in Norwalk where the Lassermans attended irregularly. "I told him we didn't want to have a wake or memorial service for Emily. He said he understood, especially given the circumstances, but suggested that perhaps we have a brief, unpublicized, service as part of the regular church service tomorrow and then an extended social hour dedicated to Emily for the benefit of the parishioners. I agreed. I hope you're fine with that."

"I think that's perfect," Don agreed. "Emily wouldn't want any fuss and it will be good to get this done quickly before the press gets wind."

True to his word, Father Lane did keep the service brief, and, as a welcome relief, it appeared that the media had not learned of the event. Don and Maria, along with daughter Jasmine and son-in-law Greg, were busy greeting church members in the church basement when they were surprised by an unexpected, approaching guest.

"Don, Maria, we are so, so sorry for your tragic loss," said the man with outstretched arms as he moved in for an embrace, first of Maria, then Don.

"How did you know we were here?" stuttered Don after the long, warm embrace.

"Never underestimate the powers of a former president," said former President Adamo with a slight smile. "I also know you're about to be retired again, and I might have a second career prospect for you."

"How could you possibly know that?"

But the former president just smiled. "This isn't the time or place to discuss that, Don. Today is about Emily. Makayla and I will stop by tomorrow morning around eleven if that's okay," said Adamo referencing his wife at his side. And with that, and within minutes, the Adamos and their retinue disappeared as stealthily as they had appeared.

Monday morning arrived, as did the small caravan of black Cadillac Escalades promptly at 11 a.m. Former President Richard Adamo and former First Lady Makayla Adamo exited the middle of the three SUV's and strode to the art deco glass and chrome double front door of the Lasserman's contemporary North Stamford home. After warm and sincerely heartfelt embraces reflective of their long-standing friendship, Don and Maria lead their visitors into the home's bright and airy two-story library with views overlooking the rear patio and Emily's beloved koi pond beyond the swimming pool. After several minutes of catching up on old times and old acquaintances, the former president got down to business.

"Don, I'm founding a new research institute, and we're going to need someone with administrative skills, a dynamic personality, and a shared vision and supporting values to lead the organization. I believe you are that person," began Adamo. Don started to interject his initial concerns about timing, winding up his job, staying under the radar while his brother's actions were dominating the news headlines.

"But, Don, you haven't even heard our mission yet. I believe the time is right for an innovative and forward-thinking manifesto and strategic game plan to combat racism. And, yes, even though I've been thinking about this for quite some time, your brother's actions have catapulted this initiative to the forefront of my thoughts and actions," continued Adamo while patting the back of Don's hands resting on his knees. Don was sitting on the white leather Mies van der Rohe Barcelona chair, perpendicular to Adamo on the matching sofa.

Don contemplated a moment and then stood, started pacing and said, "Richard, it sounds like a great initiative, and obviously very much needed.

And I am extremely flattered that you want me involved, but I just don't think I'm the right guy. Look at what my family name means to America right now!

"Don, don't you see," implored Adamo, "what your name connotes right now is an asset to our cause, not a detriment. Think about it. A prominent outspoken black politician joining forces with the twin brother of one of America's foremost racists! How powerful will that be? We can do this! We can make a difference."

"I'm not sure he is one of America's *foremost* racists," Don said somberly. "We're still not sure what he was thinking or planning."

"Don, you're right, of course, in the macro sense. Your brother probably doesn't hate black people. He didn't have a grand plan to kill black people. He's not part of some conspiracy or organized hate group. But it's clear he is a racist. He holds a view that many white people do and that is that black people can be tolerated as long as they aren't interfering with your life and don't rise above the expectations that the white people have for them. He may not be a racist in a technical sense of hatred, but he is a racist and the most talked-about racist of this day. His actions have tapped into the just-below-the-surface tensions of both whites and blacks. He is the face of racism at the moment and we can leverage that to move forward."

Don had tried to interject a few times as Adamo spoke, but it was difficult to interrupt the great orator and Don found that his budding objections were merely knee-jerk responses to uncomfortable truths. The two men talked some more for another thirty minutes. Adamo assured Don that he wasn't reaching out to him specifically because of Daniel's shooting rampage, but he admitted he did think the connection would resonate well with the public and generate greater acceptance. Don was still hesitant when Maria and Makayla returned from their walk in the gardens. Don updated her on the discussion of the racism institute.

"Don, I don't know why you're hesitating," Maria said. "You're about to be unemployed, and I don't need you moping about the house underfoot. But, more importantly, this should be a wake-up call for both of us. We can't sit idly by and expect others to do the heavy work that needs to be done to overcome the forces of racism. Richard is right that you are in a special position to bring the root causes and evils of racism to light. I want you to do this. I want to ensure that Emily is not forgotten."

So, Don agreed to become the executive director of the Adamo Institute on Race Relations, or AIRR, and Adamo himself would be chairman of the board. They would begin working on rounding out a full twelve-member board and hiring staff. They agreed to physically house the Institute in nearby Bridgeport, Connecticut, a city with a large minority population and convenient to Don's Stamford home as well as Adamo's post-presidency Mt. Kisco home in neighboring Westchester County, New York.

A little after one o'clock that afternoon, the Adamos and Lassermans were having lunch in Don's library when one of former President Adamo's aides stepped into the room and suggested they all gather around a television set. Lester Holt of NBC News was just announcing that President Haight would be holding a press conference at any moment, and he was expected to address the mass shooting rampage of Daniel Lasserman. That national tragedy occurred last Friday, and it was now Monday afternoon. President Haight had not yet made any comment on the shootings, but to be honest, he was in France on Friday and then stopped in Bermuda on the way back to Washington to participate in a charity golf tournament. At least he respected his priorities. He had just arrived at the White House earlier in the day. As the President entered the Cabinet Room just off the Oval Office, Lester Holt yielded the TV screen and audio feed to the president.

"My fellow Americans," the President began, "I want to share with you my sorrow about the tragic loss of lives in Arkansas and Tennessee last week, but first I want to update you on my state visit to France last week. France has long been a friend to America dating back to the time of the Revolutionary War. They helped us then, and we saved their behinds in World War II, so I guess you could say we're even, but even so, we continue to be very, very good friends. I believe we're going to do very good work together in the months ahead."

"What is he talking about?" murmured Maria.

Makayla said, "I just hope he doesn't say something about French fries." Just as the four of them snickered at that thought, the president did indeed say they don't have French fries in France, but they do have something called 'frites' which looked like French fries to him. The two couples groaned in unison. And then, thinking it couldn't get any worse, President Haight brought up his golf scores for the rounds he played in Bermuda over the weekend and rambled on for several more minutes about the course, his foursome mates, the weather. Finally, he returned to the topic of Daniel's race-driven killing spree three days earlier.

"It is such a tragedy," President Haight intoned. "Thirteen people lost their lives in three incidents last week. Several more victims remain hospitalized. Their families have much to deal with right now. Our thoughts and prayers are with them all."

After a brief pause for the thoughts and prayers to take effect, the president continued, "The gunman should not have taken such actions. Violence is not the answer. But this doesn't mean he is a bad person. Think of the level of frustration that he must have experienced that drove him to these actions. I know many Americans share this frustration as Congress continues to prove incapable of passing the various initiatives I promised the American people during our campaign for this great office. Let us pray for all the victims and their families. Let us pray for an end to the Congressional ineptitude that leads to such frustration. And let us pray for the great United States of America." With that, the president ended his telecast.

Don Lasserman sat in his chair with his mouth literally open in shock. Maria held a hand over her mouth. Makayla was slowly shaking her head back and forth. And former President Adamo was tense with anger. He finally broke the awe and silence.

"This is exactly why we need the Institute, Don. He didn't label this as domestic terrorism. He didn't call it a hate crime. He didn't even mention the topic of race," the former president was on a roll, but Don interrupted him.

"The worst part, Richard," Don seethed, "is that he didn't unconditionally condemn Daniel's actions. Quite the contrary. He seemed to acknowledge a certain justifiability of his actions."

Makayla Adamo not known for being shy with her opinions or timid with her choice of words spoke up, "This is going to be bad. Real fucking bad."

And Maria piled on, "I'm afraid the idiot has just awakened a simmering racist monster. God help us all."

They didn't have to wait long to see the effects of the racist monster or God's reluctance to help. By the time Lester Holt returned with the Nightly News four hours later, there were initial reports of breaking news from Pittsburgh and Buffalo where vigilante 'patrols' had taken to the streets. In Pittsburgh's Hill District, three pickup trucks had careened down Wylie Avenue with 'militia men' in the truck beds strafing the neighborhood buildings with random and rampant gunfire. In Buffalo, two men had driven a truck into a restaurant predominantly patronized by African-Americans, setting it on fire as they bailed from the pickup turning it into a large, mobile Molotov cocktail. The restaurant immediately erupted in flames and quickly engulfed the adjacent neighborhood barbershop. At the time of the Nightly News report, it was too early to identify any casualties, but that evening, the Nightly News simply did not go off the air. Breaking news continued to break with similar acts of aggression in Cleveland, Chicago, Knoxville, Denver and working its way to the west coast with armed assaults in Reno, Los Angeles and Sacramento. By the time Don and Maria turned off the television shortly after midnight, two hundred and thirty-three Americans, almost all black, were known dead, with hundreds injured and dozens of others missing.

By morning, the violence had grown to unprecedented proportions. The initial wave of attacks primarily against black communities in nearly every major urban area was now being countered by attacks on primarily white enclaves, such as Buckhead in Atlanta, Carlton Woods in Houston and Lindenwood Park in St. Louis. Riots were ubiquitous. Businesses were being looted, vandalized, and burned. Even private residences were being torched and drive-by shootings were too numerous to track. As Don watched the endless stream of violence and despair on television that morning, he noted that thus far, incidents in Boston, New York and Philadelphia were minor. That gave him a small glimmer of hope that eventually enlightenment and tolerance would win out.

His tepid hopes for calm and peace quickly flickered out. By week's end every major city was experiencing outright street warfare, including New York. Tempers flared even greater when Daniel Lasserman was arraigned on Wednesday on multiple counts of premeditated murder and endangering the lives of others. His location was being kept secret and Don was grateful for that. He and Adamo moved quickly to recruit board members for AIRR, but due to the prevalent violence, there were no face-to-face meetings, only phone and video conversations. Other than Don and Richard, the AIRR board included ten other members: three former corporate CEO's, two university professors, a media mogul, a former head of the National Football League, former vice-president Clayton Andrews who had been vice-president under Adamo's predecessor, a high-profile black fashion model, and a white, male action film star.

Over the next month, unprovoked random attacks and sporadic rioting continued, but fortunately, the intensity and frequency diminished a fair amount. Four weeks after Daniel's rampage and the weak response by President Haight that sparked this wave of overt racism, the official count of victims was four hundred eighty-two fatalities, two thousand three hundred twenty-six injuries requiring hospital-ization, and $4.8 billion in property damage. During this time, Don was able to secure and retrofit suitable office space in Bridgeport for the AIRR offices. They would be holding their first in-person board meeting in just four days' time. Given the composition of its board, AIRR had reached out to major corporations, entrepreneurs, sports teams, the fashion industry and Hollywood and received significant commit-ments for funding. Don and his staff of three: a con-troller who was really not much more than a book-keeper with serious Quick Books skills, a marketing specialist formerly with the Children's Television Workshop, and an office manager who really served as an all-round administrator manning the reception desk, fielding incoming calls, working with vendors, maintaining schedules and travel requirements. The office manager position was a natural fit for Claudia, Don's secretary at the investment firm, and she was happy to leave the hectic pace of Manhattan behind to begin the final act of her impressive career. Their first-year budget was an impressive $35 million and AIRR had already been busy with education collat-erals, public service announcements, and university outreach programs.

Former President Richard Adamo convened AIRR's first in-person board meeting in the glass-walled tenth-floor conference room overlooking Long Island Sound and the city's Seaside Park at promptly eleven o'clock Monday morning. When the group took a bio-break around 12:30 and lunch was being brought in, the former president excused himself to take an important phone call, as did several of the other board members. They were expected back in the conference room at one o'clock to finish the business of their agenda. However, at one o'clock, Richard Adamo was still on the phone. The rest of the board took their time finishing their lunches and fiddled with their own phones while waiting for their chairman to rejoin the meeting. When he finally did, at twenty minutes before two, his face was grave, perhaps even alarmed. He sat at his place at the head of the conference table and just seemed to stare into space for many, many long seconds. Finally, when Don prompted him by calling his name three times, Richard Adamo looked around the table into the faces of the eleven other board members of AIRR.

"Ladies and gentlemen," Adamo finally said to the gathering, "I'm aware of some very interesting and potentially troubling news. And it will likely have an effect on the work we are doing here at AIRR. I want to share the news, but you have to swear to absolute confidentiality. You can share nothing of what I am about to tell you." He waited and looked around the room while each individual nodded concurrence. "According to sources, which I can't reveal, the president will resign by the end of this week."

There had always been speculation about an early end to President Haight's presidency since the election nearly two and a half years ago. There was a Senate special investigation focusing mostly on Haight's ties to a foreign government and that government's illegal influence on the U.S. election that often showed promise of bringing the president down, but so far, no smoking gun and no conclusion to the investigation. There was also an SEC investigation into insider trading allegations, but it too had been stymied due to numerous adroit legal maneuvers by Haight's lawyers and the untimely death of a key player, Haight's primary financial advisor, Vincent Posner. There had been ongoing, and growing, allegations of sexual harassment, but these too seemed to be gathering no purchase. And, since shortly after the inauguration, there had been rumblings of a potential impeachment based on incompetency and some just really bizarre behavior by the sitting president. But these rumblings had never come to fruition. Everyone in the conference room was speculating as to which of these anti-Haight initiatives was finally bearing fruit.

Adamo continued after a few seconds. "I don't want to share the specifics with you as this knowledge could put you in an uncomfortable position, but I can tell you that the president will voluntarily resign in just a few days in order to alleviate pressure stemming from one particular inquiry. That is not our concern. Our concern needs to be on the likely resurrection of racist terrorism that will surely occur when Haight leaves office."

Many of Haight's most ardent and most vocal supporters were individuals with ties to white supremacist groups or outright avowed racists or right-wing Christian fundamentalists. And several of the white supremacist and Christian Right leaders had made statements during the rocky Haight presidency that if Haight were impeached or forced from office there would be consequences. Some even boldly stated that there would be a civil war unlike anything the world has ever seen. It was this backdrop that was of concern to Adamo as he addressed his fellow AIRR board members in Bridgeport that Monday afternoon.

For the rest of that day and well into the evening, the AIRR board brainstormed ideas to get ahead of the racist insurrection that would surely occur when Haight stepped down. They had dinner brought in from nearby Joseph's Steakhouse. They had planned

on going to the restaurant for dinner, but considering the confidential strategy they were discussing,
it would not have been possible to maintain their
secrecy in the restaurant. By the end of the evening,
they were united in their approach and would launch
execution in the morning.

CHAPTER *Eight*

Tuesday morning, former president Adamo awoke in his Mt. Kisco home and placed a call to the current vice president, James Shilling. He reached an aide, but the vice president returned his call within fifteen minutes. Adamo suspected that Shilling was as aware of the situation regarding Haight unfolding this week as he was, but he didn't know for certain, so he didn't mention it during the call. He began cautiously after just a few seconds of social banter.

"Jim," the former president began, "we, meaning AIRR, want to broadcast a public service announcement, and we want to do it this week. We need to make a bold statement against the racism that is tearing this country apart. I believe a joint PSA featuring you and me will be most effective." Adamo waited for Shilling's response.

"Sounds interesting, Richard. Are you sure you want it to be from me? Wouldn't Alexander be more appropriate?" queried Shilling. Adamo thought he detected a bit of a tease in Shilling's tone, but he had prepared for such a response.

"Normally I would agree with you, Jim, that the president would be most appropriate. But, quite frankly, I believe his laissez faire, off-the-cuff approach in speaking, especially regarding racial matters, is at least partially to blame for the current high tensions. I worry that he would only make things worse. I'm counting on you to bring a more civil, professional and constructive tone to the table," implored Adamo as matter-of-factly as he could.

The vice president said he understood and asked for a few minutes to have an aide check his schedule. Adamo hung on the phone for seven minutes before Shilling returned to the line.

"Richard, if you can be in Washington tomorrow evening, we can do the PSA live from the Cabinet Room at 9 p.m. I can arrange to have it teed up with all the major networks for broadcast," stated Shilling.

"That's perfect, Jim. I'm in New York right now, but I can be in DC in a couple of hours. Our marketing team has created a rough framework of what we'd like to say. I'll have it emailed to your staff communications people right now, and we can fine tune it before the broadcast. As I said earlier, we're targeting just three to five minutes of script," replied Adamo.

Adamo flew to Washington's Ronald Reagan Airport from the Westchester County Airport on a private jet belonging to one of the CEO's on the AIRR board. Traveling with him were that CEO, a Hollywood actor who was also on the AIRR board, and AIRR's executive director, Don Lasserman. By 5 p.m. Tuesday afternoon, they were settled into the Hay-Adams Hotel at H Street and 16th NW across from the White House. Shilling had arranged a dinner for the AIRR entourage at the hotel's Lafayette restaurant in a private dining room. The vice president brought along his communications director and after dinner she and Don Lasserman went to work fine-tuning the script for the now scheduled public service announcement. Adamo and Shilling would meet at the Cabinet Room in the West Wing around 7 p.m. Wednesday evening for a dress rehearsal and then be in place for the live broadcast.

When Adamo arrived at the White House Wednesday evening at seven, he and Don Lasserman were escorted to the Cabinet room. After a few minutes, Shilling and Sheila, his communications director arrived. After pleasantries, Adamo and Shilling performed their sections of the PSA. Everyone agreed it was poignant, professional and hopefully effective. Shortly before 9 p.m., as technicians were double-checking the audio feeds, an aide stepped into the Cabinet Room and conferred briefly with Vice President Shilling. The vice president nodded in ascension a few times and then the aide disappeared.

"Richard, I'm afraid we'll have to move the broadcast down the hall to the Roosevelt Room. Apparently, some issue has come up, not sure what. Anyway, as you know, the Roosevelt Room is much more intimate and regal. I should have thought to use it from the beginning." explained the vice president.

Adamo was a bit surprised. Last minute changes like this were not commonplace in the White House, but he did have to agree that the Roosevelt Room, directly across from the Oval Office, would be an excellent backdrop. Promptly at 9 p.m., an off-screen announcer informed America that the vice president would now speak.

"Good evening, America. Thank you for welcoming me into your homes and hearts this evening. I am joined by former President Richard Adamo who will be speaking with me, and to you, about the state of race relations in our country today," intoned Shilling rather coldly.

"Thank you, Mr. Vice President, for having me here today. I am honored to be playing a role to help address this vitally important issue," cooed Adamo warmly.

"President Adamo," began Shilling, "since leaving office you have been working on strategies to improve the state of racial relations in America. Please tell us more about how this work came about and how it is progressing."

"I'm afraid the origin of our work at the Adamo Institute for Race Relations is rooted in the tragic events of this past March when an individual, a white man, chose to take out his frustrations in life against a primarily black group of victims. That rampage ignited weeks of racial violence that claimed hundreds more lives, both black and white," explained Adamo to Shilling but for the benefit of the television audience.

On cue, Shilling said, "And this race relations institute has an interesting board, doesn't it?"

"Yes, indeed. We have a board of twelve: myself, three former CEO's of major corporations, two university professors, a newspaper publisher, the former head of the National Football League, former vice president Clayton Andrews, a fashion model, and a movie star. We selected these board members in order to get insight into numerous industries and ways of life and also to reflect racial equality. Nearly half of the board represents minorities of color, but we also have very high-profile white individuals who can help define the issues and concerns from a white perspective," explained Adamo smoothly.

Following the script strictly, Shilling interrupted, "Pardon me, Mr. President, but you said there were twelve board members and I believe I only heard eleven."

"Yes, of course. Our twelfth member is our executive director, Don Lasserman. He is the brother of the alleged shooter at the National Civil Rights Memorial last March. We hope, with his help, we can get better insight and understanding of the frustrations being felt by many white Americans," said Adamo also following the script.

"That's a very interesting approach," said Shilling. "I think it shows a lot of promise to get all views at the table. Maybe this will get us past talking *at* one another and work together towards real progress."

"That is precisely the basis for our approach, Mr. Vice President. We can never solve this problem by blaming others or refusing to acknowledge concerns and perspectives of others. We need to have a unified approach to rebuilding our communities and living harmoniously," replied the former president.

"Please share with the American people the platform for improving race relations in this country as currently designed by your institute," implored the vice president.

"Well, first of all, Mr. Vice President, we need to acknowledge the problem collectively and not blame others. We need to move past finger pointing, name-calling, and blaming the other party. We need to affirm that we want to live in peace with one another. We need to recognize our differences and celebrate our differences together. And we need to eradicate groups that espouse values that do not reflect our American values. We need to eliminate hate from our society and, at times, we may need to do so forcefully." explained Adamo passionately.

Again, according to script, Shilling said, "We have a chart here that summarizes the key planks of this strategy and approach." And with that a chart appeared on television screens across the country. Shilling continued, "The four initiatives are: One, stop the violence. Two, revitalize the Civil Rights Commission. Three, make education inclusive of historic facts, good and bad. Four, enact a federal hate crime law that will be strictly and uniformly enforced."

Adamo picked up the thread, "We can't begin to make progress while we're still shooting one another, so that first step is extremely important. The Civil Rights Commission needs to be better staffed and better trained to address potential civil rights issues earlier in their development, including the disenfranchisement of some white Americans. Our schools need to address the evils of slavery and oppression but also show the context of such behaviors. We should not judge the actions of men or women two hundred years ago by today's standards. And, with a federal mandate to eradicate hate, we can move forward. Part of that federal mandate will be to define hate via a statute that will make clear what is, and is not, acceptable."

Shilling continued, "As of today, we are committed to these four initiatives. A task force will be assembled within forty-eight hours to spearhead the execution of these actions. There will be more information available on the Institute's website as well as forthcoming press releases from my office."

"Thank you, Mr. Vice President, for addressing this serious problem," said Adamo.

"Thank you, Mr. President, for your service and hard work on this issue. And thank you, America, for your attention and commitment to working with us to solve the problem of racism in our country," concluded Shilling.

While both men were still staring directly into the cameras, and while the cameras were still rolling, there was a minor commotion in front of them and behind the cameras as the door to the Roosevelt Room burst open. One intuitive camerawoman swung to the noise and caught the action as the sitting president, President Alexander Haight, marched determinedly towards the front of the room where Adamo and Shilling were still seated. Haight sat in a chair closest to Shilling and made sure the cameras were now trained on him.

"Good evening, America. I trust you have listened intently to the plan of action former President Adamo and Vice President Shilling have laid out before you. Racism is a nasty problem and one that requires the most adept leadership on such issues. I am not that leader. Vice President Shilling will be much more effective at leading our country on anti-racism initiatives than me. Therefore, effective at midnight tonight, I am resigning my position as President of the United States. I wish nothing but the best for Jim Shilling and for all Americans," blurted the president, while maintaining direct eye contact with the cameras and ignoring both individuals seated in the room with him. And with that, he got up from the table and strolled directly across the hall into the Oval Office; all of which was captured expertly by camerawoman Marlene Leja.

Waiting just long enough to ensure the cameras had stopped rolling, Adamo turned to Shilling. "You set us up. You planned this."

"No, no, I had no idea this was happening. Not tonight. Not this way," pleaded Shilling.

Not wasting any further time with the vice president, Adamo strolled defiantly into the Oval Office with Shilling close on his heels. Haight was at his desk, the Resolute Desk, barking orders at some unseen aide via the intercom. Adamo launched into a verbal assault. "What was the meaning of that? You had no right to derail our initiatives aimed at bringing peace and stability to the nation."

"Fuck you," blurted Haight to his predecessor. "I'm the president. I can do whatever I want. You guys are finally getting what you want. I'm leaving. So shut the fuck up."

"But why did you have to make such a spectacle during our anti-racism plea? You've taken all the focus off the issue and placed it squarely on your fall from grace," fumed Adamo.

"Exactly!" shouted Haight in return. "This way Americans will see me as the bigger person stepping aside to let more competent people handle the tough work of this race thing. They won't be talking about any other reasons that I might step down. Thanks for the friendly cover." Adamo detected an evil sneer on the president.

"Or," countered Adamo, "they'll see you walking away from the problem as affirmation that you don't believe in the values we've been talking about. The white supremacists will interpret that you're giving them free reign to remake America in their image. You've just unleashed the devil."

"Well," said Haight calmly, "I guess we'll see how it goes down within a day or two. One of us will be right." And with that, the smiling soon to be ex-President Haight, strode out of the Oval Office for the last time, leaving his predecessor and his successor dumbfounded and speechless. Their solitude was soon disturbed as various White House aides began the flurry of activity necessary to prepare for the swearing in of President Shilling at midnight. It was a small ceremony administered by the Chief Justice of the Supreme Court, filmed in the Oval Office by camerawoman Marlene Leja, and witnessed by half a dozen dignitaries, Shilling's wife, Penny, and former President Adamo.

CHAPTER *Nine*

The next few days were a blur for Don Lasserman and, indeed, for most Americans, but fortunately, the streets remained quiet. There was simply too much other news to distract the attention of nearly every citizen. There was, of course, much controversy over President Haight's abrupt resignation and subsequent disappearance. Like someone skipping out on their latest overdue rent payment, Haight and his family skulked away in the middle of the night following his televised resignation. Their exact whereabouts were not known with certainty until the weekend when it was confirmed that they had taken up residence in Namibia in southwest Africa. Namibia is certainly a beautiful country, but perhaps the greatest allure for the Haight family was its notoriously difficult extradition process. Though no members of the Haight family had yet been charged with any crimes, there was endless and colorful speculation. Haight family properties in Utah, New York and Florida appeared to be simply abandoned.

There was also the distraction of getting to know the new president. As vice president, Shilling had been known to the media and the people, but as president a greater level of curiosity and scrutiny was applied. President Shilling, fifty-five years old, average build, pasty skin, mild facial blemishes, and a ring of marshmallow around his round, perpetually stern, face, was a deeply religious man. This had been known for years, but as president, his strongly held religious beliefs became more troubling. First, his religious views were pre-emptive; they mattered more to him than anything else, perhaps even the upholding of the Constitution. Second, his religious views were supremely intolerant, meaning he not only did not recognize any alternate religions, he condemned anyone or any belief or non-belief that conflicted with his own religious views. Third, he believed it was God's will that he should wage a campaign to convert all of America, if not the world, to his own religious beliefs. And fourth, his religious views were extremely narrow and singular. He believed, and intended to enforce, arcane religious tenets that prohibited divorce, the mixing of races, gambling, homosexuality, equality of women and various other modern-day perversions of the Bible's stately laws as perceived by him and his flock.

Another significant distraction was the volatility of the country's stock markets. Sure, there was worldwide volatility, but it was most pronounced in New York. As with any transition of leadership, there are many unknowns, and unknowns drive market uncertainty. But there were added factors at play in America at this time. For one thing, tens of billions of dollars of capital had fled the U.S. markets and gone on to other places of investment and security. Some investors preferred the perceived security of precious metals, like gold and platinum. Others went offshore in search of more stable and lucrative markets, like Hong Kong, Tokyo or London. It would be several weeks before the media pinpointed that the Haight family alone had pulled nearly $19 billion out of the U.S. economy. And there was upwards of another fifty billion withdrawn by close allies and advisors to the former president. Beyond that, money was moving haphazardly from one industry to another. What would the Shilling presidency mean for defense spending? For healthcare? For media companies? For entertainment companies? For the automotive and steel industries? For technology leaders? No one really knew, but they were busy hedging their bets and placing their chips.

In the midst of this, Adamo, Don Lasserman, and the AIRR board were stymied as to what their next steps should be. Haight's manner of resignation during their carefully and thoughtfully scripted public service announcement on combating racism had caught them off-guard and effectively undermined their message, but President Shilling's subsequent actions had an even more devastating effect. After some contemplation, the AIRR board decided to proceed with its four initiatives as outlined at the ill-fated PSA from the Roosevelt Room; however, when Adamo requested to meet with Shilling to strategize the revitalization and funding of the Civil Rights Commission, the new president responded by not only refusing to meet with Adamo, but by also announcing the outright termination of the commission altogether. Adamo placed another call to the White House to follow up on these actions, but also to inquire about the promised, inclusive federal hate crimes definition and legislation, but that call went nowhere, as in literally never acknowledged by the White House. Highly annoyed, but not totally dissuaded, Adamo then reached out to the Secretary of Education to begin talks on the education plank he and Shilling had outlined. But that call, too, went unanswered by the Secretary or anyone on her staff. The AIRR board was flummoxed and frustrated and couldn't understand why and how President Shilling could so easily and so absolutely, reverse course on what they believed to be a firm commitment to addressing the problems of racism in America. But former President Adamo could understand perfectly well. He'd been there himself; in that seat of power. He could attest to the fact that there is a fundamental shift in a man's perspective and strategy when given what is perceived by many to be absolute power. Adamo confided in his board that it takes a very strong individual to not fall victim to the allure of power, and neither Shilling or Haight were particularly strong in that respect.

The first month of the Shilling presidency was remarkably unremarkable in spite of all the confusion, chaos, and controversy. Shilling himself fueled much of the controversy with public statements about changing the U.S. Constitution to reflect the supremacy and infallibility of the Christian God and ensuring that any man-made laws are subservient to the Word of the Lord. He also spoke about the need to make same-sex marriages unconstitutional, in fact, make homosexuality illegal and punishable by death; eliminating divorce; and working to ensure that women did not work outside the home. All these positions caused a great deal of concern and alarm, but due ostensibly to their extremism, no concrete action towards realization of any one of them was occurring. Congress was hopelessly divided and becoming more so every day and with every new bizarre pronouncement by Lord Shilling.

For his part, former President Haight was also contributing greatly to the sad state of affairs in America. Apparently, from his lofty, reclusive perch in Namibia he felt invincible and proceeded to comment via social media outlets and interviews with obscure, right-wing blogs, on anything and everything he wanted without any thought as to repercussions or consequences. The Senate investigation into his alleged ties to a foreign government had been dragging on for three years and had not yet borne any fruit. A smarter man would have left that annoying, but apparently benign, situation alone; presumably dead or dying. But not Haight. Nearly every day he would make statements about the ineffectiveness of the Senate and its investigators or personal attacks against individual senators, likely prodding the investigation to continue out of spite if nothing else. The SEC investigation into insider trading, however, had borne plenty of fruit with many stock traders and financial advisors already under indictment or having pled guilty and their precarious situations being leveraged to get to the necessary evidence and testimony to bring charges against the ex-president and members of his family. Again, the former president couldn't resist some sort of daily goading, referring to the SEC as a bunch of Nazis one day, faggots the next. The closer the SEC seemed to get to the smoking gun of Haight's involvement, the more vile, personal, and crude his public attacks became. Of course, the SEC investigation had long been hampered by the various dead ends in their audit and evidence trails due to the untimely and highly suspicious death of Haight's chief financial advisor, Vincent Posner, three years earlier.

Six weeks after Haight went into exile, an SEC staffer leaked some information regarding their investigation into Haight's financial dealings. The leak specifically concerned a string of related text messages, beginning with one from Haight to his daughter Melinda. The text messages were obtained from a search of a former CIA agent's government cellphone by the F.B.I. Nearly three years earlier, the day after the presidential election in which Haight was victorious, he apparently sent a text message to his daughter Melinda who was, in essence, the Chief Financial and Administrative Officer of all Haight family businesses and endeavors.

"The heat will now rise exponentially.
Cover what you can. Tie up loose ends.

Vincent is likely to be a weak link.
Terminate now."

The message was somewhat cryptic and could be interpreted to mean that financial advisor Vincent Posner's link to the Haight family businesses should be terminated, but it could also be interpreted to mean something much more sinister. Melinda forwarded the message to Robert Jones, a retired CIA operative and close friend of the president-elect, with the following additional message.

"Bob, this is urgent. Meet me at 1 p.m.
tomorrow at our usual place."

Agent Jones agreed. He boarded a flight from his home in Seattle and flew immediately and directly to Salt Lake City where he checked into The Grand America Hotel on Wednesday evening. Hotel records show that Mr. Jones had room service late Wednesday evening and breakfast in his room the following morning. The next day, Jones had lunch in the hotel's Garden Café for two patrons. Jones did not have any more meals at the hotel during this stay and he checked out early Friday morning and headed for the airport and back to Seattle. All of this information was documented via FBI investigative files relative to the suspicious death of financial guru Vincent Posner.

Additional information from the FBI files showed that Jones took a four-mile Uber ride from The Grand America Hotel to the Bonneville Golf Club at 4:00 that Thursday afternoon. There is no record of Jones playing golf at the course or making any credit card purchases at the snack or gift shop. There is no more record of his whereabouts until 8:00 p.m. that evening when he called an Uber to pick him up at a Wendy's fast food restaurant on Foothill Drive and take him back to The Grand America Hotel. Coincidentally, Haight's financial advisor and close friend, Vincent Posner, lived on E. Laird Drive midway between the Bonneville Golf Course and the Wendy's on Foothill Drive. The gardener found Posner's body Friday morning around 7 a.m. when he showed up for his normal workday and opened the garden shed on the grounds. The medical examiner estimated that Posner had been dead about twelve hours when the body was found. The apparent cause of death was inhalation and dermal absorption of toxic pesticides, which were kept in the gardening shed.

The FBI investigation was aided by an anonymous tip from an employee of the Larkin Sunset Lawn Cemetery, which sat at 1300 S in the Sunnyside section of the city. He said he remembered passing a man on the street that runs in front of the cemetery when he left the cemetery grounds for the short walk down the block to get a hamburger. He was walking west on 1300 S when he saw a handsome, tall, mature black man with short curly white hair wearing a sharp, dark suit walk across the street from Laird Way shortly before 8 p.m. The employee and the stranger then both walked to Wendy's at the Foothill Drive intersection, with the stranger being about fifty feet ahead of the cemetery employee for the entire two block walk. The witness said he remembered the incident so well because he thought it was unusual to see someone walking in the neighborhood so well dressed, especially late in the evening. His attire just didn't fit someone out for an evening stroll and it wasn't like there were business activities going on anywhere near there at this time of day. The witness also said that when they both reached Wendy's he recalled that the stranger went into the restroom and was in there a long time, long enough that the cemetery employee ordered his meal, sat down and ate it. He was just about to leave the fast food establishment when the well-dressed man exited the rest room and headed directly to a private car that had just entered the parking lot. He didn't order any food at the restaurant, and the cemetery employee thought that it was rude to come into an establishment and just use their bathroom facility. The employee didn't think much more about the strange encounter until the next day when local police visited the cemetery office requesting any surveillance recordings the cemetery might have of the street at the cemetery's entrance. That's when he spoke up.

The FBI investigation into Posner's death had continued for three years without any hard evidence until just recently when they had accessed the cellphone records of Melinda Haight. Now that she was suspiciously out of the country, and no longer on the government payroll as an advisor to the president, the FBI had gained access to her phone records with an approved court order. The FBI had not yet completed this phase of their investigation when the leak of the connection with CIA operative Robert Jones broke. For some time, they had been tracking Jones' whereabouts and activities, which were somewhat limited and dull. Jones had been retired for just over two years and widowed for seven. He lived in a modern condo complex on Second Avenue in downtown Seattle and seldom ventured far from his home. The FBI noted a ritualistic daily jog around the Central Waterfront area then moving north along the Elliot Bay Trail. Jones also visited the Seattle Art Museum often, just a few blocks from his home, and did most of his shopping at the Pike Street Market also just a few blocks walk from his home. The only times the FBI surveillance ever noted Jones leaving his immediate neighborhood, were weekly excursions, usually a Tuesday or Wednesday evening, to Pandora's Adult Cabaret club just north of the city's central business district and weekend outings to either the Jackson Park Golf Course north of downtown or the West Seattle Golf Course southwest of downtown. For all of these weekly activities, Jones traveled by Uber. He did not appear to own a car of his own.

Now that this information had been leaked to the press, the FBI felt they had no choice but to confront Jones with the circumstantial evidence they had gathered thus far. They had documentation placing him in Vincent Posner's neighborhood at the time of his suspicious, accidental pesticide death. They had text messages between Jones and Melinda Haight referencing a meeting at their usual place and the need to terminate Posner. They had a witness that placed him at a Wendy's restaurant in Posner's neighborhood apparently washing up there but not eating. That was about it in terms of factual evidence. But now the story was out there, so the FBI showed up at the Second Avenue condo unit at eight o'clock that morning. After entering the unit following no answers to their knocks or commands, the FBI team found Jones' naked body swinging from a yellow nylon noose tied to one of the overhead beams in the loft-style, high-ceilinged open central space of the home. Other than the FBI intrusion, there did not appear to be any other signs of forced entry or any other human being in residence or even having visited recently. There was, however, a sleek, black ASUS Zephyrus GX50 laptop on a nearby glass-and-chrome table open to a Facebook post where Jones stated, "I'm sorry for what I've done. I thought my actions were helping to make America a better nation. This has not turned out to be true. We've been duped, and I'm the biggest dupe in the bunch."

The media attention to Jones' death and the implications that he likely committed an act of murder at the request of the former president, or at least, his daughter, was insatiable. Every aspect of retired CIA agent Robert Jones' sixty-two years of life was explored, analyzed and divulged, not always in that order. The FBI found six offshore bank accounts, two in the Cayman Islands, two in Cyprus, and two in the Seychelles, all linked to Jones and each account holding more than one million dollars. It would take months to trace all the incoming wire transfers, if even possible due to international bank privacy laws, but that certainly didn't stop the speculation that he had been paid by the Haight family for loyalty and miscellaneous 'odd jobs,' as the press euphemistically referenced unpleasant clean-up activities.

True to form, former President Alexander Haight simply could not resist launching personal attacks against anyone or anything that cast him in bad light. During his three years of presidency he never learned that sometimes, probably most times, it is best to let an issue run its course rather than intervene, interrupt, deflect, distract, condemn, deny, or outright attack. And with the Robert Jones suicide and fallout, his style did not waver. When word of the FBI investigation first surfaced, Haight piled on with his usual vitriol about how the FBI had been out to get him, with no basis whatsoever, since he was elected president. The animosity between Haight and FBI director Mantis was legendary, and Haight would have loved to replace the director when he was president, but political forces always prevented him from doing so. Aides and party power brokers always defended Mantis and convinced Haight that Mantis' reputation for integrity and thoroughness could be used to their advantage when appropriate. A long-time adage in Washington political circles was, "If Mantis says the moon is green, then by golly, the moon is green." Mantis, at 6 feet 3 inches, gaunt of frame, and with a full head of close-cropped silver hair, always spoke in an even and measured tone and never in anger or disgust. His appearance and manner conveyed statesmanship and solicited respect from nearly everyone he ever encountered, in person or on television. But this never prevented Haight from launching personal attacks against Mantis and it only escalated now with the probe into Jones' death.

Another usual behavior tactic of the former president was his penchant for, and ready willingness to, outright lie to the media, or to anyone. That was no different in this circumstance. Haight's reference to the former CIA operative evolved daily as additional information was discovered and revealed. When the story first broke, Haight said simply, "I've never heard of him;" the *him* in reference to Robert Jones. When the story persisted, Haight attributed the matter to Mantis' ongoing persecution of him, the president. When reporters pressed the former president on the meaning of Jones' apparent suicide note, Haight responded with, "You could never trust that lying black bastard." This, of course, sparked renewed interest in Haight's thinly disguised racist tendencies, but it also increased confusion as to whether or not Haight was personally familiar with Jones. His comment implied some sort of history with the agent, but was it real or imagined? Subsequent attempts to get clarification from Haight did not result in any clear answers. Haight returned to his previous position that he did not know Robert Jones, had never met him. When pressed to explain what he meant by the part of his statement that said, 'you could never trust...' which implied familiarity, Haight said that was just a general statement. Naturally, the underlying racial implications of this latest 'clarification' were severe and tensions in America's urban centers were on the rise with increased protests and some arson and looting along with innumerable public statements of condemnation from noted black civil rights leaders and several prominent white human rights activists as well.

As the case unfolded, almost simultaneously with media disclosure, the picture became clearer of the former president's familiarity with CIA agent Robert Jones. There were photos of Haight and Jones on a golf course in Salt Lake City from a decade ago. Haight's response was, "I golf with a lot of people." There were letters and other documents in Jones' personal effects at his condo and in a bank lockbox that indicated very strong connections with Haight and his family. Haight's response was, "Fabricated evidence planted by Mantis and his goons." There were White House guest log records that showed that Jones visited the presidential mansion four times during Haight's tenure. Haight's response was,

"Didn't come to see me." And, finally, there were text messages saved on Jones' phone regarding a communication between him and the president that included a text from Haight to Jones saying, "If I can ever get these spineless assholes to let me move on Mantis, the job is yours." Haight's curious response was, "That text was meant for someone else. I don't know how it got on Jones' phone."

Haight's strategy was simply to deny, deflect and distract. And that strategy seemed to be holding up well with his historic base; mostly white and male, rural, poor and poorly-educated. His base also seemed to be deeply religious, at least in theory, and mostly Christian evangelical. Other than their love of God, his base had deep love affairs with their guns and their flags. Even in light of the mounting and damning evidence that the former president was likely involved with foreign government interference in the presidential election, was likely involved in corporate fraud, money laundering, and insider trading, and was likely involved in directing the murder of a long-time friend he perceived to be a weak and vulnerable link in the SEC and FBI investigations into Haight family activities, Haight's supporters remained steadfast in their devotion and belief in the man. In fact, if anything, the more Haight came under suspicion and attack, the more entrenched his supporters became in their belief that he was being unfairly persecuted by an elite and envious cadre of political opponents who would do anything, especially unethical or illegal, to take down or tarnish their messiah.

CHAPTER *Ten*

Four days after Robert Jones' suicide in Seattle, Lamar Williams received a small, padded mailing envelope at his post office box in Baltimore. Lamar, dark as ebony, wrinkled as seersucker, and frail as peanut brittle, was just fifty-five years old, but looked much older than his only known partial sibling, the recently deceased, former CIA agent Robert Jones. Lamar was the product of a never-acknowledged tryst between Robert Jones' father, Owen, a Baltimore city police officer, and Dominique Williams, a popular, and frequently arrested and harassed, Wilkens Avenue street worker.

When Robert's mother, Fiona, died of emphysema at the age of fifty-nine, Robert, an only child, was just twenty-seven years old. After her funeral, the task of going through her belongings, putting her affairs in order, and disposing of the house, car and personal effects fell squarely on Robert's shoulders. Fortunately, he had the help of his new bride, Janice Williams-no relation to Lamar or his mother. Robert and Janice had been married only a year, and their marriage would last for the next twenty-eight years, full of love and devotion to one another. That love and devotion got an early test as they combed through his mother's personal effects. They found a letter written to Fiona twenty years earlier and included in the envelope was a newspaper clipping of the account of Owen Jones' death in a street drug deal that didn't go as planned and some follow-up stories on the incident. Aside from the death of his father, of which Robert was painfully aware, although he was just nearly eight years old at the time of the fatal shooting, was another disturbing revelation about that fateful night. Although it appeared to be unproven, there was rampant speculation that Owen was somehow in on the deal or, at least, enabling and profiting from it. The night of the botched drug deal, Owen slipped away from his patrol car partner simply saying he had something personal to attend to for half an hour or so. What happened from there was unclear, but an internal affairs investigation showed that Officer Jones' gun was missing from the scene, and it was the apparent murder weapon, indicating that Owen was not on guard or alarmed when confronting the street gang. Also, there was five thousand dollars in cash, in twenties and fifties, in an unmarked envelope in Owen's pocket at the time of his death, along with a bank lockbox key where investigators found another $12,000, all in cash. Robert was shocked at this. Shortly after his father's death, Fiona had moved back home with her mother and father in Fredericksburg, Virginia, perhaps for economic reasons, but perhaps to help shield Robert from the taint of his father's alleged sins.

After he read the newspaper clippings, Janice handed Robert the handwritten note that had accompanied them. Janice had read the note, so she cradled Robert with her left arm while she read the newspaper clippings in her right hand and Robert read the note. As Janice expected, Robert's tears began to flow freely. The note was not long on words but brimming with unexpected surprises and more unanswered questions.

"Dear Owen's wife,

I am a business associate of your husband. On the night he was shot, he was on his way to give me some money. He had promised me $5,000 to get rid of the baby. Now I do not have any money and do not know what to do. Will you

help me? You can reach me through
Frankie. He knows me.

Dominique Williams"

Robert was sobbing, but then he stiffened with resolve and hope having rationalized the new facts in his head. To Janice, he optimistically said, "That explains the money in his pocket."

Janice, not yet on the same page as Robert, said, "Yes, it does. He wanted her to get an abortion."

"That would be like him to help out an indigent person," said Robert who had been raised believing his father was one of Baltimore's finest and greatest police officers.

"Robert, I don't think," interrupted Janice before he again interrupted her.

"But where did the money come from?" wondered Robert drifting off in thought.

Janice wisely let her new husband percolate the obscure pieces of information for at least thirty seconds before positing her theory. "Robert, it could be that your father was getting payoffs from the drug gang and it could be that he was willing to pay for the abortion because the baby was his."

Janice feared she had gone too far because Robert said nothing for two long minutes. She decided not to push the topic and chose to go into the kitchen and prepare some tea for both of them, leaving him deep in thought. As the teakettle began its whistle, Robert plodded into the kitchen and heavily sank into one of the kitchen chairs of his childhood. In his mind, he could see his mother seated at the table and even his grandparents who had lived long enough to see him graduate high school with honors, but not long enough to see his graduation from Howard University where he had met Janice. When Janice sat in Fiona's usual spot, set two cups of hot tea on the table, Robert calmly, and abstractedly stated, "We need to get more facts."

Janice knew what Robert meant and patted his hand reassuringly.

It didn't take Robert long to get the facts he desired. Dominique's letter to Fiona referenced Frankie, and Robert knew Frankie well. Frankie Stankowski was his father's patrol car partner at the time of the shooting, and Frankie was still very much alive. Frankie had traveled to Fredericksburg for Robert's birthdays, Christmases, and other occasions throughout his childhood, and in fact, Frankie had just been at Fiona's funeral the previous week. Robert drove to Baltimore to begin his quest to fill in the blanks of his father's life and death.

At first, Frankie was very reluctant to say anything to Robert other than the puritanical pablum that he had been fed for the past twenty years. His father was a fine officer who served his city well and lost his life defending his city and its citizens from the bad guys. Frankie pleaded with Robert to leave the past alone; that it would be best for everyone, especially Robert, but Robert persisted, and Frankie eventually gave into Robert's resolve. Frankie walked Robert through the night of the shooting. They had stopped on Wilkens Avenue in the city's Curtis Bay neighborhood at a coffee shop around 10 p.m. Frankie was working on some paperwork in the passenger's seat while Owen went into the shop for two cups of coffee. When Owen returned with the two cups, he passed them through the window to Frankie and said he had something personal to take care of and would be back in fifteen or twenty minutes. Frankie nodded in acknowledgment without giving Owen's statement any more thought and continued with the paperwork on his lap while sipping some coffee. When Owen had not returned after half an hour, Frankie left the patrol car and walked in the direction he had last seen Owen walking. Frankie turned down an alleyway between the coffee shop and the laundromat. At the end of that alleyway was another small alleyway at a right angle. As Frankie turned right entering that dark passageway, he instinctively drew his revolver as he could feel the danger in the air. Some forty feet away, Frankie could see the standoff between his partner and three or four thugs. Owen had his revolver out and trained on one of the gang members and Frankie could hear shouting by Owen and the gang leader, but nothing of contextual insight, just name-calling. Frankie knew this was an explosive situation and did what he believed was best. With his revolver steady in both extended hands, Frankie shouted, "Freeze." The next five seconds flew by in cacophonous slow-motion. Frankie had indelible recollection of every action and reaction.

As Frankie shouted his command, Owen turned towards him with a mixture of surprise, fear and anguish on his face. At the very same time, the silent thug to the gang leader's left, and slightly to the right of Owen, kicked at Owen's revolver hand, and the gun fell to the ground, as did Owen. Simultaneously, Frankie's gun exploded with deadly accuracy and found its target in the neck of the ballet-kicking thug. Before Owen could recover, the gang leader had rolled and scooped up Owen's gun. He shot once at Frankie who dodged briefly for cover and then the leader took his second shot directly into Owen's head. With that, the shooter and another gang member ran into a doorway and disappeared. Frankie thought he saw another youth farther in the background, but then they were all gone, and Frankie could never say with certainty if there was a fourth gang member there or not. After the shots the gang leader and at least one sidekick had disappeared into the building. Frankie ran to the spot where his partner and a low-life lay. Frankie quickly assessed the situation while barking furiously into his two-way radio. He first checked the status of the gang member to assure he was not a threat. While still breathing, he was of no danger. Frankie's shot had caught the boy while in his mid-air kick and had gone through his collarbone and exited through his neck eviscerating the carotid artery. He was rapidly bleeding out and was already essentially comatose. Frankie then turned to his partner and friend and saw instantly that there was no hope.

Robert listened intently and silently. He noted the well of tears in Frankie's eyes as he recounted this horrific night. Frankie sighed heavily, dabbed at his tears, and then continued with the chain of events. While looking forlornly over Owen's crumpled body, Frankie noticed the thick envelope protruding curiously from his partner's right, front pocket.

"I was shocked, Robert, truly shocked, and I didn't know what to make of the situation. My first thought was to take the envelope and hide it, not to keep and it, but to keep it from the crime scene team already on their way. I knew what the situation looked like I didn't want to believe your father was capable of that. But then I thought of what would happen if they found the money on me and I remembered one of our lessons from police academy that the cover-up is always more risky and telling than the actual crime, so I left the envelope where it was." explained Frankie, now openly weeping. Speaking for the first time in several minutes, young Robert just said, "You did the right thing, Frankie."

Frankie continued, "Within three minutes another unit was on site and the crime scene geeks were just a few minutes after that. Before I knew it, Captain Flynn was there hugging my shoulder and probably saying some comforting words, but I was in shock and not paying attention. Not physical shock, although the adrenaline rush had left my body weak, but mental shock. I just could not process what I saw."

Frankie then went on to explain how internal affairs conducted a very fast investigation and basically swept the whole matter under the rug. The department did not see much good to come from airing more dirty cop laundry at a time when Baltimore PD already had such a negative public image. The money in Owen's pocket and his lockbox disappeared somewhere into the evidence caverns and then probably into someone's pockets. Finally,

Frankie stopped and said there was no more to tell. The retired police officer was as drained as Robert had ever seen anyone, including his mother in her final days.

Robert let the air hang heavy for several seconds before inquiring, "What do you know about Dominique Williams?"

Frankie was perplexed, but thought for a while, then said, "I don't know. The name sounds familiar, but I can't place her."

Robert took the envelope his mother had received from Dominique Williams twenty years earlier from the pocket of his blazer and placed it on the coffee table in front of Frankie Stankowski. The aging police officer eyed the envelope suspiciously at first, glanced into Robert's determined face, and then picked up the envelope. Frankie read Dominique's handwritten letter and with each word there came some recognition. He didn't need to read the newspaper clippings, he knew what they were. By the time he reread the short note, his hands were shaking.

"Oh Robert," Stankowski began, and then looked into the distance as the tears returned to his gray eyes. "Your poor mother. This must have gnawed at her for years. I never knew about this. She never said a word to me, or ever asked me anything about it."

Robert nodded, "That would be like her. She was good at compartmentalizing and locking things away. I imagine she added the newspaper clippings to the envelope and sealed it back up as though it was just something else to be put in its place."

"Yes," Frankie said, "but she never threw it away, so it must have always been on her mind. I can't imagine her living with this secret for twenty years."

"But what can you tell me about the secret?" implored Robert. "What does 'business associate' mean and what about the money and the baby?"

Frankie's face drooped with sadness as he looked at the pleading young man before him. A young man he had known since he was born. A young man for whom Frankie had been a father figure for the past two decades. A young man who seemed to have no recognition of who his revered father truly was. Or, at least, a young man who had not yet been emotionally able to piece together the facts before him.

Frankie sighed, then stood and walked around the room, searching for something to focus on, searching for some place to start the story that would be most digestible for Robert. After two or so minutes of introspection, Frankie sat down in the same chair across from the troubled young man; really still a boy in the eyes of Uncle Frankie. With one more heavy sigh and another loving and sorrowful look at Robert, Frankie began his tale.

"Robert, I can't be one hundred percent sure of all the pieces, but given this information and my knowledge of your father, as a partner, as a friend, and as a man, I feel fairly confident that what I'm about to tell you is as close to the truth as we can get.

"Your father was undeniably a wonderful man. I'm sure you have some fond memories of him from your childhood. He loved being a father and especially your father. He would be so proud of who you've become; a man with a college degree, a man with a promising job with the federal government, a man with a beautiful and intelligent young wife, a man with so much hope and promise for the future. You have become exactly what your father would have hoped for. I can feel his pride beaming down on us in this room right now." Again, Frankie's eyes brimmed with moisture. Then, after a breath, he continued.

"And Owen loved your mother so much. She was his world and he would never do anything to intentionally hurt her. But a man sometimes has needs that are difficult to control and those needs can be a weakness." Frankie cleared his throat. "Your mother wasn't the same after losing the baby, and..."

Robert interrupted, "What baby? The baby in the note?"

"No, no. I didn't realize how much you don't know. As you said, Fiona was good at keeping secrets. I'm talking about your sister. Your twin sister." Frankie paused to let Robert absorb this, and then pressed on. "Your mother had a difficult pregnancy. Had been confined to bed for much of the time. When the time came, it was a difficult and painful labor and childbirth. The labor was more than twenty-four hours and then you finally came out, screaming your little head off according to your father. Ten minutes later, your sister arrived, but she was blue, not breathing. I'm not really sure what happened, but she never took a breath. Other than what your father shared at that time, neither your mother or father ever spoke of the baby girl again."

"Oh God, I had no idea," Robert moaned, then continued, "But this is not the baby in Dominique's note?"

"No, I'm getting to that, Robert. And it might be painful for you, but we've come this far, so you might as well hear it all. Let me return to your birth. Owen told me that Fiona was deeply despondent after the delivery and the stillborn death of your sister. He said when the nurses brought you to her, she refused to hold you. Even when your father was holding you, she would look away. I imagine she was suffering from what today we would call post-partum stress syndrome, compounded with the simultaneous death of a second child. I guess you may not even know or remember that for the first two years of your life, your Grandma Mae took the train from Fredericksburg to Baltimore every week to take care of you and your mother. Anyway, by the time you were two, maybe three years old, Fiona was psychologically and emotionally stable enough to be your mother, and I'm sure you'll agree she became a wonderful mother." Robert just nodded, now with tears filling his eyes. But Frankie had more story to tell.

"Your father still loved your mother. Was still totally devoted to her, but after the trauma of childbirth and the death of your twin, Fiona was never the same," Frankie searched for the right phrase before saying, "in the bedroom. Your father said she was there, but sort of lifeless, just going through the motions, often crying after, and sometimes during sex. It was painful for both of them, so your father became vulnerable to the charms of other women; prostitutes. He wasn't looking for a replacement for your mother. He just wanted some good sex." By now, Frankie was pacing around the room and avoiding eye contact with Robert as he recalled his world with Owen of twenty-five years ago. For his part, Robert sat silently just staring at the envelope still on the coffee table as Frankie continued dismantling all the images he held of his father.

"Perhaps I should have said something, but I didn't. It wasn't something we would talk about. It wasn't something he was proud of; nothing to brag about with his buddy. But there were many times when we would pick up a prostitute, and I'd want to book her, take her in, like we were supposed to; but your father would just look at her, and then tell me that she's obviously a victim of unfortunate circumstances beyond her control, and we could do her more good by giving her some advice and hopefully pointing her in the right direction in life. He would get out of the car and pull the young woman aside, away from the car, and just talk with her for a few minutes before getting back in the car. Initially I tried to rationalize that your father had missed his calling as a social worker and was perhaps being instrumental in steering these girls off the street, but as repeat incidents occurred, it was obvious that he was cutting a deal; not busting her in return for a favor after his shift was over.

"Dominique was your father's favorite for probably two years before he was shot." Frankie was speaking rather matter-of-factly now, almost as if Robert were not in the room. "I didn't recognize her name at first because we always referred to her as 'Mamba.' I don't really know why, but that's what we called her. She was a Jamaican immigrant, probably illegal, outstandingly beautiful, vivaciously sexy, and definitely messed up. She always seemed to be strung out on something, but always happy…just one of the most joyful people I've ever encountered. It always struck me as remarkable that she could always seem so vitally alive and full of joy in the midst of her sad and pathetic lot in life. But I suppose that was one of her traits that kept your father coming back." Frankie paused in deep thought; Robert still staring through the coffee table. Stankowski continued in his patrolman tone, "After your father died, I'd see her around occasionally, but much of that joy of living seemed lost. Eighteen months or so after your father, she wound up in the morgue; another overdose victim from the streets. Another nameless person from a hopeless situation." Frankie stopped and did not speak again until Robert looked up from the table with a lost look in his eyes urging Frankie to go on. So Stankowski pulled some more resolve from his gut and his memory and went on.

"I didn't know this at the time, but Mamba was about three months pregnant when your father died. When she died, the boy was just an infant, around a year old. There were no other relatives, so the child became a ward of the state and probably wound up in a foster home somewhere in Maryland. Your father never mentioned the baby. I don't know if it was his, but this note from Dominique makes me think it probably was. And I had no knowledge about the source of the money. If he was dirty, I wasn't aware. Most likely it was something recent, something he felt he needed to do to take care of the baby or Mamba or get rid of the baby. I just don't know." Frankie stopped his tale, sat back down and pondered his own thoughts and memories wondering if there was anything else he knew or should know. As Robert lifted his head, heavy with shattered memories and newly forming images, he met Frankie's eyes. Frankie now burst into open crying. "Robert, that night plays through my nightmares every night. Things should have gone down differently. If I hadn't walked into that alley, if I hadn't drawn my weapon, if I had shot first, your father might still be alive."

It was Robert's turn to comfort the police officer, so he got up from his chair and sat beside Stankowski on the sofa. With his arm around Uncle Frankie, Robert said, "It's not your fault. It is what it is, and you did exactly what a reputable police officer would do. My father is dead because of circumstances he created, not you. And not my mother. This was his own doing." Frankie could see that Robert had moved beyond the shock of his revelations and was focusing on something else, something in the present.

Robert looked into Frankie's eyes and said, "Help me find the baby. Help me find out what happened to this child. Help me find the missing pieces to my father's story." Frankie sobbed, but nodded in affirmation.

So, Robert and Frankie, using their own contacts and resources, along with help from Robert's wife, Janice, who was a medical researcher at Johns Hopkins University, set about finding the story of Mamba's baby. Due to their collective skills and the fact that there was nothing about the baby's life that was intentionally disguised, they were able to ascertain rather quickly that baby Lamar was now a grown young man of twenty with an already lengthy rap sheet for petty, but troublesome, crimes. Lamar had never been adopted and bounced hopelessly and carelessly in and out of foster homes until the age of fifteen when he sought refuge on the streets and in crack houses. Lamar was a skinny, scrawny, almost sickly-looking boy that the street gangs seemed to have no interest in. He got by running errands for gang leaders, drug lords and bookies as well as occasionally hustling for older, creepy white men from the suburbs. When Robert tracked him down, Lamar was in city jail awaiting arraignment on shoplifting charges.

Lamar was shocked and suspicious of a stranger posting bail for him, but figuring he could leverage this dupe into something lucrative, Lamar went along with the stranger's request for a DNA test; most importantly, a DNA test not linked to any crime. Lamar's shock and suspicion turned into awe and bewilderment when the stranger assured him that they were brothers, well half-brothers. Lamar's good fortune continued as the stranger, now his brother, took over the role their father should have played.

Thirty-five years later, Lamar was now sitting at a massive, polished wood conference table in a high-profile attorney's modern and plush 7th Street NW office in D.C., about midway between the Capitol Building and the White House. Robert Jones' mailing to his half-brother contained a flash drive, which meant nothing to Lamar, and instructions to contact attorney Byron Jameson, a Howard University classmate of Robert's. Despite Robert's extensive efforts over the years to help Lamar get an education, to get serial jobs, to get off the streets, Lamar always continued to live on the edge. He never really found his moral compass, but he did genuinely love his half-brother, the only person he could ever remember truly caring about him, and so he was here, in a foreign and intimidating environment, doing Robert's final bidding.

Attorney Byron Jameson returned to the glass-walled conference room where he found Lamar finishing off yet another plate of donuts that his secretary had placed before Lamar just ten minutes before. Byron was amazed at how many donuts and how much coffee that scraggy, thin man had consumed in just thirty minutes time, but he was not concerned. He was more concerned with the man's appearance and had summoned a local tailor to come to the office for a rush fitting. Lamar was dressed in his usual crusty, ripped jeans, a well-worn t-shirt, and a grey hoodie that was missing most of the hood. It appeared to have been torn off haphazardly as if Lamar was fleeing from someone who had grabbed him by the hood of the sweatshirt. As the tailor began taking Lamar's measurements, Attorney Jameson sat down at the head of the table and began reviewing the progress they had made thus far and what to expect during the rest of the day.

"Lamar, as I told you when you brought your brother's mailing in this morning, it contains some very important and damning information against former President Alexander Haight and his family. The electronic files appear to be the private files of Vincent Posner, a former ally and advisor to the former president. Disclosure of these files will make it appear with a high degree of certainty that your brother was not only with Posner at the time he died, but likely also stole the files from Posner's computer and killed Posner. I need you to understand that and agree to disclosure of this information," the attorney soothingly told Lamar.

Lamar responded without any apparent thought or concern, "Yeah, sure. Robert's note said to bring that thing to you and then do whatever you said, so I'm good."

"Fine," oozed the attorney. "So, we'll be holding a press conference at 5 p.m. today to reveal the existence of these files and make a public display of turning them over to the U.S. Attorney on the steps of the Justice Department Building. I don't need you to say anything, just be beside me as we stage this scene. Your presence will bring a human element to your brother's death. I'll talk about your brother being a victim in this Orwellian distortion of a Shakespearean tragedy and the cameras will pan to you as the heartbroken family member carrying out your hero brother's final wishes. The press will pepper us with questions about Robert, his motives and actions, and probably even try to portray him as a co-conspirator in these illegal activities, but our job will be to keep the focus of scrutiny on Haight as the mastermind of these financial crimes and Posner's murder. Any questions, Lamar?"

"No, not really, said Lamar, "Do I get to keep the suit?"

"Yes, of course the clothes are yours. In fact, we should probably buy you some new jeans and shirts as well. Your brother has left you a substantial amount of money set up in a trust that will make payments to you each month for the rest of your life. We can purchase your new clothes from the estate, so it won't diminish your annuity payments." Even as he said these words, Jameson wondered how solid the trust would be. How much money would be left after fighting with the government to ascertain how much of Robert's assets were legitimate versus ill-gotten gains? How much undisclosed income would be subject to forfeiture? How much undisclosed income would simply be subject to back taxes? How much would it cost to bring the Haight files to light as demanded by Robert Jones in his last communication to his lawyer via the alley dog half-brother Lamar? Would Haight and his lawyers launch a full-press media and lawsuit assault on the now surely disgraced CIA agent? There just wasn't time to worry too much about these concerns at this time. Right now, Jameson needed to get Lamar presentable for their press announcement just three hours away.

The tailor did a remarkable, and remarkably fast, job transforming the street urchin Lamar into the grieving and heartbroken surviving brother. Jameson was pleased with the image that Lamar presented, thankful that Lamar remembered to stand up straight and look directly at the reporters. Jameson spun the tale of a dedicated and patriotic hero who was conned by the former president, a CIA-trained operative who was willing to put his skills to work for the promise of the greater America that Haight had described. The questions from the reporters went pretty much as anticipated, although Jameson felt they were even more sympathetic of Jones as a victim than he could have hoped. Jameson was physically excited looking forward to the evening news programs. He and Lamar would no doubt be the top story on all networks and news programs. And they were.

CHAPTER *Eleven*

The former president should have seriously weighed and considered the excellent legal and publicity counsel he was paying for and receiving, but his over-sized ego and unrestrained narcissism would not allow it. Alexander Haight took to social media with a frenetic fury never seen before. He slammed the FBI and its director, Ronald Mantis, for their "bizarre, unfounded and unending persecution" of him and his family. He slammed the SEC and its staff for their "fabricated speculations" into his business dealings, his taxes, and his "unprecedented financial successes that dwarf anything ever accomplished by any other individual in the business world." He slammed the CIA for its "inability to instill basic integrity into the heart and soul of its operative" in reference to retired operative Robert Jones. He slammed the deceased Robert Jones, a

man he still claimed he didn't know, for all manner of crimes, including, "stealing personal data"
meaning Vincent Posner's financial files, killing "an
old friend and confidante" meaning Posner himself,
and "showing extreme cowardice" meaning Jones'
manner of death; suicide rather than face the consequences of his actions.

As the evidence kept mounting and the FBI
was able to verify and corroborate nearly all of the
damning and incriminating information provided by
Robert Jones on the flash drive mailed to his brother
Lamar Williams, Haight continued his personal
attacks, alternating with direct outright denials. He
claimed the Posner files were fabricated. He claimed
Posner was merely someone he had done business
with, but did not know well. He taunted the media
and the authorities by saying they were wasting their
time investigating him because even if they proved a
successful case based on their lies and fabrications, he
was untouchable. Finally, in desperate frustration to
redirect the spotlight of scrutiny away from him, he
took a swipe at the man most in the media right now,
Lamar Williams, and his attorney Byron Jameson.

The former president posted, "Lamar Williams
and his black attorney are the enemies of America.
We need to put them behind us and take our country
back."

History will probably never know Haight's true intent with those exact words. Perhaps he, himself, did not even know what he meant when he sent them, but the reaction was sudden and violent. Did he intend to reignite the already-simmering racial tensions in the country he used to rule when he referred to Jameson as "the black attorney?" Did he intend to deepen the racial chasm when he referred to the two black men as "the enemies of America?" Did he intend to place a target on their backs when he said we need to "put them behind us?" And did he further intend to stoke greater discontent when he used his oft-quoted campaign slogan "take our country back;" the same battle cry that mass-murderer Daniel Lasserman quoted frequently during his racist shooting spree some months earlier?

Whatever intent Haight had, the response was sudden and unequivocal. Haight, still in protective Namibia, posted his latest rant in the early hours, still nighttime on America's east coast. So, there was plenty of social media buzz by the time Americans were waking that morning. Attorney Byron Jameson reckoned it would be wise to get Lamar out of the Washington DC spotlight and area as quickly as possible, so he called on his client at 11 a.m. at the Kimpton Hotel Monaco on F Street NW, just a few blocks from Jameson's 7th Street NW office. Twenty minutes later, Jameson exited the hotel lobby and started the short walk down the half dozen front stairs to his waiting silver Mercedes S500 sedan and driver, Walter, with Lamar and his one duffel bag in tow. Walter already had the trunk lid open and was moving towards Lamar's duffel when the rapid rat-a-tat-tat bursts of gunfire strafed the luxury sedan and the hotel's façade. Lamar and Byron escaped the brief assault with only minor injuries. Byron had been shot through his upper right arm and Lamar had only sprained his wrist as he dove to the sidewalk. Lamar, being much more used to street warfare than Byron, wasted no time in his belly flop dive to the concrete. Byron, not used to such activities, stood upright and turned towards the street when the first shots rang out. Walter, however, and the nearby potted greenery at the hotel's entrance would not live to see another day.

The attempted assassination of Lamar Williams and his attorney Byron Jameson was not the only big news incident of the day. At lunchtime, a full-frontal assault by at least twenty men and possibly a few women, occurred at the United States Penitentiary in Pine Knot, Kentucky. The prison, known as McCreary for the county of its location, was the current location of Daniel Lasserman, the racist mass murderer cum racist folk hero. The intent of the assault was uncertain. Surely, the ragged band of anarchists firing from a small fleet of streaming pickup trucks adorned with Confederate flags knew they had no chance of breaching the impenetrable and foreboding concrete block structure. Was it just a release of pent up frustration? Were they trying to make a public statement? Were they putting the institution on notice that they would be back?

Fortunately, the National Civil Rights Museum in Memphis, where Daniel had done much of his killing, foresaw the potential for violence and was on lockdown with all employees and volunteers kept away for the day. It was early afternoon when at least a dozen Molotov cocktails rained down on the buildings and grounds, having been launched from the back of four pickups encircling the motel and adjacent building and waving their Confederate flags and shouting war cries as they sped by. Extensive damage was done before the fire could be contained nearly two hours later. This inferno nearly obliterated what little was left after Daniel Lasserman's previous arson at the site.

At the same time, in Atlanta, gunfire and incendiary devices burst into action at the Ebenezer Baptist Church on Auburn Avenue where Dr. Martin Luther King, Jr., preached and rose to prominence. The building was totally destroyed. The adjacent

King Center for Nonviolent Social Change incurred minor damage. In Philadelphia, a group of about a dozen white supremacists entered and occupied Independence Hall, hanging a large Confederate flag from the window just below the clock on the building's tower face. As of the evening news, the group was still in residence.

As word of in the insurgencies got around during the day, the number of incidents blossomed. Sightings of Confederate-adorned pickup trucks were commonplace across the South by mid-afternoon and several were sighted in northern areas as well, including Detroit, Chicago, Buffalo and Hartford. More than fifty predominantly black churches had been set afire as well as ten inner city community centers and even two schools; a high school in Baltimore and an elementary school in Macon. There was no waiting for the evening news. All networks and news outlets were broadcasting all day reporting on the non-stop incidents of violence.

By the time President Shilling was ready to go on the air at 8 p.m. that evening, a protest group near Independence Hall in Philadelphia had transformed into a vigilante freedom brigade. The mostly-black group of nearly two hundred individuals stormed the historic cradle of liberty with guns and torches intending to rout the white supremacists from the building. The police force had only been able to rally about thirty well-armed and armored staff to the scene as there were so many other skirmishes going on around the city. When the assault began, the police officers opened fire on the storming citizens, but, shocked that they did not give up in retreat, the police officers backed off rather than take any civilian lives and waited for reinforcements of personnel and heavy equipment. They did not foresee what happened next. The vigilante group, minus a couple dozen fallen comrades, smashed through the front doors of the historic and emblematic site and set it on fire. It was not known if the fire was started intentionally or accidentally, but others in the vigilante group had surrounded the building and as anyone from inside attempted to flee, they were shot or stabbed to death on the spot. Within an hour, all twenty-two white supremacists were dead, eighteen vigilantes were dead with another ten hospitalized, and three police officers were dead and five injured. Independence Hall was a mere shell of itself, mimicking the tragic and eerie effect of the Kaiser Wilhelm Memorial Church in Berlin, Germany, following extensive bomb damage in World War II.

Due to the timing of this unfolding event in Philadelphia, President Shilling delayed his public address until 10 p.m. when he was able to show a live video of the ruins of Independence Hall. Shilling chose to not only open his remarks with the tragedy in Philadelphia, but he focused entirely on the illegality of the vigilante mob that stormed the building.

"My fellow Americans, we are at war. We are at war with ourselves and within our own borders. We are at war for the future of our great nation. We are at war for decency and civility and for God's grace. Earlier this evening, an illegal, vigilante mob stormed and burned Independence Hall in Philadelphia with twenty-two American civilians inside. All those inside were killed. Furthermore, three police officers, simply doing their duty to protect the citizens of Philadelphia, were mercilessly gunned down and killed.

"This type of violence and brutality has no place in America. It must stop now. I have mobilized the National Guard and the Armed Services to immediately restore the peace throughout the nation. There is a midnight curfew in effect until further notice. Gatherings of more than five people will be subject to questioning and search for weapons. Anyone on the streets after dark or in suspicious circumstances is subject to frisk and detention if warranted.

"Additionally, I have empowered a technical taskforce to monitor and assess social media postings. Any statements that indicate insurgency, illegal gatherings, or intent to incite instability will be taken seriously. All social media platforms are expected to fully comply with the requests of this task force or be subject to confiscation by the federal government.

"And, finally, it is my belief that the relentless and largely unfounded pursuit and persecution of President Alexander Haight has been one of the main drivers of our current societal instability. Accordingly, by virtue of Article II, Section 2 of the Constitution, I am granting an immediate and comprehensive pardon to Alexander Haight for any wrongdoings that may have occurred. We need to put this blame game behind us and focus on our America of the future. Any continued pursuit of known allegations relative to President Haight will be considered acts of treason and will be dealt with accordingly.

"May God bless the United States of America, forgive us our manifold sins, and allow us to become better individuals and reflect His will."

The broadcast ended with the ghostly image of the smoking remains of Independence Hall on the screen with an audio overlay of "The Battle Hymn of the Republic" playing softly. Shilling made no reference to the eighteen individuals who were killed in the effort to rout the white supremacists from the national historic site. He made no reference to the dozens of other incidents of extreme violence across the country that resulted in over two hundred fatalities just that day. And he made no reference to the nearly three thousand Americans who had lost their lives in civil violence since Daniel Lasserman's mass-murderous rampage unleashed the barely-restrained racial tempest just a few short months ago.

The next day was yet another one full of confusion and disarray. Political pundits worried openly about Shilling's imposition of martial law, for that's what it felt like, even though the president never used those words. Many wondered about the constitutionality of such an action. Other pundits and analysts focused on Shilling's use of a presidential pardon for his friend and predecessor. Was it really a pardon? Or more like a blanket amnesty? What did it cover? And would it hold up? Evidently Haight believed so, because by the end of the week, he and his family were back in residence at his Salt Lake City estate. Very few journalists ventured into the forbidden area of Haight's alleged crimes, and the handful that did found themselves swiftly under house arrest or in confinement. Some members of Congress protested Shilling's abuse of power, but their voices were quickly silenced due to the continued massive protests and violence which most members of Congress believed demanded quick, decisive and stern responses. In other words, they were willing to give the new president substantial leeway in combating a problem which they themselves did not want to address.

The violence was unlike anything seen before, and the country had seen a lot in the past months. There were civil disturbances in every major city. Peaceful marches were generally snuffed out by the new police state tactics or by armed militias which the police did very little to restrain. Drive-by assaults and fire bombings were commonplace and too numerous to tabulate. Emergency rooms were overwhelmed and injured or dying individuals were being left on sidewalks near hospitals or urgent care centers. Many hospitals themselves were victims of drive-by shootings, Molotov cocktails, even grenades in two incidents.

President Shilling was forceful with his responses, but not judicial. Troops were numerous and prevalent at sites where good, God-fearing white folks might be harmed. Federal forces were present at white supremacist events, at mostly-white churches, at suburban shopping malls and schools, and protecting national monuments and treasures. Such forces were typically scarce or absent at many inner-city protests, at mostly-black churches, and at most college campuses. Accordingly, violence reigned unabated in nearly every major city ghetto and adjacent neighborhoods. Protests were rampant on nearly every college and university campus. And black churches throughout the country were burning every day.

The death toll over the next week exceeded twenty-five hundred. Thousands of buildings, including homes and businesses, had been burned or otherwise destroyed. And even the presence of federal troops did not protect two notable national monuments. Mount Rushmore had been peppered with projectiles from high-powered, long-range sniper rifles containing corrosive acid and paint. The effect was to make it appear that Washington, Jefferson, Lincoln and Teddy were crying tears of blood. The other historic site to not survive the week was the John Quincy Adams Birthplace in Quincy, Massachusetts. Firefighters were able to save the adjacent John Adams Birthplace with only minor damage.

Haight's ardent supporters had long vowed 'a civil war' if their cult leader was ever forced from office. Now that he had been, and his successor was not effectively deterring them, the threat of a civil war was being fully recognized, albeit, as of yet, without a declared leader, but that void would soon be filled.

CHAPTER *Twelve*

Three weeks of total societal disarray, random and uncontrolled violence, ineffective, or at least, unbalanced policing, and mixed messages from the president and Congressional leaders lead to over six thousand fatalities and much of the country on fire, both literally and figuratively. Colleges and schools were closed. Many businesses and banks were closed. Many public transportation systems had been shut down to protect workers and assets, but also to limit the movements of vigilantes and protestors. In an attempt to rise to the occasion in a presidential leadership role, President Shilling went to the airwaves once again with his plan to stem the violence, restore order for all Americans, return the country to commerce and education, and build a better America for the 21st century. This plan, coincidentally, would move the country towards fulfilling

Shilling's blueprint for a truly Christian democracy. At the heart of his proposal was a Constitutional Convention to bring clarity and simplicity to the nation's governing foundation. What he wanted to accomplish via this convention was outright elimination of all Constitutional Amendments beyond the original ten, which comprised the Bill of Rights. Furthermore, the only other 'improvement' to the venerable document would be to add the authority and Word of God as omnipotent and infallible. The simplicity and implicit patriotism of this plan resonated tremendously with Haight's core base, and overnight, the movement rallied around its new leader — President James Monroe Shilling.

However, on the other hand, a large number of Americans were alarmed by President Shilling's bold, retro proposal. Many of the Constitutional Amendments were vitally important, even necessary, for modern American society to function. Gone would be the prohibition of slavery and the voting rights provisions guaranteeing Americans the right to vote regardless of race or religion. Gone would be the government's ability to collect income taxes. Gone would be the right for women to vote. Gone would be term limits for the president and the ability to remove the president from office based on inability to function effectively. And without the thirteenth

Amendment in place to prohibit slavery, many wondered what Shilling's true long-term agenda might be. President Shilling assured naysayers that appropriate Amendments could be passed later to address real concerns in a more logical and rational manner than their current form.

The NAACP was quick to condemn the president's bold and simple plan. They immediately took out full page ads in *USA Today*, *The Washington Post*, *The New York Times*, *The Los Angeles Times*, *The Chicago Tribune* and many second-tier city newspapers in print and online. While the text of the ad was clear on supporting any and all actions to stem the rampant, senseless violence, the tagline made their position on Shilling's proposals even clearer, *"Any man, woman or child who has ever known the suffering of discrimination, marginalization or outright oppression knows the path to a better future does not begin with a giant step backwards."*

The League of Women Voters also did not hold back in its social media campaign against the patriarchal proposals. In a tribute to the famous three wise Japanese monkeys of "See No Evil, Hear No Evil, Speak No Evil," their online campaign featured a trilogy of photographs showing women in chains; one with her eyes burned out, one with her ears cut off, and one with her mouth stitched shut. Their tagline simply said, *"Don't let Evil win!"*

Two days of President Shilling's address to the nation, after taking sufficient time to digest and analyze the Constitutional Convention proposal, former President Richard Adamo and Don Lasserman in his role as Executive Director of the Adamo Institute on Race Relations, penned an editorial that ran simultaneously in dozens of newspapers and websites across the country. It was conciliatory in nature while proposing an alternate path forward.

"We applaud President Shilling's focus on the strife and mayhem that currently paralyzes our country, divides our citizens, and forces many individuals to stay away from their jobs and other essential activities while they hope and pray for safety within the confines of their homes. The current situation is certainly untenable and must be changed. Too many Americans are living in fear. Too many Americans are dying in the streets or in their places of worship or as they try to live their lives by going to work or shopping.

The United States Constitution is not a perfect document as evidenced by the twenty-seven Amendments to it over the past two hundred thirty years. The Amendment process exists to support the continual improvement of our core, governing document. We should not discard what has worked well for us and we should not look to the past for a simple solution in a complex world. We should address the fundamental root problem once and for all.

Racism is a prevalent, and to some extent, a natural phenomenon. As a species, it is inherent within us to seek safety and find comfort with those who are most like us. And we are taught to generally distrust those who are different than us. Our task, as a society, is to elevate those traits to a higher level where the differences between us as human beings become irrelevant and our focus on differences is based on a common set of values and ethics, not skin color or religion. We implore all Americans to reach within themselves to find empathy, compassion and forgiveness. We beseech all Americans to put aside their firearms and other weapons, other than for the purpose of self-defense, and support one another. We call on all citizens to practice tolerance and embrace a common set of values and principles that bestow equal rights and protections to all.

Let's stop the violence now. Let's engage in meaningful dialogue now. Let's rebuild America to be even greater than before and let's do it now."

The op-ed piece had two unintended outcomes, but not the intended outcome of reducing violence and restoring order. The first unintended outcome was that the flowery and egalitarian words resonated well with the country's liberal and progressive constituents. Their fear and concerns, as well as their hope and idealism, were brought into focus around the reluctant leadership of Dr. Richard Adamo. He felt he had done his part, had served his time in the public limelight, but the resistance movement needed a face, a leader, and in the former president they found a face and voice they knew and trusted. The second unintended outcome was quite a surprise for Richard and Don and the entire AIRR board and their creative marketers who had worked so carefully on the message. The Haight base of supporters latched onto one phrase with such feral intensity that it rendered the rest of the message impudent. All the Haight and Shilling supporters could see was an attempt by Adamo to get them to "put aside their firearms." Don Lasserman grew up in a gun-tolerant culture and was the brother of the current poster child for unregulated use of firearms. He should have realized the potential effect of those innocent words, but he too was blinded in their collective zeal to bring an end to the shootings.

It was difficult to assess whether or not the violence of the undeclared civil war was getting better or worse. Some weeks, a thousand or more people died. Other weeks a little less. Some weeks a hundred or more buildings were bombed or burned. Other weeks a little less. Some weeks saw half a dozen or more historic sites under attack. Other weeks there were no such incidents. People tried valiantly to return to normal lives, either out of a sense of patriotism or just basic economic needs. They could not afford to stay away from their jobs indefinitely. And they needed food, so they had to go shopping. Most food delivery services had been terminated as such personnel had become favored sniper or drive-by targets. There were many documented cases of elderly and other shut-ins dying in their homes due to lack of food or medicine. On the other hand, a cottage industry had sprung up where armored bank vehicles, fortified prison transport vehicles, even discarded military Humvees and tanks, were put into use as public transportation vehicles and taxis. Workplaces were altered to accommodate overnight stays of workers so that incidents of coming and going were minimized. The new norm for work shifts had become three days and nights at the office, store, or warehouse, followed by four days away from work taking care of one's family and property.

President Shilling and former President Adamo dominated the news outlets. Not only were they now the defacto leaders of opposing positions, but there was a dearth of capable and qualified leaders from any other party or political establishment willing or able to take on this tremendous challenge of literally working for the survival of the nation. Former

President Haight, for his part, was not helping either camp. It wasn't that he was remaining silent; quite the opposite. His social media posts seemed to vacillate between supporting Shilling positions and Adamo proposals. Only after careful dissection of his cryptic and often caustic words, could one conclude that Haight was neither for nor against his predecessor or his successor. He was only interested in how any action, or lack of action, would reflect on him, his egocentric legacy, and his self-centered, self-absorbed, self-serving view of the world. Before long, journalists were only including Haight in their reports for comic relief. And with the state of affairs in the country at this time, comic relief was sorely needed.

CHAPTER *Thirteen*

Three months into the war for America's soul, the AIRR board sat around the conference room in their Bridgeport, Connecticut, headquarters. Bridgeport, like all other American cities, had seen its share of violence, but it was certainly not among the worst war zones. Most of the violence in this city seemed to be acts of opportunity and survival; not premeditated acts of strategic advantage or societal disruption. The board was here in person at the request of its chairman, Richard Adamo. Adamo had been using his board as a sounding board throughout the crisis, but they had avoided traveling to meet in person due to the turmoil. Only one board member was missing. Harriet Bernstein, the CEO of a Silicon Valley tech company, had been killed less than a week earlier when her private plane was hit with a rocket-propelled grenade while sitting on the tarmac at the airport in San Jose. It appeared to be a random attack against another wealthy elitist, but one could not be sure. Investigatory activities by law enforcement had been reduced to near extinction due to all available forces being utilized for response and rescue operations.

Chairman Adamo began his remarks. "First, let's take a moment to remember our fallen colleague, Harriet. She was a visionary voice on this board and worked tirelessly to make our world a better place. It is truly regretful that she will not be with us to see that vision come into focus." Around the table, heads were nodding solemnly, and occasional tears could be seen dripping from eyes of even the most stoic among them, including the male action movie star.

Adamo continued, "I need to inform you that I held secret talks with President Shilling over the weekend." Those few words prompted audible gasps from everyone around the table except Don Lasserman who had already been briefed on his friend's activities. The current president had reached out to the AIRR Chairman late last week and arranged the private get-together at Camp David, the presidential retreat in Maryland, where there would be less likely visibility than in DC or New York.

"The current state of affairs cannot be tolerated. Even before Harriet's tragic death, I believe each and every one of us has suffered a personal loss in this war. Your brother, Stan. Your agent, Belinda. Neighbors. Friends. Family. Employees. The number of dead, now approaching twenty thousand, makes it impossible that we are not all touched directly by this senseless bloodshed. It has to stop." He paused and let the weight of the message linger in the air for several long seconds. Then he continued, "President Shilling is singular and resolute in his quest for a Constitutional Convention. And I believe the only way to break this deadly stalemate is to support his desire for such a convention." The uproar in the room was immediate and cacophonous. Adamo tried several times to get order before anxious silence and attention was restored.

Adamo returned to the story he was eager to deliver. "President Shilling and I already held a conference call with the governors and attorneys general of all fifty states. We just completed that this morning, while you were getting settled in here. On that call, we asked every state to begin the process of calling for a Constitutional Convention. Due to the crisis we are currently enduring, all governors and attorneys general promised rapid action on this request, even allowing for certain legal short-cuts where needed to get this convention convened as soon as possible." The board members started to get noisy again, but Adamo pleaded for calm. "I know you view this as a concession, perhaps even defeat, but I want to share with you a revelation I had when talking one-on-one with Shilling. And I've had similar conversations with Haight. It's a small club, this presidential perspective club. And with both men I tried to find some common ground. Something we both can relate to. Something to build upon in order to make a solid working relationship. With both men, I found that our common ground is mutual respect and admiration for one particular past president... Abraham Lincoln. And let me tell you, if three men as different as me, Shilling and Haight, can share a mutual love for one singular person, well, that must be a truly remarkable person. So, I got to thinking about ole Abe and the circumstances he faced and how, in many ways, we are facing a similar time right now. Lincoln took on the tough challenge of slavery, the ultimate expression of racism, and made his go-forward decision based on the premise of preserving the union of the young United States at any cost. That cost was high indeed. During the course of that conflict, over six hundred thousand soldiers lost their lives. We are nearing that rate now, my friends, but with the lives of civilians, not soldiers. It's our children, our parents, our neighbors and friends, our colleagues.

"One of my favorite Lincoln quotes, and one of the most poignant for the time, goes like this. 'A house divided against itself cannot stand. I believe the government cannot endure permanently half slave and half free I do not expect the Union to be dissolved — I do not expect the house to fall — but I do expect it will cease to be divided. It will become all one thing or all the other.'

"As much as I admire the great Abraham Lincoln, I doubt he foresaw the extensive toll his actions would ultimately take on this country. Six hundred thousand men died and set this country on a direction which never truly solved the underlying problem. It took another hundred years before we enacted the Civil Rights Act. We are more than fifty years past that milestone and look at the situation we have today. We are now as divided as we were when Lincoln made a commitment to keep the house together. We are going backwards, and that road to the past is slathered in blood. And the blood keeps coming. The cost of keeping this nation together in spite of itself is too great and an issue as entrenched and emotional as racism cannot be solved by force. Through use of force, or victory, we are merely suppressing the symptoms, not curing the cause.

"I have given my support to President Shilling's Constitutional Convention with one significant caveat. The new Constitution must have a secession clause; a way for states to opt out of the Union. A forced marriage is never a happy marriage. I believe, I hope, with the option of divorce on the table, we will find a way to live in peace together or to live in peace separately."

Adamo finally stopped talking and sat back in his chair, feeling that the weight of his message brought on great fatigue. A fatigue so palpable that it subdued everyone else in the room as well.

Adamo nodded to Don Lasserman who stood and took over the task of explaining what they thought would happen next.

"As we all know, many states have floated trial balloons regarding secession over the years. Texas, once a proud republic on its own, has boasted great pride and desire to be free from the shackles of the federal government. California, too, has talked about outright secession or dividing itself into three or more smaller states and letting the prospect of secession fall on the shoulders of the smaller players. These wild schemes have never really materialized in any sub-stantive manner because the potential dissolution of the union is a daunting and foreboding enigma. We realize it's quite a gamble to allow the Constitutional Convention to occur, but it's our best opportunity to bring an end to the street carnage. And, we believe the potential of secession will serve as a deterrent precluding any unreasonable or drastic alterations of the existing Constitution." Lasserman sat back down and the room remained still for several minutes.

As Adamo expected, once he threw his support behind the drive for a Constitutional Convention, actions happened in rapid-fire succession. As promised on the conference call with governors and attorneys general, every state followed through with its support for the convention and began the process of selecting delegates. The convention itself was held in the U.S. Capitol Building in Washington, DC, under intense security and scrutiny. All organizing parties had shared a desire for transparency, so all the proceedings were televised via C-SPAN.

As desired by President Shilling, all Amendments to the Constitution were scrapped. The original ten Amendments, collectively known as The Bill of Rights, were updated to be more proscriptive and rigid and then written directly into the Constitution. Furthermore, the preamble was modified to acknowledge the humility of man in the presence of God Almighty.

The original preamble read: *We the People of the United States, to form a more perfect Union, establish Justice, insure domestic Tranquility, provide for the common defense, promote the general Welfare, and secure the Blessings of Liberty to ourselves and our Posterity, do ordain and establish this Constitution for the United States of America.*

The new document was modified to read as follows: *We the People of the United States, meek and humble of heart, beseech the Lord Almighty for His Grace, to grant us the strength and wisdom in order to form a more perfect union, establish justice, insure domestic peace, provide for the common defense, promote the general well-being, and secure the blessings of liberty to ourselves and our posterity, do ordain and establish this revised Constitution for the United States of America.*

Much of the rest of the convention reflected similar goals by Shilling and his cohorts. There was a lot of focus on States' rights. The Full Faith and Credit clause was amended to reflect subservience to the Word of God. "I can live with adding 'the Word of God,'" exclaimed Mathew Bommer, a delegate from Pennsylvania, but I can't abide by adding the supremacy of Christianity exclusive of all other religions." His objection was noted but eventually out-voted by a significant margin. The proposal which ultimately passed not only codified Christianity as the religion of the land, but it codified rights for unborn fetuses. Many opposing delegates stormed out of the convention hall during these ultra-conservative waves, but that only made it easier for the Shilling camp to push through its agenda given the way the rules of the convention had been adopted upfront.

Likewise, as the original Bill of Rights was being dismantled and embedded in the new constitution, several other objections were formally noted, but then significantly out-voted. Robert Wagner, a delegate from New Jersey protested vehemently about one particular change, "The original 'right to bear arms' was to ensure that each state could defend itself against tyranny of the federal government. This proposal to specifically grant individual, unlimited gun ownership rights will lead to chaos."

"Mr. Wagner," a delegate from Arkansas drawled, "the right to individual gun ownership will be unlimited in the new federal constitution, but still subject to the laws and provisions of each individual state. I foresee no chaos under such governance."

The most intense and specific debates and yelling matches occurred when discussing the rights of secession for states. It had long been understood that states did not have the right to leave the Union. Now, with so much tension and division, it was apparent that some secession mechanism was necessary to prevent further division and loss of life. Former President Adamo addressed the convention early on relative to this matter. "It is clear to me now, that forced preservation of our Union, will only exacerbate our situation of racial tensions and further fan the flames of hatred and violence. We have learned much since the great Civil War over one hundred and fifty years ago. For certain we have learned how strong we are when we work together. But we have also learned that a forced solution is temporary at best. For this reason, I am fully supportive of the constitutional changes that will allow for a short-term assessment by each individual member state of our great country and provide an exit plan should any state determine it is in its own best interests to leave our Union. It is my fervent hope that once each state takes the time and effort to conduct a responsible assessment of their strategic future, they will reach the same conclusion that I have. That we have more in common than not. That we are stronger together than apart. That our future is brightest when we are united than divided."

In a surprising show of unity and common goals, President Shilling also address the convention delegates on this important issue of secession. "I want to thank President Adamo for his support of our many constitutional improvements. Together we are making a more perfect Union as originally envisioned by our founding fathers. I too agree that we are stronger together than apart and I believe our revised constitution provides a foundation that all states, all citizens, can rally behind and provide the path forward for a greater America."

After the Shilling Constitutional Convention, Article IV of the revised constitution read in part as follows and incorporated what they believed were the relevant parts of the former Bill of Rights.

Section 1.

Full faith and credit shall be given in each state to the public acts, records, and judicial proceedings of every other state for all such acts and laws that are consistent with the Word of God and this Constitution. Neither Congress or the states shall make any law prohibiting the free exercise of Christianity or infringe on the rights of the unborn or limit the freedom of speech or the press other than in regards that such expression contradicts the Word of God or this Constitution.

Section 2.

The citizens of each state shall be entitled to all privileges and immunities of citizens in the several states. Each state shall maintain a well-regulated and fully-functional militia and every individual shall have the right to keep and bear arms in accordance with definitions and regulations of arms within that state.

Section 3.

New states may be admitted by the Congress into this union; but no new states shall be formed or erected within the jurisdiction of any other state; nor any state be formed by the junction of two or more states, or parts of states, without the consent of seventy-five percent of the legislatures of the states concerned as well as seventy-five percent majority of the Congress.

No state may secede from the union without a seventy-five percent affirmative vote of the eligible voting constituents of said state and a seventy-five percent consent vote of the remaining state legislatures and a seventy-five percent affirmative vote by Congress. For one year only, following

the ratification of this Constitution,
secession may be affected solely by
the first requirement described in the
preceding, namely, a seventy-five
percent affirmative vote of the eligible
voting constituents of that state.

Throughout the convention period, domestic violence had dropped off dramatically. Now that the new Constitution was being ratified, there continued to be a tenuous peace. All affected parties and constituents were taking time to digest what effect the new Constitution would have. Haight and Shilling advocates were delighted with the document's heavy emphasis on God and guns. Adamo and his supporters were pleased that the convention process had a significant dampening effect on the uncontrollable violence; they were somewhat heartened that the opportunity to secede included a rather high threshold, that the ability to engage in war had been better clarified and also carried a high threshold for approval.

However, there were some significant casualties from the bastardization of the original Bill of Rights. Gone were the protections against unlawful search and seizure. Gone were the guarantees for trial by a jury of one's peers. Gone were the protections against self-incrimination and double jeopardy. Gone were the prohibitions against cruel and unusual punishment. Gone was the preservation of individual states' rights. And without the other subsequent seventeen amendments, the new Constitution was still lacking protections for women, the preservation of guaranteed, equitable voting rights, and any substantive protections against potential tyranny of the president.

But, for now, peace and stability were the watchwords of the hour, and all Americans were enjoying the respite, while holding anxiety about the future at bay.

CHAPTER *Fourteen*

The blueprint for the future did not take long to reveal itself and it was moving the country in a direction that neither Adamo nor Lasserman nor Shilling nor even Haight could have, or would have, predicted. The draconian nature of the new Constitution was frightening to far more citizens than either party had estimated. The God and Guns theme resonated well with many Americans for living their own everyday lives, but far fewer of them embraced the notion of governing the country this way. Calls for secession were prompt and numerous, but mostly noise, until the first state rallied successfully to do so, and the era of the great divorce was underway.

Surprisingly, it was Florida that was first to vote for, and approve, secession. Just three months after ratification of the new U.S. Constitution, the

Legislature of Florida had arranged for a referendum vote on the topic of secession. The measure passed easily with eighty-one percent of the registered voting base approving secession. A U.S. Supreme Court ruling in the week following the Constitution ratification clarified that the Constitution wording 'eligible voting constituents' was equivalent to registered voters because if one wasn't registered, then one wasn't eligible to vote. This ruling made it a bit easier for states to satisfy the voting requirement for secession. Political analysts cited all sorts of reasons that Florida was able to rally its voting base for secession so quickly and effectively. An important factor enabling the quick action by the Florida legislature was the substantive and pervasive improvements the state had enacted in its voting records database and election process following the great 'hanging chad' debacle of 2000.

But there were many other contributing forces to cause the momentum for secession to move so quickly and successfully. For one thing, both Presidents Haight and Shilling had greatly alienated Florida citizens with their constant ridiculing of the Sunshine State's population. Florida had been the decisive swing state that put President Adamo into office nearly twelve years earlier and neither Haight nor Shilling were willing to be forgiving. President

Haight frequently spoke disparagingly of the state's elderly population, and, at one point, even suggested that voting rights be capped at age seventy-five. For his part, President Shilling said he would never visit Florida again after the Florida legislature voted to remove all remaining Confederate War statues and enacted a comprehensive statewide hate crimes law that included 'pro-Confederate' and 'pro-white' speech in the hate crimes definition along with the other categories of race, religion, sexual orientation, gender, gender identity, political affiliation, ethnicity, origin of birth, age, and physical and mental disability. It was one of the most progressive hate crimes laws in the nation at the time of its implementation.

The population of Florida had changed quite a bit over the past few decades, and this also played well for the specter of secession. As expected, the state's large Jewish, Hispanic, Black, Gay, and Elder populations were all horrified by the potential implications of the new Shilling Constitution. But two other constituencies also played a significant role in tilting the vote in favor of secession. The state's younger population viewed secession as an opportunity to drive the state's economy into a high gear, thus creating new jobs and perhaps even whole new industries, such as eco-tourism and environmental reclamation technology—both areas that had been overtly undermined by Haight and Shilling. And the state's middle-aged, mostly-white, deeply-religious, conservative base, which was widely expected to prevent Florida from succeeding at secession, was actually instrumental in swinging the vote towards secession. Post-mortem analyses showed that this demographic was concerned about the removal of unlawful search and seizure from the new Constitution, but also energized by the prospect of a free nation of Florida wherein they believed their freedoms would be better protected. Political marketers promoting the benefits of secession had pulled out all the stops to find something to resonate with nearly everyone, and one of the ploys that worked well with the 'crackers' was the nostalgic nod to Florida's history when parts of eastern Florida had declared independence from Spain in 1812 and existed as the Republic of Florida for several months with their capital at Amelia Island. This proud, but brief, history proffered hope for a brighter future as an independent governing entity.

Once the Florida secession campaign proved successful, many other states jumped into the fray to ride the momentum. Louisiana was next to approve withdrawal from the union. The stern positions of the new Constitution did not sit well in the bayous or the Big Easy, so with just over seventy-six percent of eligible voters saying yes, Louisiana found its voice for the first time as a truly independent nation. Texas, the historic poster child advocating secession, rushed into a secession vote sort of assuming it would not require much background work or salesmanship. Just one week after the Louisiana narrow victory, the citizens of Texas did not vote for secession. In fact, on thirty-two percent of the eligible voting citizens of Texas voted for secession. The loss was attributed to two primary causals. One was the faulty assumption that it was a no-brainer. And, two, was the fact that the Shilling Constitution embodied more or less exactly what many historic secessionists had been advocating — God and Guns! Why vote to leave something when you're finally getting it your way?

California had jumped on the secession bandwagon immediately after ratification of the new Constitution, but secession advocates there were taking their time to wage a thoughtful and rigorous education campaign. Their vote was still two months away. While waiting for the California vote, secession referendums came up in several other states. Wisconsin and Minnesota fell short of the required percentage by five and seven percent respectively. Michigan was not nearly as close. They fell short by thirty percentage points. Illinois was considered likely to secede, but in the end, was unable to come up with a majority to vote for secession. Washington and Oregon held their votes the same week and both referendums passed fairly easily.

Washington voted in favor of secession with a seventy-nine percent affirmative vote. Oregon voters, however, even exceeded the early Florida margin of victory with eighty-four percent of eligible voters taking the opportunity to secede from the new union of states. Two weeks later, California finally held their referendum and the lengthy promotion campaign paid off. Citizens of the Golden State approved secession with a seventy-seven percent affirmative vote.

The opportunity for secession, a strictly domestic issue, was not without external influencing factors and parties. One of the major concerns of state citizens when contemplating secession was their post-secession vulnerability. Surely no other nation would seriously consider invading the great United States of America, even in its present condition. But, without the mantle of protection afforded by the Constitution, could individual states be tempting prey for foreign invasion? Also, how difficult would economic trade be when vying for attention on the world stage? Individual states could not wield the same economic clout as the United States, so would a vote for secession be tantamount to an economic shot in the foot? Japan was one of the first foreign entities to recognize the American chaos as an opportunity for future leverage. The Japanese government proactively reached out to the state government of Hawaii offering two primary benefits should the citizens of the Aloha State vote to leave the United States. Japan offered unconditional defense protection and a free trade agreement. Naysayers suggested that Japan was only making such an offer as a prelude for future annexation of the Pacific islands, but either voters didn't see it that way or they didn't care, because Hawaii voted for secession with just over eighty percent choosing to secede.

Russia, Canada and Mexico also got in on the action attempting to influence the secession votes. Mexico made defense and trade overtures to California, Arizona, New Mexico and Texas, similar to what Japan had successfully extended to Hawaii. Californians did not agree to the offers from Mexico, but voted for secession. The government of Texas did agree to the offers from Mexico, but the citizens did not vote for secession. And neither Arizona or New Mexico ever got a secession initiative off the ground, so the matter became moot. Russia and Canada launched competing proposals to the citizens of Alaska. There was great interest in the oil-rich territory as well as the extremely lucrative fishing industry. Initially, the offers from Canada and Russia followed the pattern set out by Japan and Mexico; an unconditional defense pact and a comprehensive free trade agreement. But as the two nations eyed the Alaska territory with lust and each other with distrust, the offers were embellished. Canada actually offered to make Alaska Canada's eleventh province. This offer made many Alaskans more comfortable about the defense protections, especially sitting in such close proximity to Russia and China. The Russians wisely knew that any offer to annex Alaska as part of their Federation would be viewed negatively, so they actually offered cash to the citizens of Alaska to vote for secession. The Russian offer said that should Alaska vote for secession, they would provide defense, free trade and cash payments of twenty-five thousand dollars for each voting citizen. The move was highly skeptical, but understandably tempting for many. Interviews with some citizens indicated that quite a few Alaskans were considering voting for the Russian offer, but once they had their cash they would relocate elsewhere. When President Shilling heard of this, he issued a proclamation that immigration visas would not be available for Alaskan citizens post-secession. The Alaskan referendum was a two-tiered ballot. The first question was whether or not to secede. This measure passed with just shy of eighty percent of the vote. The second-tier matter was relative to the status of Alaska if secession was successful. The ballot was structured such that only citizens voting for secession had access to the second-tier question. The second-tier question had three options. One was to remain independent and reject defense and trade offers from both Russia and Canada. Second was the option to remain independent and accept the pacts with Russia. And, third was the option to accept Canada's overture to become a province of that nation. The Alaska legislature had voted to allow the second-tier result to be binding based on simple majority. In the end, the vote tallied as follows. Twenty-two percent voted to become independent with no Russian or Canadian pacts. Six percent voted to accept the Russian offer. And seventy-two percent voted to become part of Canada.

The other major drive for secession was understandably in the Northeast. Former President Adamo and Don Lasserman, his aide-de-camp, initially believed the looming prospect of potential secessions would be too intimidating to allow for a seventy-five percent vote in favor of any secession. However, once Florida proved that assumption wrong, both men then switched their belief to an assumption of opportunity; meaning that any state that had previously harbored dreams of independence would take this opportunity to become their own nation. Adamo and Lasserman were then shocked when Texas overwhelmingly voted against secession. They then assembled a small team of political analysts and behavioral psychologists to work with the AIRR board to better understand what was truly driving the secessionist engine. While both men personally found the new Shilling Constitution troubling, and even a bit scary, they had completely underestimated how well everyday Americans would understand the potential effects of the new Constitution and what it would mean for their freedoms—the freedoms they valued as Americans. So, once they understood that, it made perfect sense that the Northeast would harbor great desire to secede from the evils of Shilling, Haight and their ilk.

So, former President Richard Adamo, working closely with Don Lasserman, cobbled together a proposal to keep an impressive portion of the crumbling United States together in a new construct that could provide mutual security, leverage a natural trading bloc, and restore the traditional freedoms and American values that this region of the country had taken for granted for far too long. Similar to the two-tier referendum employed in the Alaska situation, a dozen states in the Northeast and Mid-Atlantic developed a secession and go-forward plan. The plan, as promulgated by former President Richard Adamo, would, in essence, create a new mini United States. The states that agreed to go along with this proposal were Maine, New Hampshire, Vermont, Massachusetts, Rhode Island, Connecticut, New York, New Jersey, Pennsylvania, Maryland and Delaware. Having recognized that security and economy were the two primary inhibiting factors to voting for secession, Adamo proposed that these twelve states pool their interests and commit their futures together. They decided on a common voting day, sort of like a super primary, wherein eligible voters in all twelve states would vote on the same two referendums at the same time. As in Alaska, issue number one was whether or not to secede. Issue number two, available only to those voters who voted YES on number one, was whether or not to create a new nation, tentatively to be call New England. All twelve states voted in favor of secession and subsequently created the new New England.

One year after ratification of the Shilling Constitution for a good, God-fearing, nation of lemmings, North America looked substantially different. Canada now stretched from Greenland to Russia without limitation, north of the 49th Parallel. A new nation existed just to the south of Canada called New England, with its temporary capital in Boston. Far to the southeast was another fledgling nation, currently just known as Florida. Farther west along the Gulf of Mexico was yet another new nation now known as French America, formerly Louisiana. Along the west coast of the North American continent sat three distinct, independent, newborn nations: Washington, Oregon and California, but they were already in the planning phase of combining their forces and assets to create a stronger, unified, singular nation. When complete, that threesome would be collectively known as Californation with its capital city in Sacramento. And far out in the Pacific was the new island nation of Hawaii where citizens were struggling with multiple options for their future. Some wanted to build even stronger ties with Japan. Some wanted to restore the Hawaii monarchy. Some wanted to create ironclad alliances with other far-flung Pacific island nations. And many just wanted to exist as one of the world's newest, independent democracies.

The new lay of the land and creation of new countries and country borders created a great many new problems. One significant problem was the issue of immigration. If one wanted to move from Alabama to Florida, as Nate Lasserman now planned to do, you were, in reality, leaving the United States of America and moving to a brand-new country called Florida. How do you handle passports?

Work visas? Asylum? Taxation? Fortunately, in an unusual and unexpected spark of reasonability and common sense, President Shilling assembled an 'international' task force. It was comprised of economists, politicians, anthropologists, military advisors and others representing the remnants of the United States of America and all the new countries created by the Great Divorce of America-except for Alaska, which was being annexed by Canada and the normal Canadian protocols would apply. Having been assembled under the mantle of common sense, the New Americas Transition Council made a commitment to establish rules and protocols deeply rooted in common sense. Accordingly, they came up with several common-sense agreements to address a myriad of transition issues.

To address immigration, passport and work visa issues, the N.A.T. Council adopted a one-year rule that would allow citizens of the former intact United States to move freely between any and all parts of the former greatest nation in the world. The one-year countdown began at the completion of the one-year secession exemption as outlined in the new Constitution. At the end of this one-year period, it was expected that each 'new' country would have proper protocols and infrastructure in place in order to issue new passports and work visas as well as provide proper border control and immigrant documentation and tracking.

Currency was another issue and the N.A.T. Council developed a two-year transition plan wherein all new countries would be able to use the U.S. dollar without restrictions for a period of two years following the secession exemption cutoff. Following the two-year currency transition period, each new country would be expected to have developed its own currency or enter into an agreement with the remnant motherland to continue to use the dollar subject to certain regulations and controls.

For federal assets and liabilities, the N.A.T. Council adopted an extremely simply and straightforward approach. In principle, they simply agreed to leave all physical assets in place. This would include all federal buildings, military installations and equipment, monuments, and national parks. Furthermore, the formula to be used to allocate non-physical assets, like cash, would be based on the pro rata value of federal physical assets. This provided incentive for receivers of physical assets to ensure they were valued high in order to get a greater share of other federal assets. But the formula was also being applied for liabilities, including the national debt, so there was a natural incentive to value physical assets as low as possible in order to minimize their share of federal debt. The N.A.T. Council reasoned that these counterbalancing forces would ensure the most balanced approach to physical asset valuation, but they amazingly failed to consider the striking imbalance at the federal level between non-physical assets and total liabilities, most notably, the huge national debt. As new countries began to sandbag the value of federal physical assets in their territory in order to minimize their allocation of the national debt, the N.A.T. Council abandoned this formula approach and mandated that all federal non-physical assets and liabilities would simply be apportioned based on population. This meant that people-rich areas like New England, Californation, and Florida were saddled with unbelievably large shares of the former national debt. And this, of course, created a great deal of animosity between the surviving U.S. and the new nations.

The N.A.T. Council made no attempt to address other practical issues, like trade agreements, defense pacts, or border control. They rationalized that these matters would best be settled by the new American nations based on proximity and affinity over time.

CHAPTER *Fifteen*

J ust as the former United States was cast into an era of reshuffling and reprioritizing, so too was the overall world order. Without the assurance of the benevolent, democratic, freedom-loving republic that was the United States of America in place to ensure that menacing forces around the world were kept at bay, many other nations felt vulnerable and scrambled for any form of security and potential prosperity. Most notably, several former Soviet Union republics proactively reached out to Moscow to reach agreements on defense and trade, and in some cases, even petition to re-join Russia in rebuilding a form of the former U.S.S.R. These countries were betting that they could strike a better deal with Russia if they returned to the fold willingly, rather than wait for Mother Russia to aggressively capitalize on some moment of weakness in their future. Other former Soviet republics scrambled to strengthen their ties with Europe, which was also scrambling to consolidate its powers of protection. The European Union was concurrently expanding its reach with neighboring countries while further isolating itself from the rest of the world to become self-sufficient and self-protective.

The frenzy for long-term preservation was prevalent throughout the Southern Hemisphere as well. Most countries in South America were eager to solidify trade and defense pacts with one another and infringe a bit on their national sovereignties for the benefit of the larger good. To accelerate their efforts, they did not spend much time re-thinking how to accomplish such a feat. They looked to the north and east, to the long-standing European Union, for their blueprint and copied liberally while making minor tweaks to better suit their needs and avoid minor mistakes as noted by the Europeans. Not all of South America was on board though. Venezuela was in substantial talks with the new nation of Florida to build better ties across the entire Caribbean region. Shortly after Florida voted to secede from the U.S., Raul Castro, who had ceded power over a year earlier, died and left a power vacuum in Cuba. Cuba's new president, who came from a family with strong ties to Miami, was eager to improve relations with

Florida now that it was free from the restraints of the old American government. Cuba's President Manuel Betancourt made an initial overture to Florida's governor, now president, Willy Graham, about creating a Caribbean Coalition. Once Graham responded with interest, Betancourt began knocking on doors throughout the region. Venezuela would be a major coup for the effort. Haiti and the Dominican Republic were anxious to get in on the ground floor of the new economic trade zone. And Cuba's significant military strength was appealing for everyone in the region. Several other Caribbean island nations had adopted a wait-and-see approach, as had Suriname, Guyana, and French Guiana on the South American continent. The United States had ceded Puerto Rico and the U.S. Virgin Islands to Florida as part of the divorce activities, since those territories were not eligible to vote on secession plans of their own under the new Constitution.

As President Shilling said at the time, "I'm more than happy to let them be your problem, Governor Graham." Shilling, Haight, and most advisors around them, viewed Puerto Rico, primarily, but in reality all territories, as leeches on the backs of 'real' Americans. Shilling also dumped Guam, American Samoa and the Northern Mariana Islands into the arms of the new Hawaiian Islands nation.

The African continent also got caught up in the post-U.S.A. paranoia and insecurity. Several cross-country alliances popped up practically overnight while other nations let themselves be plundered, economically, by China and India. Both of those countries saw great opportunity in the Dark Continent's natural resources, fertile lands, and cheap labor. China took great advantage in Tanzania, Kenya and Uganda although all three of these countries remained independent and prospered greatly in the short-term from the influx of capital from Beijing and the access to new tools and technologies. India focused more on west-central areas from Nigeria to the Democratic Republic of the Congo, but countries in this region also remained independent. Although technically independent for the time being, the five nations comprising the southernmost portion of the continent were rapidly forging extremely strong ties. South Africa had evolved so much, politically, that it had become a beacon of democracy and political progress for all of Africa, if not the world. In fact, the new nation of New England was unabashedly copying the Mandela Constitution of South Africa as the model for its new democratic foundation. South Africa had been working with Namibia and Botswana on common interests for many years, such as the Kgalagadi Transfrontier Park, and now leveraged those past successes into even greater projects. Zimbabwe, struggling for direction in the post-Mugabe era, was eager to align itself with its three cooperating neighbors. And Mozambique was also keen to benefit from strong alliances with its four strong neighbors. Collectively, they formed a working alliance called the United Nations of Southern Africa. Shortly after its establishment, the Indian Ocean island nation of Madagascar and the central African nation of Zambia, along the region's northern border, were already petitioning for inclusion in the alliance.

Not all of the pact-seeking activities were cooperative, or even particularly friendly. In the midst of the U.S.A.'s great divorce, Saudi Arabia launched an invasion into Somalia and took over the entire nation in less than two weeks. There was scattered, but ineffective, resistance throughout the impoverished, violent nation, but absolutely no attempts at interference from any foreign nations. Even the United Nations, struggling to find its footing as the United States disintegrated literally around them, only issued a proclamation of concern at the invasion, but nothing stronger or more effective. Quite frankly, it was as though the world gave its blessing to the invasion, believing that the people of Somalia were better off under Saudi Arabian rule than they had been as a sovereign nation. Emboldened by the easy success of the overthrow and occupation of Somalia, the Saudi kingdom had turned its attention towards Ethiopia, but that invasion was not going smoothly. There were other skirmishes throughout the region. Egypt and Libya were now in a state of constant, but not passionate, conflict, and no one was even sure how the war started or what either party's objective was. It had become a modern-day version of the Hatfields and McCoys where they seemed to fight simply for the sake of fighting. And Yemen and Oman were regularly flexing their muscles through military exercises and fierce propaganda campaigns designed to keep Saudi Arabia and any other potential, unwanted suitors at bay. Israel was, of course, extremely nervous, but it was not alone in the region. Turkey too was anxious about the disruption of the world order and what its role in the new world hierarchy would be. The expanding European Union as well as the fledgling, but empathetic, New England, had pledged their unwavering support for both Middle East outliers, but neither Israel or Turkey believed they could rely on these friends in the event of a true crisis.

Asia also was undergoing significant changes as the world order took on new priorities and new partners. China choose to take this opportunity to wage an economic coup rather than geographic expansions while others were weak or vulnerable. Chinese leadership swiftly moved to open up free trade throughout the region with nods to capitalism, open borders, and human rights improvements, in exchange for one major concession from its trading partners. China insisted that all transactions be done in Hong Kong dollars. Don Lasserman's eldest child, Jessica, still lived in Hong Kong at this time and she marveled at the forward-thinking wisdom of the Communist Chinese leaders to realize the huge opportunity that the current world disorder, especially economic disorder, afforded them. Jessica had been in the region since her graduation from Oberlin College when she took a job as a financial analyst at Bank of China in the Central District of Hong Kong island. That was nearly a dozen years ago, and Jessica was now a bank vice president in charge of foreign exchange investments, so she had a firm understanding of the logic that the Chinese leaders were employing. It would be an insurmountable challenge to get global trading partners to agree to conduct all trade using the Chinese Renminbi, but most nations were already comfortable using the Hong Kong dollar, so it was a natural surrogate for the global trade that China now intended to dominate. Once Australia agreed to this scheme, most other regional countries followed suit, except for Japan, which was still trying to evaluate how to play in the new sandbox.

Jessica told her father that it was now common street wisdom in Hong Kong and China that the mainland leaders would further consolidate their power and further internalize the benefits of capitalism, without losing face, by phasing out the Renminbi over time and replacing it with the Hong Kong dollar. The pseudo 'borders' between the mainland, Hong Kong, and Macau, were also likely to dissolve, but in her opinion, the dissolution was bringing the communist nation closer to the ideals and successes of Hong Kong rather than the other way around. Her husband, Alex Yip, had his own metal fabrication business based in Kowloon, the Hong Kong district on the Chinese mainland; however, he also had fabrication shops in Shenzhen and Guangzhou and also traveled frequently to Shanghai and Beijing, so he was hearing a lot of buzz about the government's plan to become the world's dominate economic trading partner in light of the collapse of the U.S. economic stability. Both Jessica and Alex were excited about their futures in the evolving new world order and economy of the future.

CHAPTER *Sixteen*

Back in 'America,' changes continued to affect the everyday life of every citizen. Don Lasserman had convinced the board of the Adamo Institute on Race Relations that there was no practical role for the institute in the new America. The bifurcation of the nation's values meant that those that needed the work of the AIRR the most were now the least likely to hear the message and would most likely be openly hostile towards them. And the new nations, such as New England and Californation, already enthusiastically embraced the principles espoused by AIRR. Accordingly, AIRR was dissolved and Don Lasserman was without gainful employment. New England, with its provisional capital of Boston, was rapidly moving forwards with an egalitarian vision of a benevolent and inclusive social democracy, sort of an amalgam of Sweden and South Africa. The New

England Constitution was largely a copy of the South African foundation document, with a few minor tweaks, but the governing principles were more similar to the Scandinavian countries where no one was left behind or without.

One of the first challenges for the new nation of New England was to agree on senior leadership. There was a loud and pervasive cry for Dr. Richard Adamo, former president of the United States and chairman of AIRR, to return to service as the first president of the new nation. Adamo, however, reasoned that a new, young nation, rich on ideals and values, deserved a new, young leader rich on ideals and values. Don Lasserman had a wonderful, potential candidate in mind. Nearly two decades earlier, Lasserman had a brilliant financial analyst who worked for him at the investment firm. Michelle had come to Morgan Stanley direct from her M.B.A. program at Columbia. She was beautiful, ambitious, energetic, intelligent and charismatic. After seven years at the firm, just as she was on the cusp of making real serious money, Michelle announced her resignation to run for an unexpectedly open seat in Congress representing the 7th Congressional district in Brooklyn where she resided with her wife of two years, Chantal. Thus, Michelle Watters became the nation's first black, openly gay Congresswoman, and continued to serve in that capacity to this day. Don called his former protégé and arranged dinner for the four of them; Don, Adamo, Michelle and Chantal.

They met at Keens Steakhouse in Manhattan's Koreatown neighborhood just two blocks from the Empire State Building. The foursome shared a platter of the restaurant's famous Lincoln's Oysters, then Lasserman and Adamo each had the signature prime rib while Watters and Chantal joyfully shared the Chateaubriand steak dinner for two. They talked casually and comfortably throughout the dinner. They all spoke glowingly of their children and grandchildren. Michelle and Chantal had adopted twin boys after serving as foster parents. The twins, Jaylen and Jayden, were four years old and the obvious light of their lives. Chantal admitted that the similar-sounding names often caused confusion, but they were all getting used to it. Michelle knew that Don was a twin and was comfortable enough to ask Don how he was coping now that his twin brother was a convicted, racist, mass murderer serving multiple life sentences in McCreary Penitentiary in Pine Knot, Kentucky. Don admitted that it was an unimaginable burden at times, but mostly confusion and anxiety. He was very concerned about his brother's potential status now that Kentucky was part of President Shilling's newborn Christian theocracy with a value system that many believed cast Daniel Lasserman as a saint rather than sinner. But Don didn't want to dwell on that, so he stuck with Kentucky as the subject matter but turned the topic to his second daughter, Jasmine, who was a thoroughbred horse trainer at Claiborne Farm in Paris, Kentucky. He was proud that he and his wife Maria had raised their daughter with the proper values, and Jasmine was now quite uncomfortable in her reconstituted homeland of Kentucky. Don was happy to report that his son-in-law, Gregory, had just closed on a deal to buy an established public accounting practice in Ocala, Florida, from a family that did not want to be part of the new Florida nation. Furthermore, the Florida-fleeing family also owned a small horse farm on the outskirts of town that Gregory and Jasmine were purchasing as well. Their plan was for Jasmine to run the farm as a boarding stable and horseback riding camp for children, something that she would feel comfortable doing as a working-from-home mother, now that she was four months pregnant with Don and Maria's first grandchild. Everyone at the table congratulated Don on this momentous life milestone and Adamo shared the joy he and Makayla, his wife of forty years, found in their own five grandchildren. Eventually, Adamo steered the conversation to the point of the dinner meeting.

He began, "Michelle, we are at an important point in history and an unimaginable, stressful period of transition. This new breakaway nation needs a dynamic and visionary leader to stabilize the region as soon as possible. As you know, the party has begged me to run for president, but I have reached a compromise with them. I don't want to run, and they will respect my decision if I can proffer an equally suitable candidate. I think you are that person."

As Adamo was speaking, Chantal was bubbling with decreasing restraint. By the time he finished his sales pitch, Chantal was nearly bouncing from her seat. Watters gently squeezed her wife's hand, looked directly at the former U.S. president and said, "Obviously we speculated as to the nature of this delightful dinner meeting and we were correct. And, yes, I would love to be our party's candidate for president of New England." Chantal squealed with delight, as did both Adamo and Lasserman, although their squeals were much more restrained in keeping with the formal setting. For the rest of the meal, right through the affogato dessert, they talked about campaign strategy, potential vice-presidential candidates, and the need for a campaign manager. For the latter issue, they quickly decided on Don, since as Adamo said with a smile, "You're out of a job right now anyway."

The New America Transition Council rules were prompting a great migration of people and their talents from one region to another. Jasmine Lasserman and her husband, Gregory, were typical of the mobile, liberal professionals looking for opportunities to relocate to a more progressive environment. The Bogue family, from whom they were buying the Ocala CPA practice, were typical of those who were seeking an opportunity to relocate to what remained of the old United States and the security and comfort they perceived it provided. The N.A.T. Council transition plan allowed for a free flow of people between the surviving U.S. and the former states, now seceded, for a period of one year. Understandably, people were looking to move for a broad variety of reasons, but all reasons boiled down to getting relocated to an environment that they believed would be best for them and their families for the future. Many black Americans were concerned about the racist undertones of the new Shilling nation, while other black Americans were comforted by the new Constitution's focus on Christian values and obedience to the Word and Will of God. Many young Americans, particularly in the technology sector, were wary of the Shilling Administration's focus on old world industries, like mining and manufacturing, and felt they would have more economic opportunities in seceded states like California, Washington, Florida and Massachusetts, where technology was touted as the way of the future. Texas was struggling to keep technology talent within its cities, particularly Austin and Dallas, and the outflow of talent from the famed Research Triangle in North Carolina was causing some in the Tar Heel State to frantically reconsider promoting a referendum vote for secession.

Individual businesses were struggling with the New America political landscape as well. Many feared that tariffs and trade wars would ensue since the N.A.T. Council had decided not to decide on free trade or cross-border tariffs and taxes. General Motors took the pro-active step of spinning of its Cadillac division, which then became an independent public company based in New York. The automotive giant reasoned that this structure would be beneficial for all shareholders and consumers because the new Cadillac Transportation Company would most likely source its manufacturing from its former parent and the General Motors remaining behind in the new United States would benefit from the increased volume. What ultimately happened, however, was that the new Cadillac Transportation Company took over and revived the old Volkswagen plant in New Stanton, Pennsylvania, from the Redevelopment Industrial Development

Corporation Westmoreland for its only point of assembly. International auto companies were also in a great quandary as to how to minimize risk in the new America. Mercedes Benz and BMW had significant assembly infrastructure in Alabama and South Carolina. Nissan was prevalent throughout the Midwest with American headquarters in Nashville. Honda was big in Ohio and Indiana. And Toyota had significant operations in Kentucky, Indiana and Mississippi. They all worried about their plants, and their sales, as the Shilling Administration had telegraphed a staunchly nationalistic agenda. Would citizens in the new America be reluctant to buy automobiles from a foreign company even if the final assembly was domestic? Would some American workers become reluctant to work for a foreign employer? Could there be an uptick of violence against foreigners and their assets similar to the rampage of racial violence that prompted the great American divorce?

Retired Americans were also anxious about their future. Not only did they have to consider the economic factors and Christian values and distortions as did everyone else; they also had to consider their own income security for the future. Which new or surviving nation would be more stable for social security over time? There was a lot of speculation that one or more of the new nations might renege on promised retirement payments or even go bankrupt. But to make these decisions even more challenging, the seniors also had to consider the future cost of living relative to wherever they would relocate, if they did relocate. Property values were declining in once-lofty areas like Austin, Dallas, Raleigh, and Minneapolis where young people and families were driving mass exoduses, but they were skyrocketing in Florida and Californation. Food was another source of inflation for some areas; it was now considered an import instead of merely coming from a neighboring state. Community farms were popping up all over the seceded states in order to minimize the impact of so much farmland remaining behind in new, old America. Many seceded nations, like New England, were locking into long-term grain contracts with Canada, Russia and China, as they could no longer depend on the Middle America grain belt for supply. All in all, there was a great, chaotic, uncertain cross-migration underway across much of North America during this one-year transition period.

In addition to Jasmine Lasserman and Gregory moving from Kentucky to Florida, another Lasserman was also on the move. Daniel Lasserman's second son, Nathaniel, was a twenty-year veteran of the NASA Marshall Space Flight Center in Huntsville, Alabama, where he began his NASA career as a thermal-protection systems engineer after college. He was now a senior level project manager, which afforded him a great deal more flexibility when considering new jobs at the Kennedy Space Center in Cape Canaveral, Florida. Though he was only able to secure a project management job two pay levels below where he was in Huntsville, he reasoned it was a worthwhile trade-off in order to escape the perceived oppressive nature of the new America envisioned by President Shilling. Furthermore, Nate had grown increasingly uncomfortable in Huntsville where many of his co-workers and neighbors had taken to viewing his racist, mass-murderer father as a folk hero. He needed to escape that environment. He had even thought about changing his surname, but ultimately decided against it. Nate's wife, Donna, a hospital administrator, was fortunate to secure a very good new position at Florida Hospital in Wesley Chapel, a suburban community to the north of Tampa. Although it was slightly more than a two-hour drive between Wesley Chapel and the Kennedy Space Center, Nate and Donna figured they could make it work. And it would be easier with their twin sons out of the house. Luke was a sophomore at Emory University in Atlanta where he was pursuing a B.S. in Public and Environmental Health and Wayne was a sophomore at Princeton in New Jersey working on a B.S. in Civil and Environmental Engineering.

CHAPTER Seventeen

Every day of the next six months brought new wonder and despair. The value of the U.S. dollar had collapsed to an unprecedented low and was on the verge of being one of the least popular world currencies for trading. The Euro and Hong Kong dollar, as well as the Japanese Yen, were the top three quoted currencies now for global contracts. The stock markets were also at record low levels, especially when viewed as a percentage of gross domestic product. Many companies were barely getting by as the economy had stagnated and their American holdings became international holdings overnight, which brought new regulations and expectations into the profit equation. New England and Californation had enacted minimum wage laws designed to make every wage a living wage. This was driving up labor costs but also attracting the best workers. Shilling's new America had eliminated the minimum wage law altogether, along with many workplace laws designed to protect workers, including overtime laws and safety regulations. There were not enough American workers willing to take low-paying, dangerous jobs, and the Administration had closed the borders entirely to all outside nations other than the seceded states, so the market demand was actually driving the wages higher in order to attract qualified, competent workers.

Nate Lasserman was settled into his new project management job at the Kennedy Space Center and also settled into his efficiency apartment in nearby Wedgefield. To his surprise and chagrin, he actually liked the small dwelling much better than the small job. This was no testament to his love of the confined space or the liberty of being away from his wife during the workweek. It was a condemnation of his new assignment. Nate had severely underestimated how much a lower-level assignment, coupled with a general lack of direction at the Space Center due to uncertainty at the new government level, would affect his work enthusiasm. As if that work environment malaise wasn't bad enough, his new supervisor, Benny Franklin, a fan of Nate's father's 'good work' as Benny put it, took every opportunity to twist everyday events and problems into an opportunity that could be solved if Daniel Lasserman were released from prison and allowed to 'finish the job.' Nate had discussed Benny's inappropriate beliefs with Benny's supervisor, John Landry, but Landry was reluctant to intervene. Benny was a forty-year veteran of the government, and his dismissal would be challenging, if not impossible. Landry preferred to wait Benny out. He figured Benny would retire soon enough. Nate wasn't sure he could wait that long.

Donna was having much better success over on Florida's west coast. First, she loved her new job. The Florida Hospital bureaucracy was much leaner, and therefore more efficient, than what she had experienced at her last hospital job in Huntsville. And she loved her co-workers and management. She truly felt they were all working together as a family, united in the common goal of providing the best care for their patients. When speaking with her husband on the phone during the week, she often found herself brimming with so much enthusiasm that she'd have to tamp it down a bit so as to not make Nate feel even worse about his toxic and mundane work environment. And her living situation was far superior to that of her husband. They had found an adorable three-bedroom, two-bath, pool home in a gated community in Tampa Palms, a mere twenty-minute drive from the hospital. And best of all, Donna and

Nate felt they got an unbelievably good deal on the property because the sellers were anxious to relocate to Arkansas where they were retiring. Nate, having grown up in Arkansas, developed a good rapport with the sellers and helped steer them in the right direction for finding a community best suited for their retirement life.

With their twin boys off at college, and Nate gone for most of the workweek, Donna found two primary outlets for her newfound leisure time. She had joined a women's bowling league as a novice but was really enjoying the social interactions. A nurse at the hospital had coaxed Donna into filling in one week for an ill team member, and now, after only six weeks of bowling, Donna didn't see how she could do without it. Her bowling average had climbed all the way to 132 over the six weeks, which was poor, but gratifying to Donna as it was improving week over week. The real satisfaction for her though was the social camaraderie that came through her teammates and the competition. Each week, the girls took turns bringing a snack food to the bowling center to share after play. Her other use of her free time was in her small garden. She had always enjoyed growing herbs and some vegetables back in Alabama, but now, in Florida, Donna dropped the vegetable passion and replaced it with tropical flowers. She was notably proud of her hibiscus, bromeliad and ginger plants, but her real pride and joy were the passion flowers of various colors that she grew along the back fence behind the screened-in pool.

Just an hour or so north of Tampa, Nate's cousin, Jasmine, and her husband Gregory, were well settled in Ocala. Gregory's new CPA business was thriving as many individuals and small businesses needed help with bookkeeping and tax planning in the new post-U.S.A. environment. Florida, as a state, was a very tax-friendly environment including no income tax for most individuals. Florida, as a nation, however, was struggling with how to design a stable and balanced budget for the future, and no options were off the table. Many were calling for a minimal income tax, but an income tax nonetheless. Most Floridians were not accustomed to filing taxes at the state level, so they turned to local CPAs for help and planning. Overall, the nation of Florida's economy seemed bright. Tourism had not suffered too much during the great divorce of the states, and there was renewed interest in eco-tourism. Agriculture was actually booming as there was a drive to source more food locally since the trade environment across the rest of the continent was still uncertain. The Florida nation was also attracting technology jobs that were fleeing North Carolina and Texas with particular emphasis on environmental remediation and improvement projects.

Jasmine, who had given birth to their son, Anderson Donald Terrano, a little over a month ago, had not yet launched the horseback riding camps, but the stable was already full with horses for boarding. Jasmine had hired two college students from the nearby Ocala campus of the University of Central Florida to maintain the stables and feed the horses. Grandpa Don and Grandma Maria had come down to Ocala from Stamford, Connecticut, the week of Anderson's due date and were still in residence helping out. Jasmine remembered fondly from her own childhood when her Grandma Eva would come to visit and spend several days at a time with her grandchildren. Just as Don and Maria had purchased and renovated a second home for Maria's parents to be close to their grandchildren, Jasmine was hopeful that her fairly-wealthy parents would agree to build a second home on the ample acreage that she and Gregory had around the farm. As she watched them doting over their first grandchild, she had no doubt they would.

The birth of Anderson had come at the optimum time. Grandpa Don had been the campaign manager for New England presidential candidate, Michelle Watters. Don was a master at organizing and planning, but even had he been inept, Watters would have won easily. Her primary opponent was a capable man and worthy adversary, but his platform relied heavily on maintaining the status quo as much as possible. On the campaign trail, and through three debates, he consistently stated that the change and turmoil caused by the secession would undermine their society if not kept in check. Watters, on the other hand, artfully positioned the change and turmoil as liberation and opportunity. Her vice president, Thomas Vance, was even more artful and charismatic. A dashing, tall, blond, blue-eyed Pennsylvanian of Swedish descent, and a banker by vocation, Vance wore his character well and walked the talk. He was flawlessly devoted to his gorgeous, immigrant wife, and their three teenage daughters, and could not have epitomized the American dream and ideals any better. Yet, despite wearing the successes of the past so well, he spoke fervently about what the new changing world would bring for his children, and all children, in the future. He often referenced the American dream, but only to set up his most frequent rally cry: "There is a new dream, a better dream, and it includes all of us." One could picture him as a cult leader, and the citizenry rallied excitedly behind him and Watters. They won the election with seventy-two percent of the popular vote. Watters told Don Lasserman that there would be a place for him in her Administration, but he said he had a grandson waiting to be born in two weeks and that would be his only priority for the foreseeable future. A week later, he and Maria were on a Jet Blue flight from Westchester to Tampa to await the arrival of Anderson Donald.

Californation, on the other side of the continent, was also moving forward with its regional consolidation and governance plan. For the sake of expediency, as the three former states of California, Washington, and Oregon seceded and adopted a plan to form a new, united, west coast nation, they established a transitional structure; wherein the temporary capital city would be Sacramento, the interim president would be the current governor of Oregon, and the interim vice president would be the sitting governor of Washington state. Lively debate and campaigning ensued for several months, but in the massive, inaugural election that occurred the same day as the New England election, the citizens of Californation agreed on a number of issues. For one thing, they voted, with fifty-five percent affirmative vote, to keep Sacramento as the new nation's capital. They also approved a new constitution, very similar to Australia's in many ways. For one thing, all citizens would now be required to vote in order to avoid

tax penalties. And the referendum system so popular in California would be retained, but the criteria
for propositions was redefined in order to cut down
on abuses and nuisance ballot issues. The voters also
elected Terrence Tran, mayor of San Francisco, as
their first president, and Deborah Kent, Oregon legislative assembly senator as vice president. So, the
new nation of Californation had set itself on a course
of living its values by reflecting diversity in its first
top leadership team with a president of Vietnamese
descent and a vice president of Jamaican descent.
There had been a huge populist outcry for either
Jack Armstrong or Joe Getty of the hugely popular
Armstrong & Getty Sacramento radio talk show to
run for office, but neither personality had been so
inclined. In fact, they were on the cusp of retiring
from the airwaves, but the incredulity of the Haight
and Shilling Administrations demanded that their
common-sense perspective continued to be heard.
Their long-held tagline had been, "The Voice of the
West," and now that Californation was a nation, their
tagline had evolved to "The Voice of the Nation" and
in many ways, their common sense, practical views
greatly influenced the foundation and development
of the new Californation nation.

The Tran-Kent Administration's strategic priorities for the future of Californation included invest-

ments in agriculture, responsible timbering, tourism, technology, and ecology. They also were intent on forming a water rights treaty with Canada as they foresaw potential water issues coming from new, old America where the source waters for the Colorado river resided and any impairment of the flow of the Colorado would have disastrous effects on the southern portion of the new west coast nation. The Tran-Kent Administration was also cautiously encouraging further investments in desalination plants, but also investing in technologies that could mitigate the environmental impacts that such plants historically incur. Additionally, they had secured free trade pacts with Japan as well as the new Hawaiian nation and were optimistic about entering the Chinese free trade alliance using the Hong Kong dollar as the trading currency. They were treading cautiously, as were many other nations, because it remained unclear how Japan and China would work together on the world stage. But as of now, neither Asian powerhouse nation was forcing any other nations to choose sides.

The only troubling matters on the Californation horizon were the border with new, old America to the east and the uncertainty of future trade with its eastern neighbor. American President Shilling had announced intentions of building a wall around all borders, definitely including Californation, and also announced a strategy to minimize all imports via excessive tariffs. Californation President Tran embarked on a trade mission to Asia and Vice President Kent did the same in Mexico and the Hawaiian nation. Californation could ill afford any negative impact on its key agricultural crops, especially almonds, olives and apricots. The wine industry, from Paso Robles to Napa and Sonoma up to Willamette Valley, Yakima Valley and Walla Walla, was also understandably nervous about the future of trade. Vice President Kent, along with the executive director of the Californation Wine Growers' Association planned a global marketing tour, which would kick off in New England.

As for the Hawaiian nation, they also seemed to be fairing fairly well. Tourism was up appreciably over prior years. There was a great influx of tourists from South Korea, Japan, China, Australia and Indonesia. Visitors from the latter nation said they felt more comfortable visiting Hawaii, especially since it was no longer part of the United States; this was mainly due to the rising anti-Muslim sentiment that had tainted America in its final days. There was also an uptick in visitors from other predominantly Muslim nations, but not enough to be statistically significant. The new nation of Hawaii had also strategically decided to transform part of its island territory into a massive, global distribution hub. To the west of Kaunakakai on the southern shore of the island of Moloka'i, the government, in conjunction with several large, international shipping lines, had begun work on a massive distribution warehouse center. When the site was completed, it was expected to have three million square feet under roof with over half of that refrigerated to keep fish, fruits, vegetables and other perishables fresh as long as possible. Adjacent to the grounds of the distribution site, just on the other side of Highway 450, the nation was building the most modern port in the world. The massive and plentiful dockside gantry cranes would unload containers directly onto one of two massive concentric conveyor belts that would wind their way over the highway, through the distribution center, and back to the waterfront. Radio Frequency Identification tags were attached in duplicate to each cargo container. The RFID sensors would telegraph the next destination for the container and computerized, railroad-like turnouts would divert them to the proper aisle conveyor inside the distribution center, or leave the containers on the circular conveyor, thus returning them to the dock for immediate loading on another ship headed to a different market. The outer circle conveyor, moving clockwise, was at a higher level designed to feed the second story of the warehouse. The inner circle conveyor, moving counter clockwise, fed the ground level warehouse. The engineers envisioned a grand-scale, Amazon-style, automated warehouse, moving shipping containers around as easily and accurately as Amazon moves boxes.

Back in the new America, or the remnants of the old America, President Shilling had shamelessly set about molding the nation into exactly what his critics always said he would; a fundamentalist Christian theocracy. All forms of affirmative action had been abolished. Concentration camps had been established for avowed homosexuals. Abortions were illegal. Traditional borders had been shut down, and the new borders with the seceded states were being prepared for stringent control. Mosques and synagogues were routinely being burned or strafed with drive-by shootings, and there was typically little response from law enforcement. Even occasional, sporadic lynching had returned to the American way of life after being eradicated for nearly a century. Political opponents, the media, foreign world leaders, and any other critics were routinely chastised and taunted, including by the president himself. Shilling held true to his intents and edicts when he pardoned former President Haight and had effectively shut down any and all investigations into Haight and his family. For his part, former President Alexander Haight took to living in the spotlight as much as possible and shooting off his mouth as much as possible. To the extent his racist tendencies might have been throttled back a bit when he was president, there were no such constraints now. Perhaps most curious of all during this time, President Shilling met privately with notorious, racist, mass-murderer Daniel Lasserman at the federal penitentiary in Kentucky. They met for an hour, in private, no cameras, no reporters, but offered a photo op at the end that was a thirty-second shot of just the two of them, fingers linked across a wooden table, in prayer. And God only knows what they were praying for.

CHAPTER *Eighteen*

Three years after the great divorce, life for most citizens in the new, old America, as well as the spin-off nascent nations had settled down to predictable daily routines. President Jim Shilling had cancelled normal-cycle presidential elections on the premise of instability and turmoil in the wake of the great American divorce and thus far, no new elections had been held, nor were they in sight. Surprisingly, there was only minimal outrage when he took this action. Perhaps it was because he made the announcement as a prelude to a prayer for the health and well-being of the nation, which needed great healing following the divorce. Perhaps. Or perhaps it was because the new, old America had quickly grown used to the Administration's inflexible and strident intolerance for dissent and criticism. What remained of the Congress was mostly filled with Shilling shills.

The New America economy was doing okay but not great. The country still had very productive farmlands, and they were producing well, but market access was an issue for them. The new nation of New England was sourcing all of its food stocks from Canada, Californation, Florida, Ecuador, Chile and Brazil, unless of course, they were able to grow it on their own in New England. Likewise, Californation, in response to various border disputes with New America, was also foregoing any imports from the former motherland. New America also still contained a great deal of manufacturing capacity, but they had various issues, including market access, lack of capital--financial, intellectual and human— and insufficient materials and natural resources. The Shilling Administration had taken such a hardline stance on nationalism-essentially isolationism-that the rest of the world, including the new nations built from seceded states, had no choice but to learn to work around New America. This meant that the rest of the world was prioritizing its trade with anybody but America. Resources, including minerals and oil, were bypassing the American heartland altogether. The New American domestic oil industry was thriving and certainly helping to prop up the limited economy. The significant easing of regulations around traditional drilling and fracking made it a lot easier and profitable for the domestic producers, but the country also had no choice but to produce locally as there were limited external options for the isolated nation.

Another industry that was booming was gun manufacturing. The movement of gun manufacturing, once concentrated in the Northeast, to the South had begun years earlier. A month after the horrific, mass shooting at Sandy Hook elementary school in Connecticut in December 2012 that left twenty-six dead including twenty-one children, that state and neighboring New York passed more restrictive laws aimed at gun manufacturers. Remington promptly announced it was relocating its manufacturing to Huntsville, Alabama, and its headquarters to North Carolina. Similarly, Beretta, once manufactured in Maryland had moved to Tennessee later in 2013 after the state of Maryland also passed more restrictive laws aimed at the gun manufacturers. As the great American divorce unfolded, all gun manufacturing that remained in any seceded states, immediately relocated to territory remaining in the new, old America. The gun manufacturers could easily foresee what was about to transpire and they were correct. Californation passed a law that outright prohibited assault rifles, other than for the military and limited handgun ownership to two firearms per capable and tested adult individual. Hunting rifles were permissible, but no single individual could own more than five such firearms. New England preserved the intent of the original U.S. Constitution Bill of Rights but tapped into the Second Amendment's original focus on 'a well-regulated militia.' In the new New England Constitution, every state and municipality, had the right and responsibility to maintain well-trained and well-resourced law enforcement organizations, meaning police forces and state guards. Assault weapons were restricted to use only by such organizations. Individual gun ownership was severely restricted. The new nation had established a review board to grant handgun ownership on a case-by-case basis and it had proved to be a major deterrent as it was a lengthy and grueling process. In practice, the gun ownership board was mimicking the hunting rifle stance of Californation, but it was much less lenient when it came to handguns. In three years of operation, the board had only approved less than two thousand permits for individual handguns and no single person had been permitted to own more than one.

President Shilling and his tribe had created a self-serving and self-sufficient society, but it came at a cost. Some commodities simply were not available in America and technology had ground to a

halt meaning there was minimal new product development or process improvements. The remnants
of the once-great American nation were cast on a
course of destiny where societal development had
been retarded and economic progress was in a state
of regress. On the positive side, virtually anybody
that could work and wanted to work could be put to
work. There was such as shortage of qualified labor,
due to mass exoduses and the shutdown of any
immigrant workforce, that employers were willing
to invest in practically anyone able to be trained to
do the jobs. However, many Americans had grown
lazy and were simply not willing to perform many of
the manual and non-skilled jobs, especially in light of
the lack of a living wage.

Daniel Lasserman Junior, now known simply
as DJ, still lived in Memphis working as a nurse
at Le Bonheur Children's Hospital, and his wife,
Brigette, was an on-staff pediatrician working at the
same hospital. Their oldest daughter, Rebecca, was
just beginning her freshman year at Baptist College
of Health Sciences, where she would be studying
nursing, following the medical field footsteps of her
parents. Their second daughter, Tanya, was in the
eighth grade and an avid soccer player. Their third
daughter, Melanie, was just entering sixth grade,
and as of yet, had shown no real passion, or much

interest at all, in anything other than her friends and smartphone. Regardless of Melanie's lack of passion, the DJ Lasserman family was quite firmly rooted in Memphis and hadn't felt that they could leave the new, old America, even if they had wanted to. DJ was most certainly not a fan of his father in general and abhorred what his father had done on his racism-fueled mass-murder spree four years earlier, but he did secretly enjoy the attention that came his way at times. It was rare that anyone said anything negative to him about his father, though he was certain that many people hated Daniel Lasserman Senior. The ones that would talk to him about his father were the ones that applauded his father's 'mission.' At first, DJ would try to correct the racist supporters and explain that his father had no grand plan or visionary mission. His father had just simply snapped when he was fired from his job and the human resources manager that did the deed was black. The dominoes just sort of fell in place from there. But the backslappers didn't want to hear any of that. They were just happy to be in the presence of the son of the living martyr of the movement that lead to New America. DJ and Brigette were fairing much better than most in New America under President Shilling. True, neither of them had received a pay raise in nearly five years, but they both had good jobs and their pay compared quite favorably with most Americans. Shilling had totally undermined what little was left of Adamocare when the great divorce was final; many of DJ's and Brigette's clients were just barely getting by and were usually in quite bad shape by the time they finally presented themselves at the hospital. They knew the cost of the medical care would have to come from their own pockets or just not pay at all. Aside from Adamocare, most other social support systems had been gutted or eliminated by Shilling, or Haight before him, so crime was rampant among those who could not, or would not, work. DJ and Brigette both carried handguns with them when traveling to and from work, and they had taken all three of their daughters to pistol ranges to learn how to properly handle the guns. The family also went hunting quite often. Daniel Senior's cabin in Harrisburg, Arkansas, was now in the hands of DJ and he used it frequently for weekend escapes with his family where they could hunt deer and turkeys on the grounds. His brother, Nate, had wanted nothing to do with the cabin following their father's arrest and the new, old America judicial system had negated all civil suits against Daniel Lasserman Senior, so his property was free for transfer to his son.

Nate was finally finding happiness and fulfillment in the new nation of Florida. After more than a year of suffering in a work environment that lacked direction and working under a racist-loving supervisor, an escape opportunity presented itself. Florida had decided to significantly curtail government operations at the space center and primarily provide infrastructure for private space exploration companies. As such, the space center itself would need far fewer personnel. They offered a generous buyout plan that consisted of double the normal severance pay plus a bonus payment of ten thousand dollars per each year of service. Nate had recently passed his silver anniversary with NASA, so he received a bonus of a quarter of a million dollars. He promptly gave notice on his Wedgefield apartment and happily moved his meager belongings home to his wife Donna and their home in Tampa Palms. It only took a month or so for Nate to figure out what his second career should be. There was an upcoming election for an open senate seat, so he ran as a Libertarian candidate and easily won the contest. Nate benefitted from many factors that played well in the new Florida nation. All the major American political parties had transferred over to most of the new seceded-state nations, but the Libertarian perspective seemed to resonate well in the new Florida. Floridians were historically skeptical of big government and they liked that the Libertarian party was rooted in the principles of a government interfering as little as possible.

Nate also benefited greatly from his good looks and poise. His dark, wavy hair had touches of grey, and was also responding nicely to the abundant Florida sunshine, as was his normally pale skin. He now sported an even, not overdone, perpetual tan. His clean-shaven, square-jaw face signaled strength, as did his muscular upper body, trim waist, and tight ass. Always above normal in looks and athletics, Nate had truly blossomed into a middle-aged Abercrombie model with the support of the Florida environment and outdoors lifestyle. The third factor that greatly helped Nate win the election was name recognition. Ever since his father went on a racist, murdering rampage, the Lasserman name had been in the news. First, it was in the news because of Daniel's shooting spree. Later, Nate's Uncle Don, served as national campaign manager for Michelle Watters who was now president of New England. That type of news still made the daily news in Florida. And Nate, himself, had a certain amount of media notoriety. On the day that his fugitive father was captured, Nate was there. Actually, Nate and his Uncle Don were the ones to physically capture Nate's father and avoid further bloodshed. More importantly, most of their heroics were caught on video.

Television cameras had been rolling when Don and Nate stepped out of an FBI crime scene van clad only in their underwear and walked into Elvis' Graceland Mansion. Daniel Lasserman Senior wanted to be certain they were not carrying any weapons or recording devices. When Nate ran for the senate, video of his underwear walk was everywhere, being shown by admirers and detractors alike. He was self-conscious about it at first, but his wife, Donna, playfully told him she found it sexy, and then backed up her claim with mutually enjoyable proof. Since then, he didn't mind the footage. But, there was additional footage that bolstered Nate's image as strong on crime. When his father was holed up in the Memphis museum to Elvis, he had smashed every security camera he could find. He missed one in a light fixture. That security camera caught, in great lighting and resolution, the moment when Nate slammed his father against the wall and dislodged the Beemiller handgun he was holding. That video clip, a clip that Nate did not want shown out of respect for his father, really resonated with voters in the Sunshine Nation who viewed his actions as part vigilante, part Wyatt Earp, and helped propel him to a huge victory.

The Florida nation was generally prospering in the post-secession phase of its evolution. Cuba President Manuel Betancourt had envisioned a grand Caribbean empire when Florida became independent, but a true union appeared out of the realm of possibilities for now. What had transpired, however, was that all nations in or bordering the Caribbean, had signed on to a regional pact that afforded free trade within the zone and a mutual defense commitment. The promise of the Caribbean pact had even inspired the people of Venezuela to overthrow the dictatorial Nicolas Maduro and adopt more democratic and humane processes in order to become full members of the regional power-house. Each nation remained independent, but the headquarters for the regional pact was in Havana. In a bold and surprising move, the pact had agreed to use a common currency, the Cuban convertible peso, for all domestic and regional transactions. For its part, Cuba was modifying the peso to be inclusive of regional leaders and landmarks. For international transactions, outside of the Caribbean Pact trading zone, they had agreed to use the Hong Kong dollar and had pegged the Cuban, or Caribbean, peso to the Hong Kong dollar for exchange purposes. These actions not only brought trading stability to the region and solved Florida's need for a post-U.S. dollar currency, but also greatly advanced China's quest for the Hong Kong dollar to be the world's preferred trading currency.

The Caribbean Pact also enabled much closer cooperation among the regional nations for virtually all industries. Georgetown, Cayman Islands, long renowned for secretive off-shore banking, had worked closely with the banks of Miami, Tampa, Havana and San Juan to create a regional financial powerhouse. Georgetown became the home of the newly anointed Caribbean Stock Exchange. Most Florida companies that formerly traded in New York were now trading via Georgetown. Florida orange growers were developing modern orange groves throughout Cuba and Puerto Rico, which was greatly enhancing the region's output and solidified its position as the world's predominant citrus producer. Sugar cane and rum production were also on the rise and constituted a good portion of exports from the region. Tourism was further developed throughout the region, aided by Florida's historic successes and marketing expertise. Grand casinos and resorts once again thrived in Havana, but also in Georgetown, San Juan, Punta Cana, Caracas, Castries and Freeport. The region collectively decided to invest heavily in textile and apparel industries in Haiti and the Dominican Republic. The Pact also committed to energy production one-hundred percent fossil-free. Solar power was ubiquitous, but the power companies also developed more wave energy plants to capture tidal waves, and wind farms.

Additionally, many years earlier, Cuba had embarked on a massive, underwater, geothermal energy exploration project that was now able to be completed and brought online with the influx of Floridian technology and capital. Venezuela, whose lifeblood was oil production, was still producing massive amounts of oil for export and for use in petroleum-based products such as gasoline, asphalt, chemicals, plastics and other synthetics.

The Cuban Revolution of 1959 had promised decent living conditions for all citizens. Over time, that mission evolved to include adequate housing, sufficient food, quality and free healthcare, and unlimited education. Under the Caribbean Pact, that mission further evolved to ensure everyone had access to clean water, electricity and communications. And the scope included everyone in the region. The Cuban Revolution was predicated on the principle of restoring democracy to the island nation after the overthrow of the corrupt dictator Fulgencio Batista who had lined his pockets by aligning himself with mob-based enterprises from the United States. Now, Cuban President Manuel Betancourt was able to fulfill the democracy objective of the revolution while maintaining the social safety nets, by forging this pact throughout the Caribbean and leveraging all the best aspects of every nation member.

CHAPTER *Nineteen*

This time period had not been especially kind to the new nation of New England. Although the economy was fairly productive overall and there were no real defense threats, the region was not the powerhouse it once was. New York was still an important world financial center, but it wasn't *the* financial center it was when old America ruled the world. And, New York had lost its status as the world's political leadership center. The United Nations, headquartered since its founding in New York City, pulled out of the city two years after New York's secession from the old United States. The UN was now headquartered in Geneva, Switzerland and had reconstituted its Security Council to be reflective of the new world order, following the restructuring of North America. Due to the overall instability of the world, and the transitory state of many nations, the United Nations scrapped its structure of permanent Security Council members with veto powers.

The new structure still included fifteen Security Council members with two tiers. The first tier was intended to include the most powerful nations in terms of economic and military might and was called the Strategy Council. There were five member nations in this group at a time and they were elected for ten-year terms. They could be re-elected an infinite number of times, but they had to be elected by the entire general membership. The candidate list for this tier was comprised of the top ten powers ensuring that an element of moral leadership could be comprehended in the structuring of the Strategy Council. Pure economic and military might did not automatically ensure a nation a seat on the Strategy Council if other nations were wary of that nation's intentions. The second tier consisted of ten member nations elected for two-year terms and only one term at a time. Once a nation served on the Security Council, exclusive of the Strategy Council members, they could not be on the Security Council again for ten years. There was no veto power for Strategy Council members, however, for all Security Council votes, Strategy Council members had the weight of two votes while the other ten Security Council members held only one vote. While this structure could result in deadlocks, it also ensured that the rest of the world could not easily be bullied by too much power in the hands of the Strategy Council.

CHAPTER *Twenty*

Don Lasserman sighed heavily as he sat on the edge of his California king bed in his Stamford home. He glanced up at the coffered ceiling with its inlaid fresco copy of some masterwork of centuries gone by. Caravaggio, he remembered. Then he looked to the battered, but still ticking, Westclox alarm clock on the nightstand. And then he peered towards the partially open door to the master suite bath where his beautiful, loving wife of one year shy of forty, Maria, was brushing her shoulder-length blonde and greying hair. With another satisfying sigh, he lay back on the bed and wistfully recalled a day nearly six years earlier when he awoke in this very bed. On that day, he cursed the buzzing alarm clock as he tossed it to the floor. On that day, he respected and resented his emotionally distant wife, sleeping not too far away. On that day, he was not prepared for what would unfold during the course of that day; a day that forever changed his life, the lives of his family, the lives of every citizen around the world. On that day, he could not name one reason to continue living. On this day, he was so glad to be alive.

Other than the setting, the only thing that day of nearly six years ago had in common with today was Don's heartache for his only son who had died of an unintentional drug overdose. That ache would never leave his soul and heart. It had been profound six years ago when the wound was still fresh; Teddy had been gone just two years then. And it was still profoundly painful today, but manageable in the context of all that had become beautiful and joyous in his life.

Earlier this evening, Don and Maria had arrived back at their Stamford, Connecticut, home following their Jet Blue flight from Tampa to White Plains, New York. They had been in Florida for the past three weeks at their winter home in Ocala. Maria had designed a charming, single-story, Mediterranean-style bungalow for their second home. Don had it built on a half-acre lot carved out of their daughter's sprawling horse ranch in Ocala. Jasmine and Gregory had two sons now; Anderson nearing four years old, and Silas, just six months old. Don and Maria spent most of the winter months in Ocala now to be close to their daughter and grandsons but returned to their primary home in Connecticut for at least one week a month throughout the winter season. The past three weeks in Ocala had been especially enjoyable for Don. Not only did he get to spend quality time with his grandsons, but he was also nearing his seventieth birthday, and Maria and Jasmine had arranged a surprise birthday party.

On the day of the surprise party, Don's son-in-law, Gregory, asked Don for his help with Anderson during an errand he wanted to run. Gregory, like Don, was very interested in classic cars, so it didn't take much arm-twisting to get his father-in-law to agree to accompany him on the nearly two-hour drive to Kissimmee where there was a special preview of classic cars on display in advance of an upcoming auto auction. The three generations had a very enjoyable time strolling among row after row of vintage and classic cars. Gregory captured an excellent picture of grandfather and grandson sitting in a 1965 Plymouth Barracuda. Red in color, it was more similar to the condition of the white and weathered 'Cuda Don had as a teenager than the pristine, professionally-restored yellow one parked in his Stamford garage now. Shortly after noon, Don, Gregory, and nearly four-year old Anderson, enjoyed a delightful roadside lunch of burgers and chicken nuggets at the

Minneola Grill before hopping on the Florida turn-pike in Gregory's sleek, racing green, Jaguar XF, for the speedy drive back to Ocala. As they approached the ranch, Gregory drove around the back of the horse stables so he could approach Don and Maria's bun-galow unseen from the main house. If Don thought this was odd, he didn't comment. Don climbed out of the luxurious British sedan with the intention of grabbing a quick nap in his hammock on the covered rear porch overlooking the pond. But Maria had her heart set on walking up to the main house to help get baby Silas ready for his afternoon nap and provide motherly advice to Jasmine on an unspecified bak-ing project. Maria asked her husband to join her on the five-minute walk up to the house and he readily complied knowing he could always walk back down to the bungalow on his own whenever he wanted.

Artfully, Maria maneuvered Don around the back side of the stables, claiming she wanted to see one of the newest boarders. From the stable, she steered him through Jasmine's vegetable gar-den, claiming she wanted to check on the cucumber and squash plants that their daughter had recently planted. The five-minute walk became more than ten but achieved the desired result of delivering Don to the back door of their daughter's home, well out of sight of the half-dozen or so vehicles parked out front. Jasmine and Maria were visibly pleased that they had successfully pulled off this surprise birthday celebration.

Don passed through the massive, formal living room greeting all of his guests. Former U.S. President Richard Adamo and his wife, Makayla, were there. Travel was easier for them now that America had discontinued secret service protection for former presidents that lived outside of the new territorial borders. They had flown in from New York and driven their own rental car over from Orlando. Don and Maria's eldest daughter, Jessica, and her husband Alex, were there, having traveled all the way from Hong Kong with their two-year old daughter, Mei Lin. They had arrived the day before but stayed overnight at cousin Nate's home in Tampa Palms so as to not spoil the surprise. Nate and his wife, Donna, were there, as expected, but Don was surprised that their twin sons, Luke and Wayne, were also in attendance. Both young men were recent college graduates. Luke was now working as an environmental engineer for Mosaic in Riverview, Florida, and brought his fiancée, Barbara. Wayne was an engineer working at Bechtel in San Francisco, although his job took him around the world to various projects. He had just flown in from Santo Domingo where he was working on a hydroelectric dam project. Wayne had become a licensed pilot and had flown himself, along with a colleague, into Ocala that morning. The colleague dropped Wayne off at the home of his first cousin once removed, and then continued driving south on I-75 to visit his grandparents in Bradenton.

Also in attendance was Nate's brother, DJ, and his family. DJ, a nurse in Memphis, and his pediatrician wife, Brigette, had driven from Memphis to Atlanta with their two high school daughters, Tanya, a senior, and Melanie, a freshman, the day before. In Atlanta, they stayed overnight at their oldest daughter Rebecca's apartment. Rebecca had recently graduated from college and just started working as a nurse at Grady Memorial Hospital. This was the first opportunity for DJ and Brigette to visit with her since she moved to Atlanta. With all three daughters on board, the family completed the five-hour drive, including the border check south of Valdosta, that morning.

The group got along famously. Adamo was keen to learn from Nate, now a senator in the nation of Florida, how the governance process was working here in the Sunshine nation. Senator Nate had nothing but good news to share and was very excited about the benefits of the highly successful and amiable Caribbean Pact alliance. Hostess Jasmine was thrilled to have her only sister in attendance from halfway around the world, and it was the first time their children had a chance to be together. Lots of pictures and videos were taken. Gregory caught a particularly touching moment with his Nikon Coolpix camera of Don, eyes full of tears, with one hand on each of his nephew's shoulders, each of them locked in intense eye contact. It was an image that expertly captured the elephant in the room—the fact that it was Nate and DJ's father's seventieth birthday as well, and he was spending it alone in McCreary Penitentiary in Kentucky. Plenty of tears were also shed by Don and Maria as well as Jessica and Jasmine in remembrance of Ted, deceased eight years now, who never had the chance to know his nephews or niece.

Now, Don was back at their home in Connecticut staring at the Caravaggio reproduction on the ceiling, reflecting on the joy of his children and grandchildren. They were, of course, delightful, but it was also wondrous to him to think that his family was spread out over so many nations of the world. He and Maria were here in the heart of New England. Jessica was firmly rooted in Hong Kong. Jasmine had built an enviable life in the new nation of Florida, as had his nephew, Nate. And his other nephew, DJ, seemed to be doing as well as possible in the new, old America. Equally stupefying to him was the important roles that he and his family had played in the creation of the world as they knew it today. His brother was the catalyst for the racial explosion that lead to the downfall of the old America. Don himself had been part of the planning, along with his good friend Richard Adamo, of the framework that enabled the great divorce. And following the divorce, Don had been instrumental in getting Michelle Watters, now president of New England, elected as that new nation's first leader.

Lost in thought, Don didn't feel Maria lay down beside him and was startled when she wrapped her arm around his chest. They turned to one another and took in the entirety of each other's souls with their eyes, then kissed lightly. It was good to love and be loved. Within minutes, they were both asleep, no doubt counting their blessings and dreaming of the uncertain future.

CPSIA information can be obtained
at www.ICGtesting.com
Printed in the USA
BVHW040632261118
533964BV00034B/531/P

9 781642 374209